Léa

Léa

a novel

ARIELA FREEDMAN

.ll.

Prepared for the press by Elise Moser and Jennifer McMorran
Author photo by Lev Wexler
Cover design by Leila Marshy
Graphic design by Debbie Geltner
Cover art by Carlos Oliva
Photograph by Archie Fineberg

Library and Archives Canada Cataloguing in Publication

Title: Léa : a novel / by Ariela Freedman.
Names: Freedman, Ariela, 1974- author.
Identifiers: Canadiana (print) 20210335912 | Canadiana (ebook) 20210335920 | ISBN 9781773901022 (softcover) | ISBN 9781773901039 (EPUB) | ISBN 9781773901046 (PDF)
Classification: LCC PS8611.R4227 L43 2022 | DDC C813/.6—dc23

Printed and bound in Canada.

The publisher gratefully acknowledges the support of the Government of Canada through the Canada Council for the Arts, the Canada Book Fund, and of the Government of Quebec through the Société de développement des entreprises culturelles (SODEC)

Linda Leith Publishing
Montreal
www.lindaleith.com

To Imma

Prologue
Montreal, April 15, 1937

Léa leaves her house at dawn and the air still feels like winter. It is the time of year when Montreal is entirely unpredictable, frigid one day and sweaty the next. She thinks she sees grey flakes of snow as she wraps her thin coat around herself and hugs her arms to her chest. For weeks she has prayed for good weather. The streets are nearly empty but for a few milk carts, delivery trucks, boys on bicycles throwing newspapers against the closed doors of the sleeping city.

Tomorrow, they will own the front page of every one of those papers.

She hurries to the garment district, her head down, hands deep in her pockets. The sidewalks smell of charcoal and rain. Her coat is brown, her hat is brown; she is a city sparrow, meant to blend in on the street, flitting from corner to corner. There is no reason for anyone to stop her, but still, she is nervous, and does not want to attract attention. When she gets to Sainte-Catherine, she can see that Rose Pesotta has beaten her there, standing in front of union headquarters.

In her bright purple double-breasted coat, a gold pin on her chest like a medal, Rose looks like a general. She shares none of Léa's concern about being conspicuous. "How did you sleep?" Rose asks.

"I'm nervous," she confesses. " I feel like I'm throwing a party, and I don't know if anyone is going to come. How about you?"

"I slept like a baby," Rose says. "Woke up every two hours screaming." She smiles at Léa. "I slept just fine. Don't worry, they're coming."

Léa peers down the street, shivering. She is trying to look around corners. She is trying to see the future.

The minutes stretch like hours.

And here they are. Here they are! A myriad of women shoulder to shoulder in glad defiance, chatting and laughing. As they fill the street, the day becomes bright and loud with possibility. Hundreds, no, it must be thousands of girls, from half a dozen factories, where the doors will stay shut and the machines will lie idle on this glorious day. The sky is clearing, the sun is out, even the grimy downtown streets are beautiful. Every single upturned, smiling face is full of promise.

Léa walks into the crowd as if she is parting the sea. "Frieda!" she cries. "How are you feeling?" Frieda salutes her with a bandaged arm—just last week, it was caught in the mangle on the floor of the laundry. Those machines are vicious. Léa hears her name and turns around to see Charlotte, who was so afraid that she would lose her job if she showed up for the strike, and she pulls her into a hasty embrace. "I'm so glad you're here!" She knows many of the girls by name, and greets them in their own languages: English, Yiddish, French. For months, she has been holding them by the hand. For months, she has been pulling them along. She has been leading them right here, to this moment.

Something about Léa is hard to pin down. Her narrow face, her rawboned cheeks and china-blue eyes, can shift in an instant from inconspicuous to remarkable. Depending on how she's dressed and where she is, she can look French or English, Catholic or Jewish. Even her name, Roback: she could be from anywhere. Sometimes she is plain and seems to fade into the background. But when she is excited or enraged, she is transformed, her cheeks flushed, her eyes kindled in the sun. Right now, she is a bead of quicksilver moving through the crowd. She is luminous.

By mid-morning, they are five thousand strong, standing shoulder to shoulder. They extend for blocks. They shout and laugh and hold placards and sing songs. With the power of their bodies, they refuse their exploitation.

It takes a little while for the police to show up, and when they do, they stand in confused restless clusters, watching the girls, not sure how to proceed. In Ontario at the General Motors strike, Hepburn's Hussars rushed the lines with billy clubs; in Chicago, they used tear gas and pistols. But these are girls. What do you do with girls? Some of the protestors, wearing their new spring coats and spring hats, drift towards the horses and pet them. The cops aren't sure if they are there to flirt or to fight. As a girl strokes the muzzle of a police horse, the animal dips his head. It seems like they have all gathered, not in conflict, but in a great-hearted fellowship. The beast tamed; a moment of unexpected grace.

The mood of the crowd is not fear, it is delight. It looks like everyone is on holiday. The women are shedding their coats, moving freely, stretching in the sun. They have paralyzed the police with their beauty.

Then the reinforcements arrive, and the battle begins.

A flash of light off a cop's baton, and she is in Berlin, running down the sidewalk that bloody May Day eight years ago, through the tear gas and the shouts, caught between the orders to stop and the calls to run.

She will not run. Not this time.

Hand in hand, facing the lines, she lifts her chin, and all she feels is calm and righteous exhilaration.

I
Youth
Beauport, Montreal, 1905-1925

1.

And here comes Léa with the light brown hair, standing on the fence in a ray of sunlight.

Genug iz genug! Trop c'est trop! She leaps down into the shadows, crouches as if she has fallen, jumps up laughing to climb back again. She is gone all day long in the summertime, from dawn until dark. She comes home with her hair full of knots and twigs, her knees scraped and her skirt torn. The fields, the river, the streets are hers, and she wanders freely. "Like a boy," people in the village say, in a tone of scandalized admiration. *A maydel mit a vayndel*—a girl with a ponytail, swinging through the long summer days.

When they came to Beauport she was three years old. Five now, and she does not remember any other home. In the kingdom of her childhood, her sovereignty extends over the tall reeds and wild irises that verge the river; the roof of her palace is as high as the dome of the stars at night. Her summer crown is made of daisies and of dandelions, and in the winter, she conquers mountains of snow and flies across blue-white fields of ice.

For her parents, the move has been more complicated. Their first week in Beauport, Madame Langlois brought them *blanc-manger* as a welcome gift. Mama said thank you, took the dish behind the house, and tipped the dessert right into the chicken slops, thinking it must have lard. They were the first Jews the town had ever seen. To her alarm, Madame Langlois was still standing in her kitchen when she came back in with the empty, glistening plate. "My apologies," Mama said, her face on fire. She tried to explain about the web of laws on beasts and birds and swarming things that kept her from sitting at a table with her neighbours.

"Madame," Madame Langlois said, "it is only cream."

They are good friends now, and still laugh about that. How the poor chickens walked around with beards of pudding, and did not lay eggs for weeks. Mama's first lesson in trusting the neighbours, and also, being careful about what can and cannot go into the slop pile.

They run the general store, where everyone shops, but because they are Jews they are not allowed to own it. They stay inside during the Corpus Christi parade to avoid kneeling for the Eucharist. The centre of the town is the church, and they will not step inside it. When their uncle comes to visit from America, he brings Jewish books, and he tells his sister to keep speaking Yiddish in the house with the children. The neighbours eat pea soup, *pouding chômeur, fèves au lard, tourtière*. They eat kneidlach, roasted chicken, tsimmes, kugel, and brisket.

But Mama learns to make her own *blanc-manger*. She also makes chicken soup for anyone who is sick in the neighbourhood. They start to thread their Yiddish with French words and phrases. "He's a *goy,* but he's a *mensch,*" Papa says of his landlord, Monsieur Langlois, who teaches him to fish in the nearby streams. In return, he takes him hunting for chanterelles in the woods, those saffron mushrooms that smell of apricots and the forest floor, which he recognizes from his boyhood expeditions in the Polish woods.

That first bright yellow flag in a sun-speckled patch of pine; he felt like he was coming home.

2.

One night that winter, her brother complains of a pain in his stomach. "You're faking it," Léa says, dismissive of malingering. But Harry's face is hot, and when Mama pokes him just above his bellybutton, he screams. She is so pregnant she can barely hold him on her lap.

Dr. Paquette comes to the house and operates on the kitchen table. He pours chloroform into a handkerchief, and Mama and Madame Langlois hold Harry down as the doctor cuts into his stomach with the scalpel. It is dark outside, and the operation is illuminated with a lantern, slick belly in a pool of golden light, twisting away from the cut of the knife. In the shadows Léa crouches in a corner, ashamed of her earlier suspicion, her face covered in her hair. She digs her nails into her palms, and she wishes she could bear his pain.

Anybody, heal him.

Out comes the red and swollen appendix, and the doctor sews him back up as deftly and neatly as a housewife.

Every few days, the doctor comes to drain the pus from Harry's incision, and he needs to be held down as he howls from the pain. He sleeps in Mama's room so she can comfort him when he wakes up. Zayde Roback sends him red velvet slippers as a convalescence gift, which to Léa seem the height of luxury. She heads to the bedroom to see Harry's scar for the hundredth time. The scar looks like a centipede, a hundred black legs crawling across his stomach. She wants to touch it, and when she does, she draws back her hand as if she has been bitten. Then she wants to touch it again. She is drawn to cuts, scabs, scars, bruises—anywhere something has broken, and the tender spots where something has begun to heal.

When the baby is born just ten days later, she is put in charge of her younger sister. Without asking, she borrows Harry's slippers and pretends she is a king and Annie is her slave. "Bring me chocolate ice cream," she commands, and Annie takes the best cut-glass bowls from the kitchen and fills them with mud.

The mud drips penny-sized coins on the new slippers, and while she runs to clean them off, Annie wanders away. She spends a frantic half hour before she finds her sister playing under the porch. Her black hair is full of twigs, her bow is gone, and her mouth is ringed with dirt. Léa drags the stepstool to the sink and scrubs Annie's face with a rough washcloth, and Annie cries bitterly but only as long as the washing lasts, then scampers off to visit the new baby. None of the adults have noticed their disappearance.

All the other girls are little mothers. They can be relied on to rock a baby, set a table, or mop the floor. Not Léa. Give her a broom and she will forget she is sweeping halfway through the room, give her a pillowcase and she will turn it into a nun's hood or a beggar's sack, give her a book and she is lost for the day.

But Léa is the very best at pitching pennies, she can wrestle boys twice her size, she skips in her hard-soled shoes like a machine gun, rat-a-tat-tat. Once when she was playing hide and seek, the other children looked so long and so hard for her they assumed she must have already gone home, and she stayed hiding in the bushes until the stars came out. She wears her toughness so lightly that it does not register as strength.

"What a shame she's not a boy," Madame Langlois says, but Madame Parent corrects her: it is women who need to be tough in this world.

3.

At seven years old Léa longs to taste the Eucharist, her longing even more urgent because it is forbidden. She thinks it must taste like *pain au chocolat*. No, like the meringue they ate in Quebec City, or maybe like the *manna* which she read about in the Bible, which fell in the desert as white as snow and tasted like anything you could think to desire.

It is impossible for her to go to church. Everyone knows the Roback children. She would be out on her ear before she could even get in the line for communion.

She finds it intolerable to be deprived, even when she does not know what she is missing.

"Please, Ophélie," she begs her neighbour, who goes to church every Sunday, her curls fat sausage rolls and a stiff polka-dot bow crowning her hair. "Tell me how it tastes?"

Ophélie shrugs her shoulders. "It tastes like nothing."

"That's impossible," she says, more convinced than ever that something is being kept from her. "Nothing tastes like nothing. It has to taste like something. Even water tastes like something."

Ophélie, who is afraid of spiders, mice, dogs, cats, and ladybugs, has to be bribed with a new pencil, a square of chocolate, and a blue silk ribbon to smuggle out a piece of the wafer, which she does in her squirrelish cheek. It takes a few minutes to run out of the church and meet Léa in the bushes, and by then the wafer is a mealy mush.

She swirls it around her mouth experimentally.

"You're right," she says finally, "it's nothing."

She spits the rest into the grass, and Ophélie stares at her. She looks horrified, her mouth open, her eyes round.

"You better get back inside," Léa says. She spends the rest of the morning trying to catch little silvery fish with her hands in the brook while poor Ophélie is stuck inside with her prayerbook and not even a real snack. At the synagogue in Quebec City, at least they have herring.

Everyone shops at the general store, even the nuns, who buy white handkerchiefs for the priests. The family is friendly, the children so charming, and the father gives credit, which wins over even the hardest hearts. We have so much, Papa says. But they could have a little more. Mama hides the money for housekeeping because otherwise he will give everything away. Sometimes—though not often—they go to bed hungry, and she relies on the chickens in the yard, the cows in the field, the money she can make on the side for the eggs and milk, and a little sewing. The children help, both girls and boys. There are no aristocrats in the family, Mama says. When she is indisposed, which is a word for pregnant once again, Harry takes over the kitchen.

Half the time, the families who buy on credit can't pay it back. Her father shrugs his shoulders philosophically. "What am I going to take," he says. "Their children?"

And in that department, thank God, he has enough. There are five now, and another on the way.

He takes them to Quebec City to be photographed, the girls in white dresses and black stockings, Harry in a double-breasted coat with a large ruff collar. In the photograph, Annie is daydreaming as usual, pretty as a doll with her dark bob and white hair bow, her eyes far away. Rose looks messy and delighted. She insisted on having Mama's ring to play with during the photography session and she is grinning, triumphant at having gotten her way. In three-quarter profile, Harry is thin and delicate—he has taken some time to recover

11

from the operation—and he is holding onto the back of baby Lottie's dress so she doesn't fall off the photographer's chair as she, startled by the light of the flash, seems to float like a pale balloon with her round face and too-large dress. And Léa looks straight at the camera. Her gaze is firm, and her chin is lifted, she is serious, determined, and radiant. She is ready for anything.

4.

Five peaceful years and then, with the sudden violence of a summer storm, the mood in the village changes.

In nearby Saint-Roch, a man from Quebec City gives a lecture on the subject of "the Jew." He speaks of the strangers in our midst, who look like us but are not like us, who care only for money and worldly things, who pile up material possessions but kill the soul. The next day, an old Jewish man from the town is punched in the back of the head. A dozen people must have seen it, but none of them will say who attacked him. The windows of the synagogue are broken.

In her house, Léa's parents stay up late, sitting at the kitchen table. There is an unusual impatience in her father's voice and an extra stitch of worry between her mother's eyebrows. She lingers while clearing up the plates so she can listen to them. The half-understood allure of adult conversation in a time of crisis: something is wrong, but she isn't sure what it is. If she is quiet, they will forget to tell her to go to bed.

Papa reads out loud. "Listen to what he says. 'The Jews of Poland and of Russia have destroyed whole villages with poisoned whisky... they give whisky to children... Beware the Jewish danger! Protect the purity, the sacredness, of our rural ways of life!'" He throws down the paper. "I've seen this before."

"*Un vrai antisémite*," Mama says. "It's a pogrom." Her tone is cynical and resigned.

The paper reports that the Jews in the countryside grow rich at the expense of the French-Canadians. Inside their houses, behind closed doors, the Jews are laughing at the good people of Quebec.

"They're talking about me," Papa says, grim-faced under his beard. The next week, with satisfaction, the paper notes that some of the villagers have decided to boycott the store.

And it is true: business is down. At the end of the day, Papa is exhausted even though barely anyone has come in to buy. What tires him most is waiting for the door to open, wondering about what they will do if it does not, how to pay suppliers so they can keep stocking the shelves, what will happen if the food goes bad before it is purchased. There are no margins, none; anything they lose comes right out of the family's mouths. There will be no new shoes for school, no new dress for the holidays, no brisket for the pot.

The village is divided. One morning, there is a gift of eggs and cake on their doorstep, the next day a brick through the window.

Harry comes home with a black eye and will not talk about it. The next day, someone Léa does not recognize hisses *Jew* at her as if it is her name and throws pennies—pennies which she picks up and spends before she gets home.

Papa stays up late going over the accounts, but he was never a fighter. In the morning his eyes are red, his shoulders are round. Defeat is all the world has ever offered him.

Mama is different. She should have been the businessman; she could sell sand to the Sahara. She bakes for a full day, she puts on her best dress, and then she makes the rounds, Annie at her apron strings for sympathy.

The next day, right when the store opens, Madame Parent is there at the door, Madame Langlois right behind her. They fill their baskets and are back the next day. They're not sure what they think about *the* Jews, but the Robacks are *their* Jews and have always treated them fairly.

Besides, it is a full hour on foot to the next general store.

5.

The neighbours are shocked that the girls do not attend school at the convent, but Mama is firm: she draws the line at the grey steps that lead straight to the man on the cross. Mama will not have them trained by nuns, those sisters who stalk the street, bristling in their stiff black robes. But the children have to travel all the way to Quebec City for the Protestant school. It is a long day, and Léa is often kept late. She is ten years old and chronically, incorrigibly defiant.

The French teacher is a Scot. She has a long nose and red cheeks, and when she speaks, she exaggerates her enunciation so she seems to grimace, stretching her lips in her narrow face. "Allai-zee," the teacher says on the first day. "*Le pendule mark neuve eurre.*"

Léa laughs. "That's not French!" she says. Miss Wood has her write on the board, "I will not be rude to my teacher," five hundred times. In English! She alternates the sentence in English and French, and Miss Wood sucks in her breath and tells her she must start all over again.

She skips class and strolls along Dufferin Terrace arm in arm with her new friend Annabelle, looking at the grey-blue, ever-changing, ever-moving river. A giggle of girls, they go to a Chaplin film at the cinema, marvelling at the little man who keeps stumbling in his too-big shoes and too-small hat. Léa leans back in her seat and laughs with her mouth wide open in the freedom of the dark theatre in the middle of the day, the moment even sweeter because she isn't meant to be there. Annabelle covers her mouth when she laughs, as if she is ashamed, and later cries when they are rebuked for missing class, her curls shaking on her shoulders. Léa is unrepentant.

When she is given letters of discipline for her mother to sign, she fakes the signature without thinking twice about it. Her forgery is bold and confident, breaking the line at the bottom of the page.

This dodge lasts longer than she expects. Finally, her parents are called in, and sit uncomfortably on the edge of the hard wood chairs as the principal berates them for their ill-behaved daughter. They look like peasants and sound like greenhorns, with their heavy shoes and thick accents. Sitting between them, she squirms and burns. Her father has so many books that his library puts the school to shame—how dare this woman speak to him as if he is an ignoramus! She hates to see them through the principal's narrowed, pale-blue eyes.

Her parents mumble apologies, and when she promises to do better it is only on their behalf, so they can get out of that airless room, clutching the last shreds of their dignity.

"Just try, Léa," her father says. He sounds miserable. Once again, she says that she will try, but her instinct is to rebel. When she opens her mouth, the devils fly out. She can't help herself.

In school, Annabelle is punished for writing with the sinister left hand.

"Jesus sits at God's right side," the teacher says, and smacks the offending hand.

"But Gabriel is God's left hand," Léa calls out, forgetting that Gabriel is also, after all, the angel of death.

"Léa," the teacher says. She has never once spoken her name except in a tone of warning. Léa shuts up—she is not afraid, only unwilling to fight lost causes. Annabelle is made to stand in the corner, looking at the wall, for the entire afternoon. Léa can see her shoulders shake. At the end of the day, she walks her to the train.

"You shouldn't let her do that to you," she says. "You should complain. There is nothing wrong with being left-handed. You need to learn to stand up for yourself."

Annabelle cries all over again, her eyes raw and pink.

"For goodness sakes." She buys Annabelle a Hershey bar and Annabelle eats it all in the station, still gently sobbing, her hands and mouth covered in chocolate.

Stupid Annabelle. Who, when they checked each other's hair for lice, dug her fingers in the top of Léa's head. When Léa asked if she had found a nit, she said she was looking for the horns.

Léa doesn't miss the two pennies. Like the rest of her family, she treats money as if it is meant to be given away. Her father says, who needs to be the richest man in the cemetery? To grow up in her family is to know that what you have, you share.

Annabelle hasn't learned that lesson. Léa wouldn't have minded a piece of that chocolate.

She gets accustomed to spending long hours of detention after school in a room that smells like dust and chalk, and she daydreams out windows that look like they have never been cleaned. She imagines leading armies like Joan of Arc, dressed in chain mail, climbing mountains, a lone explorer. Her punishment is that she should do nothing, and that of all things is most intolerable to her: she would scrub the outhouse, she would wash the floors, she would happily clean those windows. Later in her life, she will have trouble sitting still, resting, even sleeping. You can sleep when you're dead, she will say, and she will think of those hours of enforced idleness as some of the most frustrating of her life.

Across the ocean, a war begins. Troops march onto the movie screen before the main feature begins and feel as imaginary as the actors and actresses whose giant faces flicker in light and shadow, a hundred times larger than life but nowhere near as real. An English war, the French papers call it. Nothing to do with us. Canada has sent troops of volunteer soldiers, but few come from Quebec. Why should we fight foreign wars, the French papers say, how dare they ask us to fight British wars? And as for France, did they fight for us? Papa, who left Poland to get out of fighting the Czar's wars, entirely approves, not because he is a nationalist but because he is a pacifist. "There is no glory in war, Léa," he says, throwing down the newspaper. "To fight is to lose." He is too old for the draft even if they enforce it, but he goes to an anti-conscription protest in Quebec City, nonetheless. That Sunday, he finds his boys playing at being soldiers. "War is not a game," he says, and discards their rifles made of sticks and rubber bands. There are few rules in their family, but on this, he is unbending.

An internment camp is constructed in the Beauport Armoury and she can hear the men speaking German on their way to the logging camp where they are made to work. When she sees them on the sidewalk she tags along after them, and because of her Yiddish, she understands some of their conversations. They are amused by this girl, with her dirty knees, constant questions, and quick smile, but eventually their foreman notices her and tells her to stay away.

She dreams of the prisoners at night. They are walking ahead of her, and though she calls to them in Yiddish they will not turn around. Then one of them does, a man at the end of line, and he wears her father's face. She wakes up crying, which startles her, and all that day she clings to her father as if he really was in danger of being taken away from her. As if a dream was not a figment, but a prophecy.

6.

As she walks home from school, she feels a sharp shove between her shoulder blades and stumbles off the sidewalk. It knocks the wind out of her. As she is struggling for breath, she watches a young seminarian stride past. She knows him; she sees him in the station all the time. He pretends not to recognize her, as casual and dismissive in his violence as if he had swatted away a fly. He spits, and glances back at her, spiteful glee in his face.

At school, there is a low hum in her ears and a constriction in her chest. She should have kicked him right in the shins, she should have stomped on his toes, she should have spat right back. Her head is loud with the retorts she did not make, her eyes are hot with shame at her own passivity, and her fists open and close on air. She feels diminished, less herself. The teacher calls her name and she does not even hear it. All day, she makes careless mistakes, misses a stair, trips over her own feet. At dinner, she pushes food around her plate until her father says, "What happened, Léa?" and she cries into her mashed potatoes.

She has never seen her gentle father so angry. "It won't do," he says. He comes to the station the next morning and tells her to point out the student priest. He's not hard to spot, with his red hair and round red face.

"There he is," Léa says, "in the dog collar. They should put him on a leash." She feels calm and righteous, holding her father's hand. He seems in this moment like justice personified.

Papa marches up to the seminarian, who is eating a croissant. The front of his cassock is covered in crumbs.

"What is your name, young man?" Papa says.

The seminarian sputters. He is still chewing, and there are flakes of pastry stuck to his lower lip. Finally, he swallows, and draws himself straight. He is taller than Papa by a head. He glances at Léa, whose chin is lifted in defiant expectation, and back at Papa.

"I'm not giving my name to a damn Jew!"

And then Papa, who loves nothing more than peace, who sailed across the ocean to avoid the draft, raises his right arm and hits the young man in the jaw.

"Let's go, Léa." He takes her back home even though it is a school day. She is so proud she feels like she is walking on little pockets of air.

But then she looks up at her father's face and what she sees is regret. He has protected her, but it has cost him something. She should never have told him. She should have handled it herself. She spends the rest of the morning throwing pebbles at a frog, imagining it has the man's fat face. Imagining she hit him with her own strong fist.

After that, she notices a change in the seminarians, who no longer seem to think that God has granted them the entire street.

"They just weren't thinking," her father says.

Her mother says to Léa, "Papa told them he'd pull their credit."

The priests have a robust account: they need to be kept in candles and watered silks. Her father is not the first Jewish peddler to trade in liturgical garments. Either way, the students from the seminary keep their distance now, and she feels emboldened; she skips down the sidewalk, singing a song that is popular in school this year, "*Au revoir et merci.*"

On the streets of Beauport one of the nuns is looking a little too voluminous in her robes, her face round like the apple cheeks of the Virgin in the statue in the church. Then one day she is gone, and so is M. Vedette, the young priest who looks like Rudolph Valentino and must slick his hair back with Brylcreem, it is so shiny and wet.

"Boys only want one thing," her mother says, but she will not tell her what it is.

There is not a boy her age in town that she cannot beat in a race or in a fair fight, and she is unafraid. When boys snatch or smack or pinch, as they sometimes do to the girls walking by, she hits them, hard. "Don't get into fights," her mother says. She does not listen.

She is distracted by the new puddles of the first spring melt and by the delicate snowdrops blooming on the edge of the road, when Théo Tremblay steps right in front of her. He is the youngest of ten boys, and she has often seen his brothers collar and cudgel him as if he was their dog. Now he is the tallest in the family and is always looking for a fight.

He breathes raisin breath into her face, opening and closing his fists as if he is uncertain whether or not to punch her. He has a mole like a dark slug on his neck. He says, "You know, on Sunday, the priest told us that you killed Christ."

She laughs at him. She has beautiful teeth, and she bares them as if to bite him.

"I didn't kill Christ," she says. "What nonsense. The Romans killed him. I wasn't even alive. You tell your priest that he's wrong. Or if you want, I'll go tell him myself."

She steps on his toes deliberately as she passes him—she is wearing her heavy school shoes. For the rest of her walk, she jumps in every puddle.

When she tells her mother, her mother shrugs and says, "Let them believe what they believe, and we will believe what we believe."

But a shrug is not enough for Léa. She is not content to stay in her corner. Léa is a roar and not a whisper. One day she will show them they are wrong.

The next time Théo Tremblay sees her, he will cross to the other side of the street.

7.

She always knows when her mother is pregnant because there is a special apron that she wears, which enfolds her growing girth until the night—it always seems to be at night—the doctor is called and the bedroom door is closed and the younger children are sent to the neighbours. She lies in bed, her eyes open and her arms rigid at her side, and listens to the deep animal roar until there is a new cry, wavering and high—a voice that has just met the world—and then, blessedly, silence and sleep. She would like to throw the apron in the fire so she would never again hear those midnight cries, but it always disappears, folded into some trunk or drawer until one day Mama is wearing it again, and her arms no longer fit around her mother's waist. Harry and Léa and Annie and Rose and Lottie and Becca and finally two more boys, Joe and little Michael.

It is not a choice. Once she overheard her mother and her aunt Rose at the kitchen table. Her aunt had only three children, which, mysteriously, was true of some of the women who lived in cities but never of the women who lived in the country.

"How do you do it, Rosie? I have children every year, and you have three, and it's finished?" her mother said.

"But I don't do anything."

They were drinking tea. This pregnancy, Mama could keep nothing down. She vomited out the world. Five months in and there was less of her than when she started.

"Please, Rosie," Mama begged, "there must be something that can be done."

"I don't do anything," Rose said. And then, reluctantly. "It's Sam. He does something."

"Aha! What does he do?"

"I don't know, you'll have to get Moses to ask him."

But she does not, and the apron comes out again, wrapped around that womb which holds all of the trouble of a woman's life.

8.

On a stormy spring evening, Léa once again hears her mother's wails but this time there is no new small voice. Instead, her mother's cries change from guttural pain to a weeping that lasts for hours. In the morning, the cradle by the stove is empty.

The younger children come home with Madame Parent in the afternoon. She brings a new apron for Mama, ironed and folded. She brings a casserole for dinner, she boils water and makes tea and sits with Mama—who shuffled from the bed to the kitchen table around midday, and has been sitting there ever since, her head in her hands, as if she is turned to stone. The action of the small house moves around her as Joe and Michael tug on her skirt and try to get her help, her attention, her affection. Madame Parent puts her arm around Mama's shoulders. She whispers in her ear and holds both her hands on the table as they sit together in silence.

Madame Parent, who had eleven pregnancies but only has five children.

Her father covers himself with a tallis to pray that morning, and under the shawl Léa hears sobbing, not praying. When he takes off the straps of his tefillin his arm is bruised red and purple.

Her mother sits in the rocking chair for days, cradling her grief.

After the dead baby, Léa thought that certainly her mother was finished having children, but it takes more than saying you are finished. She was always such an active woman—all the women in the town had to be active. It was a requirement; just to keep a family fed and clean you needed to have enough tenacity and strength to clear the Augean stables. You needed to be ready to saddle the sea. Now her mother seems hidden in herself. She trails off in the middle of sentences, lies down in the middle of the day, lights the stove and forgets about the fire.

The baby is an abstract loss; Léa never even saw him. But she misses her fierce and competent mother.

Dr. Lachance comes to the house even though it is Christmas Eve. He knows Mama is not sleeping well, in part because it is so difficult to find a comfortable way to rest, in part because when she closes her eyes, she sees her baby's perfect, blue-tinged face, the full lips pursed as if to nurse.

"You're lucky to have children, Madame Roback, many women cannot have children," he says. "You must be strong for them. And do not despair, there will be another child soon."

Mama looks like she wants to weep. Instead, she says meekly, "But I have eight."

"And soon will have nine, I promise," he says, as if that were helpful.

The nine fruits of the spirit! Which are—Léa has memorized them at her school: Love, Joy, Peace, Patience, Kindness, Goodness, Faithfulness, Gentleness, Self-Control. And Jesus died in the ninth hour.

There is diphtheria in the countryside, and Dr. Lachance brings serum and injects them at the kitchen table, one by one. The spectre of illness so soon after the loss of the baby terrifies Mama, who alternates neglect and desperate, clinging care, which Léa minds much more than being left alone. She is too old to sit on her mother's lap.

When the special apron comes out again, Léa is furious and terrified. She cannot even look at her father, that gentle man, who has put his wife through this cyclical, brutal, precarious labour. This baby, thank God, does not die, though it takes her mother a long time to recover, her eyes always very far away, as if seeing not this baby, but the last one.

The baby's face is white and red when he cries, and lined like an old man's, but very, very soft. To cry means that you are alive.

Mama now stays up at night to make sure he is still breathing.

This time the doctor says, "Mrs. Roback, you mustn't have any more children."

"What can I do?" she says. "Talk to my husband."

He says, "No, no, no, you know what to do."

"Believe me," she says. "If I knew, do you think I would have ended up like this?"

Mama knows a woman who slept with her little daughter every night to keep from getting pregnant again, using the one child as prophylactic against another. Her priest told her she would go to hell for that. *Le bon Dieu* demands you open your legs and you shut your mouth. Mama saw her pushing an enormous stroller the next year—twins, can you imagine— and as she walked, she cried. The stroller was so cumbersome she didn't even have a free hand to wipe her own face.

The doctor looks around. Mama is still heavy from the birth, of course, but her face is a death mask, her eyes smudged with lost sleep. The house is squalid because they are too many—drying clothes hung on every surface, dirty dishes stacked, books piled on the floor, the smell of feet and the sour tang of dried milk.

"Very well, Mrs. Roback. Send me your husband, I will have a talk with him."

And there are no more children after that.

The new baby is Leo, the little lion. Golden Leo, last born, most beloved. Still, when Léa sees him swaddled in the crib by the stove, she thinks of the other one.

Mama won't leave this baby for an instant. She listens to him breathe when she is sleeping. When other people hold him, she watches with an untrusting, ravenous look, as if they will snatch him away. She sits long hours in the rocking chair, singing to him in a tuneless drone. It is as if she has forgotten she has a family outside of the infant she cradles in her arms.

Mama was only sixteen years old when she got married, eighteen when she had her first. Since then, her life has been only labour, from when she wakes up in the morning to when she falls into bed at night. Léa can see that everyone wants everything from her mother, all the time. The only time she can rest is when she nurses Leo, and then she looks like she is rocking her way in and out of memories, holding Leo's fingers, which are nearly translucent, and watching the pulse beat in the warm soft top of his head. She seems to breathe in his sweet and musky scent as if he could bring it all back—the dead baby, the lost years, and most of all that stupid girl of sixteen who walked into Oddfellows Hall wearing a white lace veil and had her whole life signed away, five thousand six hundred and sixty-one years after the day of creation.

9.

In Montreal, a landlord is suing his tenant for subletting his property to a Jew. A priest testifies in court that he has instructed his parish to ban Jewish tenancy. And at the church in Beauport, where daily miracles are reported, the *curé* repeats the same ban, forbidding his congregation to sell or rent their property to Jews, knowing there is exactly one Jewish family in town.

When it comes time for Monsieur Langlois to renew the lease on the general store, he delays. At last, the truth emerges: he is afraid of the priest, who has promised repercussions for those who defy him. Papa goes to the *curé* to ask for a deferral or exception, but the *curé* refuses.

Despite his gentleness, there is a passive stubborn defiance in Moses Roback which surprises his family: he will not be chased out. He finds another store to rent in the village. But he never feels as welcome.

Over Easter weekend, there are riots in Quebec City. Since the draft was first enforced in January, there is furious discontent in the streets. The military is called in; the rioters fire on the troops, and the troops fire on the crowd. Mama is afraid to send the children back to school, even after the protests have calmed down. These days, she is afraid of everything.

She is not doing well. She stays in bed most of the day, her skin has a greyish tinge, she forgets to gather the eggs in the yard, to do laundry on Thursdays, to put supper on the table. The children run wilder than ever, they eat bread dipped in sugar for supper and their clothes are dirty.

After a little while Harry takes over the kitchen again, but the house is a mess and Léa is useless as a housewife.

"It's too much," Mama keeps saying, and her eyes can't stay open.

Dr. Paquette comes and shrugs his shoulders. "I think she might just need a rest."

Uncle Abe comes from the city and says, "I think she might need a change."

It feels like a failure to pack up their lives to return to Montreal, with not much to show for it except so many more mouths to feed.

To spite the priest, Papa sells the business to a Jew from Quebec City.

10.

What Léa learns in Beauport.

To love nature. Spring summer autumn winter. And the countryside when the cherry trees are blooming and the wind blows pink confetti in her hair.

That you are the sum of your actions.

That most important in life is to do something. Not just to write a cheque, but to do something, anything good.

That she never wants her mother's life.

To speak French like a *Québécoise de souche*. Later on, in Montreal, when she speaks French, no one can believe she is a Jew. But the Jews don't speak French like that, they will insist. They will treat her as a miraculous curiosity, a wondrous pet, like a parrot that has learned to talk, and she will pretend to be flattered and not offended.

And when you are around priests, watch your ass.

Their last night in Beauport she goes outside, and it is the kind of cold that feels like purity. There is late frost on the ground, the sky is an endless black, each star a portal to another dimension. So beautiful, she thinks, how is it so beautiful? It isn't possible that the world is so beautiful.

She stays outside until the cold has turned her feet to fire.

11.

They can't afford a store in Montreal, so Papa starts a new business as a travelling salesman—a peddler, Mama says with some disdain—and is away all the time. Their new landlord does not want to rent his apartment to a large family, nor to a Jewish one, so Mama uses her substantial skills of persuasion and tells her she has only four children. When it's time to move in, she shows up with all nine. The landlord complains but leaves them alone. It is not hard to find tenants, but it is hard to find tenants who can pay. The apartment is small and in disrepair. There are holes in the ceiling and mice in the walls. The windows won't open and the doors won't close.

It is good to have Mama distracted inside the sweet fog of early motherhood, because it turns out that they have arrived in a city under siege. The flu from last spring has come back, this time bearing sharp teeth and claws. The first cases are reported around the Navy barracks in September. The sailors have brought the disease from Europe, and then they disperse all over the country by rail, vectors of an invisible illness which targets the young.

"Look at this, Léa," Harry says. He stabs at the newspaper with his fork. "You mark my words, Léa. This is only the beginning."

He thinks of himself as a doctor already. At sixteen, he is the proxy father, and at fourteen, she is the default mother. It doesn't suit either of them, though they both like telling people what to do.

Léa says, "Stop imagining the worst."

She loves Montreal. She can spend all day walking up the mountain to the lookout and through the winding paths of the cemetery, or down Saint Lawrence, watching the endless theatre of the street—a woman yelling out her window, leaning so far forward Léa is afraid she might tip herself out, a child learning to take his first steps in the crowded aisles of the fruit market, two dogs who have tangled their leashes and when released move like serpents, in sinuous ellipses, unlike any dogs she has ever known. Summer flies by in a parade of open hydrants and ice cream cones, overgrown yards and shady alleyways.

"I'm a natural cosmopolitan," Léa declares, and switches her allegiance from the country to the city, lording it over the younger ones that she was born in Montreal. She is a chameleon and takes on the texture of the busy streets and verdant alleyways the way she once inhabited the spirit of the river and the apple orchards. She is intoxicated by the life of the metropolis.

But the next week, the paper reports the first case in the schools.

"I told you," Harry says, and Léa sighs. It is tiresome when he is right. "The children should stay home," he says.

"And who's going to look after them?"

He shrugs his shoulders.

"Léa," Mama calls from the curtained cave of her bedroom, "Léa!" and Léa runs in alarm. "Léa, look at the funny face the baby makes when I do this," she says, and blows straight into Leo's face. He screws up his eyes and catches his breath, then dissolves into laughter.

Eight months old, and he shows no signs of crawling. Mama carries him in her arms like a lapdog, and he is at the peak of his chubbiness, round and dimpled, with golden hair.

"Mama, you scared me, I thought something was wrong," Léa says.

Mama replies, "What should be wrong? What's the problem? Whaaaaat's the problem?"—she is addressing the baby, who has puckered up his face as if contemplating a cry, and then starts laughing as soon as he has her attention again.

"Nothing's wrong, Ma," she says. "Everything is fine." She trips on a diaper, picks it up to wash, and listens to her mother babbling as she closes the door.

Nothing is fine, but her mother is in no state to know about it.

All week she reads the newspaper, and there is not much about the flu. There are more cases of the illness, but only among the military. The front pages are all devoted to the war, which they are winning, and she can feel the hum of anticipation in the streets.

On Monday, the front page of the paper shouts that Germany has asked for peace, but inside there is alarming news. The schools in Westmount have closed.

"I'm not going to say I told you so," Harry says, which is just like him.

The next day the city closes all the schools, the theatres, dance halls, the concert halls and movie houses. The churches are still open, and that will turn out to be a mistake. There is a Eucharistic Congress in Victoriaville, with 25,000 attendees, and as they drink the blood of Christ they take the infection into their bodies, bringing it back to their homes and congregations.

Their father is God-knows-where buying God-knows-what in the countryside; they're not even sure when he will be home.

"I'll break it to her," Léa says, and knocks softly on her mother's door. Mama is blowing rubbery kisses onto her baby's belly, so blind with love for her new child she cannot even see the rest of them.

"The schools are closed," she says, "there's a flu. The kids will be home, I'll keep them out of your hair. And you should be careful going out with the baby."

"We're always careful, aren't we, baby?" Mama says, and Léa shakes her head. This odd childish behaviour has something to do with the last pregnancy. It is unseemly, her mother so girlish and foolish, but the way she was after the dead baby—that was so much worse.

She has just discovered the city, and it is becoming a ghost town. It feels deeply unfair. She goes into the closet to cry quietly—it's rare, in that house, to have the privacy to cry—and then she washes her face and scrubs it dry a little too roughly, to punish herself. The groceries must be purchased and the kitchen must be cleaned. The dining room will be a schoolroom. And she will be a nursemaid and a teacher and a cleaner and a mother.

She rolls up her sleeves and gets to work.

12.

In the golden October sun, the sidewalks are busy and there is an air of carnival, despite the flu. Léa lingers at her errands. She has more liberty on the street than at home, where the demands are constant. Barbershops put their chairs out on the sidewalk, because fresh air is the best remedy against infection, and she passes a dozen men loitering and waiting their turns as the barber, with a bowl of foamy water at his feet, shaves his customers with a straight razor. They are talking about what everyone is talking about. She slows down to listen.

"Soak a cotton ball in alcohol and add chloroform. Put it between your teeth and breathe in for fifteen minutes. That'll knock out the infection."

"I heard a mustard poultice helps. You have to apply it when it's very hot and have another ready for when it cools."

"There's only one thing that will do the trick, boys. Two quarts of warm water and a tablespoon of salt. You'll need a syringe—a big one. A copious enema! Continue until the pain is gone."

"I have a better idea to take away the pain," says the barber, "and it rhymes with quicker." He picks up the glass of water he's been using to rinse the blade, mimes a shot, and they fall against each other, laughing.

Liquor licenses were suspended last May, but those who know, know.

That night, she and her sisters walk over to the Windsor Hotel to hear the man with the megaphone voice. They don't have tickets, but he was going to perform outside before the official show. They are met by a disappointed, milling crowd. The event has been cancelled in order to keep people from gathering in groups, but this is no better, as they breathe frustration into one another's faces.

Lottie is beside herself with disappointment. She is only nine. Léa gives her a piggyback ride most of the way, and she can feel her falling asleep, Lottie's wet face pressed between her shoulder blades, her heels banging against Léa's hips. So heavy to carry, and it's a long way home.

Many of the windows they pass are marked with a seal of red.

The next time she visits the fruit and vegetable market, supplies are low. Some shoppers are wearing saggy fabric masks, and their narrow eyes look around the crowded aisles with fear and suspicion. Léa feels the nakedness of her unmasked face. She buys a dozen soft, worm-eaten apples from the bottom of the barrel and a bag of potatoes, pays quickly, and hustles home, hugging the potatoes to her chest.

"There is nothing to eat!" Lottie roars, and Léa tosses her an apple just to keep her mouth shut. Papa is still not home. They are starting to hear worrisome stories about the countryside, whole families found collapsed around the stove. In the streets she can smell camphor, though there is none to be had in the pharmacies. When she gets home, the table is sticky, there are crumbs all over the kitchen floor, Rose and Becca are fighting, and little Michael has managed to shut himself in the closet. Harry has gone to study—where, she doesn't know, the libraries and the university are now closed.

"I can't go on like this," she says, but she rescues Michael, who is sleepily oblivious on a heap of clothes in the closet. She pulls the girls apart, gets the broom, wipes the table down with a wet cloth, and starts supper. Mama walks in the front door with Leo, blithe and carefree, with roses in her cheeks.

37

"I'm going to put him down for his nap," she announces, and vanishes into her bedroom.

This is the new pattern of the days: Léa gets up, makes breakfast for the children, tries to get the older ones to do their schoolwork, forages in the barren city for supplies, and comes home to cook and clean again. Harry comes and goes on his own schedule, just like a man. Annie helps, Rose and Lottie fight the whole day long, Becca cries, Joe is quiet and an angel, and everyone forgets about Michael until he is found under the table eating fallen crusts of bread, or in the bathroom throwing onions into the toilet and spilling talcum powder all over the floor. Everyone tries not to think of Papa and what a bad time it is to be a door-to-door peddler.

On the fifth day without school, right before the Sabbath, there is a knock at the door. It is Papa, dusty and panting. Léa opens her mouth to ask where he has been, but he is too excited to listen.

"Look at what I found!" He has lugged a gramophone up the stairs; the cabinet is as tall as his waist. "There's a box of records downstairs," he says, and Lottie runs down to see.

"I found it in a village outside Quebec City, I couldn't believe how little they were asking! You don't even want to know how I got it home."

"Papa," Léa says, and then she swallows. She cannot tell if the ache in her chest is disappointment, anger, or relief. "Papa, we were so worried." He chooses not to hear her, and Lottie is back upstairs with the records, and they are all on their knees leafing through them. She gives up, sits with the others, and takes a turn looking through the albums.

"The concert halls are closed," Papa says, "but we have our very own concert hall!" He is parroting the ads for gramophones—they have never been to a concert. Léa bites her lip at the sweetness but also the futility of the ways he cares for them, when the pantry is getting empty and they are down to a final fistful of quarters.

But in the coming weeks, while the weather is poor and they are stuck indoors, it is soothing to have the gramophone playing. The music is like the picture book they have of Orpheus taming the hearts of wild beasts. Annie and Lottie waltz around the living room; Michael lies in front of the machine, asks for Beethoven, and falls asleep on the floor.

13.

The churches and the synagogues close. The archbishop has agreed to limit the tolling of the bells for the dead to before noon, or they would ring all day. There are hourly processions of hearses winding their way up to Mount Royal cemetery. Léa runs the makeshift schoolroom and also scrubs potatoes, chops onions, scours the city for milk, which is nowhere to be found—too many farmers and delivery men sick. There is less learning every day, and she lets it go; the hours and the lessons trickle through her fingers, they no longer seem important. She allows the children to play in the alleyways until dusk and insists that they gargle with warm water and salt when they get home. Mama has emerged from her fog just enough to look after the littlest ones. Papa goes out every morning with his sales case, but it's unclear where he goes and why. Sometimes when he comes home his pockets are filled with apples and onions. He has a robust cheerfulness that often looks like denial, and he has rebranded his stock: wool underwear to keep you from the chill, quilted jackets for convalescents.

He adds Bovril to his case, claiming it increases the defensive forces of the body against epidemics. "Then leave some for us," Lottie demands.

"I have something better," he says, fishing a chocolate bar from an inner pocket. Léa holds the square on her tongue and lets the rare sweet bitterness dissolve very slowly.

Every day, in Montreal alone, there are more than a hundred dead. There are rumours of a shortage of coffins. The papers say it is better, then worse, then the same. The police have prepared little leather satchels for the houses of the sick, the kind schoolchildren carry, each equipped with a gingham smock, a cotton mask, a bottle of disinfectant. When they deliver them, they stay to help build a fire, and leave as quickly as they can. On Sunday, the churches ring the call to worship at half past nine, and the priest of each congregation enters an empty sanctuary to offer Mass to the silent pews. After Mass, they take to the streets, bringing the host door to door. Their automobiles are their chapels, doorways their altars.

Half of the obituaries in the paper are for boys killed in action, the other half for those taken by the flu. Léa monitors temperatures, stuffy noses, coughs. In a house of nine children, it would be more surprising to find everyone well.

"Thanks God," her father says, but his eyes are dark wells of fear. He has brought home smelts wrapped in greasy newspaper, and the house stinks of fish for two days. She is grateful for the open windows and the good weather; she is glad to be able to send the children outside. Conditions of perfect hygiene, the health officer instructs, but that's a laugh.

Harry catches Michael and his friends sharing a peashooter in the alley, passing the straw back and forth, taking turns shooting each other with little balled-up wads of paper. Michael has a fit when Harry snaps it in two. "It's not mine!" he shouts.

"Then don't put it in your mouth! You need to be more careful!" No bobbing for apples and no public gatherings this Hallowe'en. The children were so looking forward to their first Hallowe'en in the big city.

The following afternoon, Michael comes home complaining of a headache. His skin is warm and dry, and he is shaking with chills. Léa tells Annie to boil water for a compress and wraps him in blankets. There is nowhere to isolate him so she makes him a bed on the floor of the closet; she has heard about families where the sickness spreads quick as a wildfire. She gives him a teaspoonful of castor oil, puts mustard powder into a bucket of hot water and has him soak his feet.

"Do we have lemons?" she calls to Annie in the kitchen, but they do not, so she has him gargle with water and salt and sends him to lie down, telling the other children to stay away. She feels very distant from herself as she lays the back of her hand against his forehead again and again and brings him glass after glass of water, as though these small actions might save him. She feels the pressure of all of the deaths behind the closed doors of the city, knocking on her own doorway. A tunnel in her memory opens up to the night the baby died, and she refuses, she refuses to enter it.

He sleeps twelve hours, and in the morning his eyes are clear and he bounces right out of his makeshift bed. She feels like the spirit of death has brushed their house and has decided to pass over. She watches him carefully that day, and startles at every sneeze, but he really does seem well. Miracle.

The streetcars run, but they are mostly empty. There are restless knots of people in front of their apartment buildings trading rumours and swapping eggs for sugar. The grocers have taken their bins and racks of fruits and vegetables off the sidewalk, on the instructions of the health authority, and the streets look deserted. The stores close early.

She passes a cluster of delivery boys. Their white cotton masks are hanging from their ears as they share a cigarette.

"They're lying," one says. "It's not a flu, it's the plague. It's the Black Death."

"The purple death," another says, taking a long drag on the cigarette. "I saw them taking out a body and the sheet slipped off her face. She was bright as a plum." Léa backs away.

That night she has amethyst nightmares. She dreams of the dead baby, but his skin is violet and he is so small he keeps slipping out of her arms. She dreams that her parents are walking away from her, and that the distance between them keeps growing, and that she calls and calls to them, but they do not turn around. She wakes up exhausted and soaked in sweat. She will need to do a wash today, alongside everything else.

And still the front pages of the newspaper shout war, war, war, and so the world outside goes on and fights, even as soldiers collapse in their barracks in febrile sweats and Navy ships carry home sailors who survived the trenches only to lie down in their bunks and never rise again. They are claiming that the peak of the plague is near. If this goes on much longer, she will lose her mind.

Montreal has its first snow of the year, wispy meagre flakes that melt as soon as they hit the ground but nonetheless are the first portents of winter.

Léa has her birthday in a city suspended. People are not even mourning yet, just holding their breaths. She is fifteen, but she feels a hundred.

14.

It is difficult to care about the war when an invisible enemy is breathing down your neck. The city decorates Sainte-Catherine Street to bolster patriotic feeling and raise money and morale, hanging bunting from the lights and decorating the storefronts with the colours of the allied nations. They walk over to see the Birks window, where there are two enormous panoramic paintings, one of soldiers going over the top and the other of a solitary Frenchman standing beside a shattered stone house in the countryside.

"He looks constipated," Harry says, and leans over to read the artist's name, a Mr. Dwight Franklin. "Victory loans to keep the bowels moving!"

There are a lot of people in the streets, maybe too many. Something about this national display leaves Léa cold. What a waste of time and effort. Isn't there enough suffering in this life without needing to play at toy soldiers with real lives?

"They say they are opening the schools again in Toronto," Harry says.

"Thank God."

Delivery vans are being used as ambulances. They advertise their business on the side: Crown Laundry, McKenna Flowers, Superior Coal, Society Clothes. But their speed gives them away. They are carrying the sick and the dying through the empty streets. By contrast, hearses continue to wind their way slowly up the mountain path; the dead are past the need for haste. The funeral homes ask people not to order large and elaborate shells for their coffins, it doubles the time for the burial and creates too much work for the already overburdened gravediggers. They sell only plain caskets, and limit the size, but nonetheless there is a shortage, and some bodies are wrapped in sackcloth and put straight in the ground.

But the cases are slowing down. The snow has receded, and the air has the crisp brightness of a fine November; the city stretches tentatively in the sun. There are more people on the street again, and fewer masks. She walks the girls to Dominion Square and sees a motley parade of children on tricycles and scooters. There must be thirty of them, different ages, all under ten. Lottie and Becca run to join them. There is a nun watching, arms folded over her grey habit, and Léa says, "What's this, then?"

"It's the emergency children's home," the nun says. "Their parents are too sick to look after them. We take them here to play every afternoon."

Becca finds a bicycle and pedals in circles as fast as she can. Lottie grabs the hands of a little girl, and they jump up and down just for the pleasure of it. Children will play. Léa feels sick, watching them spin.

When they get home, she sends them straight into the bath, and Lottie cries because she confiscates the velvet ribbon that one of the children gave her and throws it in the trash.

The city is disinfecting the schools in anticipation of opening them again. They worry if they open the cinemas first, the theatres will be full of children and the epidemic will feed off their festive proximity, their infectious laughter. They mandate open windows on the streetcars even though the drivers complain of drafts.

The Victory Loan campaign has wanted a parade for months, but the health authorities have hedged on permission. But for a week now, flu cases have dropped. The churches will reopen for Thanksgiving and the parade will be allowed to proceed. There will be live music, and mounted police, there will be Indian chiefs and the Grand Orange Lodge in full regalia. The Zionist Society of Canada will have their own float. The children pore over the list, strategizing about where best to stand, but when Monday comes the crowds are so thick it takes an hour just to walk to La Fontaine Park. They go slowly, shoulder to shoulder in the mass of marchers, sirens blaring and horns honking, flags at every window. Léa has Joe by the hand, Michael on her shoulders; he keeps banging her head like a victory drum. Over the shoulder of the man in front of her, she sees the big black letters on the headline, EXTRA EXTRA, and with her free hand she taps him on the shoulder. His breath is already thick with whisky, at ten in the morning.

"What does it say?"

"It's over," the man says. "They signed the armistice. We won!" He sighs. "What a morning."

An airplane is somersaulting over the park, diving so low it threatens to hit the treetops.

On their way home, they pass the Zionists' float and Léa cannot believe it. A group of men dressed as Maccabees; she recognizes their faces from the neighbourhood, feels mildly shocked by their naked knees and loose tunics. Behind them, they have built a replica of the temple of Jerusalem. The warrior Bar Kokhba jostles elbows with General Allenby. Mr. Balfour struggles for balance at the top of the steps as he unrolls a giant scroll.

"Hail Britannia, Liberator of Palestine!" the banner reads.

And there, finally, is her father, whom she's been looking for all day, with a shield made out of a trashcan lid, and wearing her mother's bathrobe, smiling more broadly than she has seen him smile for weeks, no, maybe since they lost the baby. She waves at him but he doesn't even see her. He is marching in step with the Maccabees and his eyes are fixed on victory.

When they get home, Becca has broken the strap of her shoe and Joe's mouth is bright blue from his sucker and Michael's gum is stuck in his hair and needs to be cut out, but they are happy for the first time in weeks and so tired they can barely keep their eyes open for their baths.

"What do we do tomorrow?" Joe says as he is drifting off, thinking of the airplanes and fireworks and costumes and floats, and imagining a parade that extends into a future in which winter never comes.

Léa says, "Tomorrow? Tomorrow you go to school!"

There is a brightness and a lightness in her chest. Far better the servitude of the classroom than this endless domestic drudgery! Joe's disappointment is no match for her elation. She falls asleep to the inconstant explosions of cap guns and homemade fireworks.

In the morning the street looks like they have lost a war rather than won it.

15.

For the first time, they live near their extended family, and that is a snarled web of obligation and delight. Papa's mother, Baba Roback, lives on Norbert Street. They can see the whole mountain from her living room window—a precious and tender emerging green in the early spring, robust and cloaked with leaves in the summer, a conflagration of scarlets and golds in the fall, and then naked and black and white in winter, which lasts as long as all the other seasons put together.

But Baba rarely looks out the window. Her eyes are turned inward, towards God. She is a religious fanatic. She will not even have her photo taken, lest the image of the divine is stolen from her face.

Léa suspects that Baba Roback believes God is made in her image, rather than the other way around.

Baba Roback is a kvetcher, a yeller, a crier, she is a whole horn section of laments. Papa is loyal to his mother, but when Léa asks him what it was like growing up in her house, a pained look passes over his face and he says, "It was loud."

She has never once heard her father yelling. She has never met a more gentle man.

Uncle Abe says when he was a boy, Baba would want him to pray, pray, pray, so he was often late to school, running through the streets of the Plateau with tsitsis and peyos, fringes and forelocks flying. Baba was a good cook but he frequently went without breakfast. *Zog vayter zog vayter*, keep saying, keep saying, keep praying, she'd urge him, even as he watched the minutes tick by on the clock, felt the hungry pit in his stomach yawn open. The apartment was covered with a gauzy layer of dust, and the windows hadn't been cleaned for so long that it was always overcast, even when the sun was shining. The apartment smelled like bread, but she wasn't baking. It was the brewery down the street, belching yeast into the air, the odour so thick you could almost taste it.

She would not read a Yiddish story or a Yiddish newspaper, she said they were full of lies. But Baba Roback had a gift for languages. She knew hundreds of folk songs in Yiddish, Polish, and Russian. She had a beautiful voice and listening to her sing was a master class.

When Avrum—now Abe—left the city to go to university, he would not trust the books he could not pack to his holy, sloppy, erratic mother, who was likely to burn them. Instead, they lived with his father on Rivard Street, in special glass-doored bookcases bought just to store them. His father was illiterate—he signed his name with an X and spoke better French than Yiddish—but still he took those books on as a sacred duty. He would not even let his new wife touch them, but every week would take them out and dust them himself, one by one, with the same reverence Baba Roback showed when she kissed the prayer book.

Léa sometimes goes with her mother to Zayde Roback's to help him write letters to his daughter, her aunt in Buffalo. He has an inkwell and a blotter on his desk and it is her job to fill the well and to clean the nib after they are finished.

Even the work of dictating the letter exhausts him. He paces up and down the living room, searching for the right words. He calls her mother by her Yiddish name, Faigele.

"Tell her, Faigele," he says with urgency. "Write it down just like I say it right now, that I hope, I hope"—he stalls, and strokes his beard as if the words are hiding in there. "Tell her that she should come by us to stay soon, *mirtz hashem*,

49

and also, if she wants, I can send her some money to make a visit."

The stale air of the apartment—has he never opened a window?—makes Léa restless. She opens up the glass bookcase to browse the shelves and little white pellets roll onto the floor. Zayde has put moth balls on the shelves to protect the books and the room now stinks of formaldehyde.

"*Lozn es aleyn,* Léa," he says, and closes the door. Leave it alone.

He keeps those books as if they were never meant to be touched or read.

Uncle Abe is at Harvard now. One day, he says, he will write an entire book of his mother's expressions. His *mamaloshen*, his mother tongue, his mother's tongue. His own book will join the others behind the glass on his father's shelves. This language, sometimes as sweet as honey and sometimes a whole swarm of stings.

16.

At sixteen, she goes to work. No choice: the family needs the money. She interviews at the laundry and Mrs. Allen, who is married to the owner, looks her up and down, confused by her name and lack of an accent. "Are you English, then?" she asks.

"No, ma'am," Léa says, "I'm Jewish." Mrs. Allen raises an eyebrow, plucked and pencilled to a needle-thin arc.

"How nice for you," she murmurs. Léa almost walks out, but she needs the work.

They start her on the floor. The ironing must be done by hand: hardest are the fashionable pleated skirts. Each fold must be straightened and starched, one by one. The girls work at long tables, facing each other in rows, and she is clumsy with the iron. She becomes accustomed to the purple welts on her arms, and to her blistered and raw fingertips.

It is always warm in the warehouse, and she likes the smell of bleach and Ivory soap, but she gets headaches from the close air and the chemical fog. She starts to see drifting spots as if those stains from the laundry have transferred from the fabric to her field of vision. She wears her hair up to prevent it from being caught in the wringer. A girl's fingers are crushed while she is feeding sheets into the mangle. These damn machines, they just keep on grinding. The bosses don't seem to care. It's cheaper to replace a girl than to make the floor safe.

She makes eight dollars working six days a week and brings it home. When they move her to reception, she does not get a raise, but the work is easier. She sits behind a desk; she can even read in the quiet hours. The nicer the clothes the ruder the client, she notices, though the most beautiful clothes are dropped off by servants and she never sees their owners at all. They are silken ghosts, visions of luxury outlined in their satin bodices, their beaded dresses, the tiny buttons on their blouses, their spotless gloves. White kid gloves by the dozen! Chiffon robes! Imagine the servants they must have in those homes on the mountain.

There are also some friendly clients, especially from the theatres nearby, who bring in their costumes as well as their own clothes, visions in velvet and brocade.

The prostitutes dress well, though not as well as the madams. At the laundry, they make no distinction. Rich and poor alike soil their clothing; their job is to take what is dirty and return it spotless.

In heaven, the angels only wear white.

Even her managers have managers, all the way up to the top, a man she has only glimpsed twice, who looked at her like she was a spot on his impeccable suit. And in turn, he answers to the priest, who answers to the bishop, who answers to the pope, who answers only to God. They tell the girls their goal in life is only to serve. To serve! Rewards will come later, in heaven. But Léa doesn't buy that pie in the sky when you die nonsense. Like hell. This life is the only life, and this life is her own.

Free of school curriculum and school censorship, she reads only authors on the Index, books banned by the Catholic Church. Flaubert. Montaigne. Anatole France. Balzac, Zola, George Sand, Stendhal. When the entire corpus of an author's work is forbidden, the index says, *opera omnia*. When it is only their body of fiction, *opera omnia fabulae*. When the authors are unspeakable, they are not listed at all: it is as if they do not exist. Nietzsche is in this category, and Schopenhauer. Karl Marx is also not on the list but she does not know if that is because he is unspeakable or because he is permitted. Anyway, she has not herself yet begun to read Marx, though what she hears about his work reminds her of her father's generosity. His socialism is instinctive and natural.

In addition to novels and poetry, she likes theatre, cinema, visits to the museum. She likes cloche hats and headbands and dropped waists and ribbon belts. She cuts her hair *à la garçonne*. She likes tennis and walks on the mountain and Outremont Park.

She reads *Madame Bovary*: "For him the universe did not extend beyond the circumference of her waist."

She reads Zola: "I would rather die of passion than of boredom."

She reads Stendhal: "I love her beauty, but I fear her mind."

Her body is late to change, and she retains the androgynous wiriness of a girl. For half a year, she washes the mottled monthly stains of her underwear in secret, until her mother finally notices and points her to the stash of belts and napkins, which she hates. At night, she presses her legs together and longs for something, she isn't certain what it is. After work, she walks the city in a restless reverie, loving it all, still wanting more.

One day at work a regular client, Adele from His Majesty's Theatre on Guy Street, sees her reading a copy of a play by Molière and tells her there's a job opening in the box office. She should bring in an application.

"Why take in the dirty laundry of these wealthy women," she shrugs, "when you could live the life of the *theatre*? You're too good for this, Léa."

Adele: grey eyes, red hair, slim as a licorice whip. She comes from somewhere outside the city and never talks about it. It's as if she was born the day she walked into the theatre. Léa has never before met anyone so self-made.

The theatre! She has been to His Majesty's for the Sunday concerts of the Canadian Grenadier Guards. They play military marches, but they also play Wagner, Meyerbeer, Saint-Saëns, and the three B's—Bach, Berlioz, and Beethoven. Since her father brought home the gramophone in the year of the terrible flu, she has loved music with an ardour that borders on worship. She likes to watch the crowds lined up waiting for the doors to open, men in top hats and women in furs, but she is even more drawn by the glimpses she gets of the musicians and the actors slipping in and out of the back doors—incognito in street clothes before a rehearsal, or truant in full paint and costume on a break during the performance, sneaking a cigarette in the alleyway.

Mr. Evans interviews her. He has grey teeth, a nervous sniff, a lopsided smile, and dandruff on the shoulders of his jacket. "I don't see your phone number on the application," he says, and leans towards her. "Is that to keep the mashers away?" She crosses her arms and does not return the smile. Mr. Evans leans back, all business again. "You can start on Monday," he says.

Adele is waiting outside the office. "Did he make a pass at you?" she says.

They both laugh.

"He's like a mouse," Adele says. "Just stomp your foot and show your teeth, and he'll go back to his little hole."

"I can handle it," she says.

"Oh, I have no doubt."

Since she was a child, she has known how to dodge stray hands, impudent stares, bold questions. How to stare at the roof of the tram car when pressed too close. How to step back with her heel, hard, on the way out the door as a small act of revenge.

She will miss the girls at the laundry, and she will miss some of the clients, especially the drivers who liked to crack jokes while waiting for their deliveries.

On Monday: The judge says to the prisoner, what did you hit the man with? The prisoner says, a tomato. A tomato! The judge says. The man's been in the hospital three months. The prisoner says, well, it had a can around it.

On Tuesday: There was a robbery in the backyard last night. Two clothespins held up a shirt.

On Wednesday: Why were the trousers not allowed in school? They were suspended.

On Thursday: Did anyone tell you, you look like Helen Black? But you'd look worse in white.

She will miss one driver in particular. He is French-Canadian and slender, with black hair that falls over his eyes, a goatee that makes her think of pirates and romantic poets, and a chipped front tooth. It is fair to say that when he comes to drop off or pick up clothes, he lingers. He leans on her desk and it seems like something is always on the tip of his tongue.

On her last day, a Friday: Do you serve lobsters? We serve everyone!

Anyway, he can find her if he's interested. Anyway, he never does.

17.

His Majesty's Theatre is a fantasy of excess a world away from the laundry floor: red plush seats and marble floors, crystal chandeliers and lights that catch and glitter on the diamonds around women's necks. The crème de la crème of Montreal society—a French phrase for an English elite, some graced with the titles of British nobility. They walk over from their houses in the Golden Square Mile or they are chauffeured in limousines. The younger and thriftier clients arrive with the Deluxe Cab Company, exclusive to His Majesty's. They fill the house on Friday and Saturday nights and often show up late, after dinner in the Palm Room at the Ritz, laughing loudly, a display to rival the stage.

Box seats cost three dollars, but Léa is accustomed to coming with the plebs on Wednesdays and to Saturday matinees, which are only fifty cents. Now, once the box office has closed, she can attend any night there is space, sliding into an empty spot in the darkened theatre. Her salary isn't much, but she gets big tips to help the wealthy find even better seats, and she is expert at locating an empty box overlooking the stage, or a vacancy in the front row.

She is not much younger than the actors and actresses. They still treat her like a kid, or like a pet. They offer her chocolates from the boxes they have been given by fans and hangers-on and pass on flat glasses of champagne that have been sitting on their dressing tables undrunk. Better yet, they offer anecdotes and advice. They sweep through for two or three weeks, arriving on special cars on the train with the sets and costumes which dress each stage for performance, and then the wind blows them to the next destination. She likes their instant shallow charisma—they are actors, after all, and take pride in the speed at which they can make you fall in love—and quickly she learns to enjoy their blandishment and their easy charm and to not take it too seriously.

The women at the theatre understand pleasure. They are specialists. Their hands are soft, their nights are their own.

Adele takes Léa dancing on the roof of the Normandie Hotel, and shows her the foxtrot and the Charleston, the quickstep and a dance called the black bottom. She teaches her to break a leg and mooch around, to reach for a Lucky instead of a sweet. Léa still lives at home, but when her family is getting up she is going to bed, when they come home she is leaving for work. She is having so much fun.

"Now all you need is a boyfriend," says Adele, who is juggling three. Léa isn't so sure. Her new freedom is delicious, and her passions are her own: words, art, theatre, she is in love with everything. But a boyfriend—a boyfriend sounds like the end of all adventure. No thanks.

Revues and musical theatre are the most popular shows. After that, operettas and the occasional opera. The shows come north right after they play Broadway. The actors stay in the Corona Hotel next door, and they drink at the Frolics, at the Venetian Gardens and the Palais d'Or. The first big show of the fall season is *Shuffle Along*, with its all-Black cast and chorus. She knows it's a hit when she hears the audience whistling on their way out—"I'm just wild about Haarry—and Harry's wild about me!"

In March, Nikita Balieff brings his Russian revue from Moscow, and every night introduces it with the same speech in broken English—"Goot efening letties and gentlemen—I spik bad English but I gif you my wort in twenty or tirty years I will spik better Eenglish and you spik Russian."

She is in the hallway outside his dressing room when he leans out, wrapped in a crimson velvet robe. "I'd like a corkscrew, please," he says, "and a pitcher of water, and some wineglasses."

His English is crisp and courteous. For a moment she thinks this is the impersonation, and the broken English of the stage must be his real voice.

"Right away," she says, as soon as she finds her tongue.

"Much obliged," Nikita says, and winks. He is in the middle of taking off his makeup, and he looks half a gentleman, half a clown.

This is the reason Léa is the perfect audience: for all that she has seen of offstage life, she is perpetually, joyfully naive. You can pull the same rabbit out of a hat a hundred times, and she will gasp every single time.

To work for the theatre is to learn to want more. The actors tell her about New York, about Paris, London, Berlin. When they see her reading at the box office, they tell her she seems smart, that she should go study. She tries acting a little, practising monologues when she thinks she is home alone. In the middle of her speech, Harry walks into the kitchen to make a sandwich. Rose interrupts, making rude comments on her performance. Michael asks her where the scissors are. It is impossible to concentrate, so she gives up, saving her practice for slow hours at the theatre.

So many of the theatre-goers are regulars; she expects to see them two or three times a week, and when they do not appear she worries about them. Lucien is one of her favourites. "What eyes," he says the first time he meets her. "Blue as cornflowers! And what a lovely little collar. Sapphire is your colour, darling." He sprinkles compliments everywhere he goes, speaks with his hands, walks like a dancer.

Lucien has a little atelier on Mackay Street, near his friend Émile Phaneuf, who makes the most beautiful hats. "You should come to our salon, Léa," he says, "it's all bookworms, just like you." He has noticed that she always has a novel on the counter or on her lap, and he has started to bring her books by authors she has never heard of before—Rimbaud, Gide, Colette. He has just been in Paris, and frequently travels back and forth to Europe and to New York City to buy the fabrics he can't find in Montreal, and to bring home books alongside the brocades.

That night, at Lucien's exquisite apartment, Léa sits between a poet in a satin evening coat and a cabaret singer in a backless gown. She eats oysters for the first time, with a silver fork, and shivers as she swallows. She can smell the sea. They stay up late, listening to records by Beethoven and Bach.

As it gets later, they switch to ragtime. Lucien dances with Émile, slim piano player hands on his narrow hips. Léa spins in circles on her own.

Lucien and Émile are both wonderful cooks, they know how to sew, they know how to dance. It takes her a few visits to understand that they are not roommates with exceptional domestic skills, they are a couple, and unlike any other couple she has ever known. Or perhaps not. A distant cousin came to visit them in Beauport once, and her parents had a whispered, intense conversation when he showed up with a man about his age, both of them wearing the most perfectly fitted suits. They were as unexpected in the countryside as a pair of peacocks striding across the corn fields, she couldn't keep her eyes off them. Her parents were, as ever, gracious, but her grandmother, who was visiting, was more rude than usual and afterwards said something Léa didn't understand: where was the little bird? She understands now, and is ashamed at the memory of her grandmother's cruelty.

Lucien and Émile are so cultured, harmonious, remarkably in love, in the little world they have crafted inside their apartment, where art, affection, and beauty are the norm. She falls a little in love with both of them. They make her world wider.

"You must see Paris," Lucien says, "you'll love it."

Émile says, "Wait! This is what you'll wear as you stroll along the Seine."

He takes out one of the hats he has constructed, a black straw fedora with silken burgundy poppies. He adjusts it on her head.

"You are fascinating in that hat, Léa," he says.

She looks at herself in the gilded mirror, Émile hovering behind her.

"Dazzling," Émile says, "as if it was made for you."

She feels a pinch of regret as she puts the hat down on the table and pats her hair back into place. She knows how much they charge for those bits of straw and silk, and it would pay rent on a nice apartment for a month. She sees Lucien's eyes flicker towards her; he smiles, and she blushes and looks away.

On her birthday, there is a square white box wrapped in a burgundy ribbon at her spot at the table. Her hands tremble as she opens it. Émile and Lucien watch like proud parents as she puts the hat on.

"I can't believe it," she says, blushing from her neck to her forehead. "For me? It's so beautiful."

"Next, Paris," Émile says.

18.

When she opens her rejection letter from McGill Léa is standing outside the theatre. Perhaps it should not come as a surprise. The university has begun to pull back from admitting both women and Jews. She tells herself she doesn't need them, gives herself a little shake, and stands up straighter. Still, it is terribly unfair.

Madame Dax, in town for a French revue, is having a smoke on the sidewalk and notices Léa struggling to compose herself.

"What's the matter?" she says.

Léa, trying to keep her voice light, says, "Nothing, just a letter." It has been a long week.

Madame Dax has been in the business for nearly twenty years and can fill in for nearly any role except that of an ingenue. She takes the letter from Léa's loose grasp, and glances over it.

"Every time you get a rejection, you need to put yourself out there, right away, before you have the time to think about it. May I?" She balls the letter up and tosses it in the gutter. "Forget them. You know what you should do?" She widens her musical-comedy eyes. "You should apply to my hometown, Grenoble! There's a wonderful literature department there, I can help you with the application, you'll love the city. You can see Mont Blanc from the streets—it's sublime."

Émile has always claimed to be a bit of a prophet. Grenoble is close enough to Paris. Léa breathes in deeply, and feels her chest expand, her heart lift.

Madame Dax is heading home to Grenoble to see her mother after the show finishes, and she sends Léa the application. Léa does not exactly decide to keep it secret, but she holds the possibility to herself over the long months. It is the first day of December when she finally gets a response. "You have a letter from France," Lottie says.

"It must be from my friend," Léa says. She snatches it away, puts it in her pocket, and won't open it until she is alone.

Shabbat dinner is the only time the entire family gathers together.

"Good news," she says as soon as the candles are lit, and there is forced cheer in her voice. "I've gotten into university! In France!" she adds, because not telling feels like lying.

Her mother has forgotten to take off her apron after cooking, and seizes the edges of the fabric with both hands, her knuckles white.

Her father says, gently, "We did not know you planned to study so far away." And then, even more softly. "Congratulations, Léa. We are very proud of you." His mildness feels like a rebuke.

Her mother leaves the table without a word and walks into her bedroom, shuts the door. The food tastes like sawdust and no one speaks through the entire meal, except for Leo, who chatters through dessert, lifting the silence as if it had no weight at all.

Léa washes every single dish in the cold, greasy water, then knocks on the bedroom door. There is no response.

Her mother is lying like a corpse on top of the blanket. Her eyes are open. She does not acknowledge Léa, who sits at the edge of the bed and covers her mother's hand with her own. Then there is movement, as her mother draws back.

"I am so sorry, Mama," she says. "I won't go. Of course not."

She leaves the room, closing the door softly, and lies in her own narrow bed in the small shared room with the barred windows, which feels that night like a prison cell.

The next day, Mama is up preparing breakfast as usual. She punishes Léa by refusing to make eye contact and slamming the dishes into the sink. Léa's father asks her to walk him to synagogue, though she hasn't attended in years. She is jittery and her stomach hurts, she has been up all night regretting her sacrifice—and she is not a person who generally indulges in regret. Her head aches and her legs are heavy.

After weeks of grey weather, the sky is blue, and the body, that betrayer, lifts her spirits as soon as she leaves the house. The meagre lawns and grimy sidewalks are covered with fresh snow, furring the branches of the trees and blurring the edges of the street, scattering diamonds of light everywhere. They walk three blocks before her father speaks.

"Your mother," he finally says, and then he stops. It is another block before he resumes his sentence. "Your mother is also very proud of you. You know, she never had this opportunity. Never imagined..." he stops again. "Of course, you must go. We wish," he says, "we wish we could help you more"—but Léa is spilling over, she has been saving for months, she does not need any help, has also borrowed money from some theatre friends, in fact has already put a deposit on the ticket, she is not walking anymore, she is almost dancing on the sidewalk and does not realize they have reached the synagogue.

He inclines his head towards the door. "I assume you are not coming in," he says, and then takes both her hands in his own. He holds them a moment. His hands are always hot, and hers are always cold. Ever since she was a child one of the ways he showed his love was by sharing that warmth.

The rims of his eyes are red and despite her excitement she wants to take it all back, how could she even think of leaving them, leaving him? But he squeezes her hands, as if to seal a promise, and walks into shul. After that, no one speaks of it again until the day they follow her down to the station to say their goodbyes.

II
Wander
Grenoble, New York, Rome, Berlin, 1925-1932

1.

She takes the train to New York and boards a ship named *Grace*. She feels no regret as she stands on the deck and watches the land fade into the line of the horizon, as if the whole world she knows has vanished. It is late January, too cold for most of the passengers to stay outside, but she wraps herself in every layer she has brought and spends hours looking at the ocean, wearing a fur ushanka that one of the Russian actors left behind, the flaps tied under her chin. At night, there are more stars than she has ever seen. She covers herself in blankets on the deck chair and drinks in the stars until she is so cold, she needs to go inside.

It is a new experience for Léa to be alone; she even has her own cabin. It takes her a while to learn to sleep without the restless night noises of her sisters, but soon she learns to like the silence. Best is being able to read a book without interruption.

When she wants company, she goes to the tourist lounge and learns how to play bridge, or heads to the dining room where she eats her meals with a family from Spain. They are on their way home from an American holiday, and seem a little overwhelmed by everything—travel, the ship, their own four children; it is a mystery they had the courage to make the journey in the first place. She takes pity on them and helps with their girls, who are exact copies of one another, just staggered in age and size, like Russian dolls, though instead of fair and round they are slight and dark. The eldest is twelve, the youngest six. One day she cuts their hair, one after another, black bobs and bangs like Louise Brooks, and when their mother, Isabella, sees them, she claps her hands and insists on the same hairdo. They speak in English over meals of lamb pot pie and roasted chicken with bread sauce, mutton chops and sirloin steak, prune compote and jam pudding, potatoes every which way—such heavy food. If they keep eating like this, they will sink the ship.

"After we land in Cherbourg, we stop in Paris," Isabella says. "We have an errand to run."

She laces her fingers on the table in front of her and leans forward.

"We are meeting a merchant to purchase a set of silverware. I don't know what we were thinking. We don't speak a word of French. I was hoping you could help us so we aren't swindled."

"Why not?" Léa says. She has never been this free.

On their last few days on the ship, the sky is blue and the air has warmed up, and she spends hours on the deck playing badminton with the girls. They have sailed out of winter and into spring; when they get off the train in Paris, the daffodils are blooming.

The silver merchant is located on Des Rosiers Street. Léa wears her best suit and fur collar and tries to look respectable, shrewd, and prosperous. Because she has never been to Paris, she is unprepared for the crowds of men in long black coats and round fur hats, beards, and peyos. It is like walking down Park Avenue on a Sabbath afternoon. The store has an ornate silver mezuzah on the lintel and out of old custom, she presses her fingers to it and brings them to her lips as she swings open the door.

"*A gutn tog!*" she says. "*Vos makhstu?*"

All the way across the ocean to barter in Yiddish with a salesman who looks a little like her own grandfather.

A wandering Jew is always at home.

2.

Grenoble: like a village in a picture book. It is an easy city to like. Madame Dax has arranged a bedsit in a neighbourhood full of Italian workmen and cheap, good places to eat. Most of all, Léa loves the view of the mountains from almost everywhere, stretched out against the sky like a stage backdrop, too beautiful to be real. When she doesn't have classes, she walks on the trails, past patches of crocus, primrose, and forget-me-not, and she takes her books to a little bench that perches over a vista of town and river, where the view competes so well with the words on the page that often she spends half her time staring into the distance.

She is studying literature and linguistics. She reads at the elegant old library, under the dome of the roof, surrounded by books stored so high they must be fetched with a ladder. One of her teachers has assigned Shelley's poem about Mont Blanc, which she can see in the distance from her bedsit window. The everlasting universe of things—the phrase ricochets in her brain as she encounters the implacable blue stare of the mountains everywhere she looks. Everything is on a different scale than it is back home, and she climbs as high as she can to look down on the miniaturized dollhouse of the city, and then to raise her gaze to the throat-catching glory of the horizon. I will raise my eyes to the hills; her father loves that psalm. The psalmist means God, but here the mountains are sufficient: their ability to bring perspective, their granite imperturbability, dear God, their beauty.

She grows stronger and more tranquil. The air is sweet, and the light so soft. She can be anyone here.

The last tenant of the apartment has left a little pile of books in the corner. Marx's *Capital*, Kropotkin's *The Conquest of Bread*, and *The Communist Manifesto*, a dog-eared pamphlet in French translation. She picks up the Manifesto first, curious. All she knows about the little book is its notoriety. Every other sentence has been underlined, and she sinks down to the floor and reads alongside the traces of the last reader, who has sometimes marked the page so vigorously their pencil has ripped the paper. Those famous first sentences catch her with their grandiose, almost gothic poetry: a spectre, a haunting, a holy alliance. As she reads on, she is compelled by the bold sweep of the narrative, the rise and fall of kingdoms and of systems as the wheel of history inexorably turns. And then: a nightmare vision, a world exploded, the vast appetite of capital unleashed, a giant mouth that will swallow all it can.

She closes the pamphlet, disturbed. No wonder it has been banned. Though not in France, where she begins to notice it everywhere: the windows of bookshops, the shelves of cafés, sticking out of the satchels of students. She keeps flipping it open, compelled by its radical, propulsive simplicity, the resolute certainty of its position, the vertiginous play between abstraction and concrete political change: free education, the abolition of inheritance, the collectivization of the means of production. An end to the oppression of workers in factories, of women and children in families. She thinks of her father, and his allergy to accumulation. Every time he made a little bit of extra money, he gave it away. When she was growing up, that made them poor. But what if it also made them just? What if the ruling principle of society was not to hoard, but to share?

Madame Dax has given her the names and addresses of clients looking for English lessons. She spends her mornings in lectures at the university, her afternoons teaching English conversation to the sons and the daughters of the bourgeoisie in their homes. The Grenoblois are informal, friendly, egalitarian, still proud that their city was the cradle of the French Revolution. At the same time, they can be stuffy and provincial, fixated on the order of seats at the table, of the right forks beside the plates.

Sometimes she meets her students at the Fountain of the Three Orders in Place Notre Dame, which commemorates the Day of the Tiles.

"Do you know the story?" her student Charlotte asks. "The aristocrats and the church wanted to tax the merchants and the farmers, and when the army came to town to collect the money, the people fought them off: they rang the bells to alert the peasants, closed all the shops and stalls and filled the streets. Men stood on those roofs and flung tiles at the soldiers. When the soldiers shot at the crowds, the peasants stormed the city until there were too many to shoot and the army was forced to withdraw their troops. It was the first victory of the revolution."

She points up at the statue.

"There they are, the three estates. The aristocracy, the clergy, the commoners—that's us. Looking together to the bright future."

Léa cranes her neck. Three men in costume, at the top of a high pillar against the pale blue sky, each with an arm outstretched. On the right, the clergyman in his robes with his hand beseeching the heavens. On the left, the nobleman in a long coat, his arm high, his palm flat, as if he is giving a command. And the workman in the centre, his hand stretched from his shoulder in a wide-fingered salute.

"In Grenoble, we say, the priest is saying, please God, let it rain. And the aristocrat is commanding the rain. And the workman is holding out his hand to see if it is raining or not."

"I see," Léa says. "So, the priest relies on faith, the nobleman on power, and the commoner is an empiricist. He believes in the world as it is, and in the evidence of his own senses."

"That's right," Charlotte says. "Though you'll find plenty of people here who think they can command the rain." She nods over at the new hydroelectric stations by the river, the "white coal" that will make the new fortunes of the city.

For a short while, Léa is also rich. She commands the rain. The franc continues to fall, and each time she exchanges her Canadian money, she gets a little more. She spends it on books and carafes of wine—which she shares with classmates who have never had to pay their own way—and on weekend trips to Paris. Three girlfriends from Montreal are studying there, at the Sorbonne: Clara, Agata, and Julia. They show her the city with proprietary pride. Julia is heading to Italy for the summer, so they offer Léa Julia's empty bed for her term break, and she has just enough money saved from her English lessons and her Canadian stash to accept.

"I am in Paris," she writes to her mother, her most faithful correspondent. "Can you believe it? It is every bit as beautiful as they say." Her mother writes back with family news. They have moved to Esplanade Street, right on the corner of Bernard. "It is a lovely house," she writes, "quite a step up. I feel so fancy! Annie has a boyfriend named Norman, they fight all the time, but they still seem serious. Rose also has a boyfriend, Caesar Goldstein, he's very handsome but can you imagine naming a baby Caesar? Luckily, it doesn't seem to have gone to his head, he's a nice boy. Lottie is heading to New York on her own to study nursing. She's only sixteen years old—I worry about her, but you know Lottie, so practical."

When good Americans die, they go to Paris, Benjamin Franklin once said, and Americans swarm the city. Léa hears as much English on the street as French. The Americans travel in packs and can be heard for blocks, raucous in their prosperous bohemianism.

She makes a point of speaking French, so she isn't mistaken for one of them.

Her roommate Clara is in a theatre production of *Edward II* and convinces Léa to take part. The lesson Léa learned at His Majesty's still holds. She's no actress.

"You know what's the matter," Clara says, watching her practise her lines. "You're too honest! You can't pretend. You are who you are, and that's a gift. But not a gift for theatre."

It doesn't matter. She has only two lines, which she delivers with wooden precision at each of their four performances. She has her photo taken professionally, in the costume for the play: a well-cut suit with a narrow skirt that reaches to her knees, a wool hat, a fur stole. There is no payment, but she gets to keep the clothing. When she returns to Grenoble, she wears it on the train, so she can arrive in transformed elegance.

Back in Grenoble, her professors recite their lectures to half-empty rooms, minutely parsing the books they study with no sense of passion or engagement. She decided to study literature because she loves it, but in the classroom there is no love, no energy, no excitement, only dry words to scratch out on an empty page. She is starting to worry that studying literature will destroy exactly what she enjoys about it, the frictionless escape, sledding down the white field of the imagination.

Though escape, too, is beginning to feel insufficient. At night, she keeps reading Marx, making her way through the thickets of *Capital*, reading and re-reading the manifesto until she has some of it by heart. *Capital* is too abstruse, but the manifesto is spellbinding. It feels almost like reading poetry, if poetry could change the world: it gives her language to articulate the everyday injustice which surrounds her, and more, to imagine one day it might be otherwise. She is getting impatient with the distractions of beauty.

If, instead of lifting your eyes to the heavens or gazing at the splendour of the mountains, you look down into the lit basements of the city, there are rooms full of women ruining their eyes by candlelight, making the fine lace gloves for which the city is famous. They make her think of the women doing piecework in the railroad flats of Montreal, their kitchen tables covered with scraps of fabric, their backs bent and their eyes sore. Léa has seen what those lace gloves cost in stores, and she is certain that the girls who so carefully crochet the fine lace are getting paid a pittance. It is fashionable to sympathize with the workers, but most of the other students will never have to make their rent by standing all day on a factory floor. Charlotte's parents, for instance, own several of the buildings that the workers occupy; the only expectation they have of their daughter is that she marries well. Léa feels more like the girls in the basement than like the students who sit in cafés between their classes and spend their days reading books. When her teacher assigns Dante's *Inferno* she remembers her days at the laundry. Wasn't it a kind of hell, working all day in the heat and in the stench of the chemicals, doing the same heavy labour again and again until their backs were ruined? What was their sin?

Studying can feel like a betrayal of those girls, and of the girl that she was, not so long ago. She loves books. But there is more urgent work to do.

Despite the strength of the dollar, her money is starting to run out. It will be a challenge to fund another year of study, and the Americans, alas, have finally discovered Grenoble, cluttering the streets and pushing up the very cheap rents which drew them in the first place. Her clients can't afford her anymore. As the franc loses value businesses begin to shutter; more than once, she arrives for a lesson only to be met with an apology at the door.

"Come home," her mother writes, "we miss you."

The letter makes her panic. At the idea of returning to Montreal she feels trapped. But staying in France is impossible. She starts to skip classes, as she did as a kid in Quebec City. She loses the feeling of freedom that she had, and for the first time in her life, she feels lonely. It is nothing like she expected. Loneliness means moving like a ghost through a world that does not see you; it means you could disappear and not leave a trace. She is unsteady in herself. She has always had so much to ground her, her large family, her theatre friends. She has nothing and no one here.

She is surprised when she catches her own reflection in the glass windows of the shops. She looks thinner, hunched. Like a nobody.

The answer arrives in a letter from Lottie, breezy and brief. "Why don't you try New York?" she writes. "You'll love Manhattan! My landlady is looking for a tenant."

Léa buys a ticket. All season, she's been hearing the same song on the radio, *I'll Take Manhattan*, which feels like a sign. She gives away most of her things before she leaves, including *Capital* which is so heavy, but at the last minute she slides the manifesto into her bag. Her suitcase is so light the porter does a comic double take as she hands it to him. She doesn't have much to show for her two years in France—no degree, no money saved—but she has a new sophistication that isn't all her Paris suit. A crispness in her French pronunciation that her family will laugh right out of her. And confidence—she has taken on this new city and this new country, all by herself, and she has survived. She can start again, anywhere.

3.

In the heart of Manhattan, Stern Brothers advertise themselves as importers of the latest Paris fashions. They are impressed by the fact that Léa speaks French, and that she has worked in fashion—her euphemistic presentation of her time at the laundry in Montreal, and three days she spent modelling in Paris. She invents a stint at a lingerie counter in Grenoble and is so convincing in her description, she almost believes it herself.

Mrs. Samuels, who will be her supervisor, has a twenty-two-inch waist. She mentions it, twice, spanning her middle with her own hands as if it were her own most outstanding qualification. Mrs. Samuels begins the interview in French to trip her up—there must be a lot of girls who pretend to know French to garnish their resumes—and then is quickly lost in the fluency of Léa's response. Mrs. Samuels's face grows red, right up to the roots of her harshly dyed black hair. Has she lost the job? It is always a bad idea to embarrass the boss. But Mrs. Samuels' supervisor is also there, a man in a three-piece suit, and he laughs and says, "Very well, Miss Roback, you are hired!"

Mrs. Samuels takes her up to the lingerie section, which is on the top floor of the building. They still sell corsets, made in Paris, though most women now wear brassieres, bandeaus, or the less glamorous girdles—they have those, too, near the back.

"No woman is difficult to fit," Mrs. Samuels lectures. "Your job is to flatter the figure. We can adjust these corsets in house, so that they follow the natural lines of the body with ease and perfection!"

She flutters her hand, outlining in air the bust, the waist, the flared hips. There is nothing natural or fashionable about her own silhouette, her pinched wasp waist—Léa has brushed by her and found it as hard as cement.

The girls in Paris are flat from chest to knee. If they have breasts, those breasts are bound so that their flapper dresses have the right shape. Waists are gone; the ideal female body is the shape of an eight-year-old girl. Léa is herself not particularly well-endowed, which means she is in fashion. She has always been content with cotton camisoles, nothing that pinches or pokes or constricts. But all day long now, she hooks, snaps, and buttons recalcitrant flesh.

The right way to fit a brassiere is to have a woman lean forward and shake those bosoms into the cups like pouring pudding into molds. She perfects the lift, smooth, and separate with a cool, dry, sexless hand so that the women look at themselves in the full-length mirror and see no unsightly bulges, no gaps or hollows, no leftover rolls. It takes soft eyes and compassion. When the women strip down, they reveal the road maps life has left on their chests and stomachs: stretch marks, lesions, scars. There are women with port-wine stains; women with scales of psoriasis, silver and red, in long angry patches; women who stand like statues as if she isn't even there, and women who smile at her apologetically, as if they are sorry she has to touch them at all.

This part of the job she likes. The part she does not like is selling. Mrs. Samuel issues her a series of instructions and rules: always show the most expensive pieces first, begin with silk, or if they insist on trying something cheaper, choose it a little small (if they are large) and a little large (if they are small) and then tell them the fit is just not as good, but that you have something else that would make their husbands very happy.

"What if they don't have a husband?" Léa says, and Mrs. Samuels looks irritated: despite her name, Léa has heard that Mrs. Samuels does not, indeed, have a husband.

And then there are the difficult customers—not the ones who ignore her, which is a favour she is happy to return, and not the ones who need constant reassurance, she can give that with both hands, but the ones who insist on trying item after item, who leave the dressing room draped in discarded clothes, who take up so much time and speak without respect.

One day, a woman comes in whose shape reminds her a little of her mother—short and stocky, an apple of a woman—except that she is wearing clothes that cost as much, perhaps, as a new dining room set.

"Miss," she says, "I'm looking for a new corset," and then she says it again, though Léa is serving another customer.

The woman needs to be squeezed into item after item. If Léa does not pull hard enough she complains it's far too loose, if she uses her strength she says, stop, you're suffocating me. It is hot on the fourth floor, despite the fans, and fitting is warm work. Her hands are slippery, and as she works to hook a fussy little catch she pinches the woman's back.

"What's the matter with you?" the woman says, and Léa throws up her hands.

"For goodness sakes," she says, "you're just too fat for this one! Size up, and it will be much more comfortable."

Around her, the other girls stop what they're doing and stare. When Mrs. Samuels marches over, her heels the rat-a-tat-tat of a firing squad, it is the first time Léa has seen her smiling.

She doesn't mind being fired. All month, she has looked in envy at Bryant Park from the store's tall windows as the daffodils bloomed, and then the tulips. She felt robbed of spring. Now the roses are in flower, and she finds a spot on a bench in the shade and watches the world go by. She takes books out of the public library and reads them in the park, she makes friends with the habitués—the girls who walk for their figures on their lunch breaks, the man who comes to read the paper every morning, wearing a straw panama hat and a white linen suit, the tramps who clump together at the corners. She gets to know them the way you know strangers in the city, by their faces, their schedules, their habits.

Two of the regulars sit on a bench right across from her watching her read. "Look at that girl read," one of them says. "I like a girl who reads. I would get a job for a girl like that."

She closes her book and smiles at them, but they startle away like the pigeons when you stamp your feet. She calls out to their backs, "You know, that's the nicest thing a gentleman has ever offered to do for me."

On Saturdays, she and Lottie take the subway to Coney Island and stroll on the new boardwalk, arm in arm. Lottie is flourishing. Nursing school keeps her busy, and she likes to be busy. She has met a boy and it's pretty serious. Léa is amazed. Her little sister, catapulting into adulthood.

New York seems to collect Montreal Jews. There is a whole little colony in Brooklyn, and new arrivals nearly every day. One of her brother's friends, Moishe Wolofsky, asks her to the movies, and when he picks her up she regrets saying yes. He is really only half-grown, his hands and feet too big for his body, gawky and thin with a hopeful but unconvincing scruff of beard. She wants to see *Joan of Arc*, but he convinces her to see the new Buster Keaton instead, and he laughs so loudly that she shifts in her seat, uncomfortable. "That was great!" he says at the end, oblivious to her silence, and before she can object he tells her he will pick her up the next Tuesday night. This time they do see *Joan of Arc*, and she sits in rapture, leaning forward in her seat, her eyes lifted to Joan's tear-stained, ecstatic, unrepentant face. This time Moishe is silent. "You liked that, hey?" he says at the end as they say goodbye outside the theatre. She nods. She doesn't want to cheapen what she feels with words. She doesn't especially want to see him again, and this time he gets the message, because the next week he does not call.

She is not attached to her virginity. Her integrity, yes. If she could shed one without losing the other, she thinks she would be game. Sometimes, when her fingertips brush the clerk's palm at the deli counter when she takes her change, or when a stranger puts his hand on her lower back as he passes her in the subway, she feels liquid and almost reckless with desire. But she has never known a woman who has loved without consequences, and those consequences are too heavy to contemplate. She sometimes thinks of the nymphs who followed Diana and swore themselves to chastity, not out of priggishness, but out of jubilation. When she was a girl, she could run faster than anyone in her village. She would hide in the tall grasses, sucking sweet clover, invisible as the boys searched for her. No one could catch her.

She is the same girl as she ever was, quick, independent, restless. Her money is running out, and she is not built for idleness—a week of summer mornings is enough time off for her, she is itching to do something. She interviews at a lawyer's office on Madison Avenue, and begins as a receptionist the next day. It is a boring job, but it is easy: that is the best and also the worst of it, there is nothing to learn, no way to grow. She is not allowed to read at the desk, she needs to be in an alert posture of constant readiness in case she is needed, although she is rarely called upon. If she were allowed a book, it would be perfect. Though she likes being paid, it feels like a sin to be paid to do almost nothing. She greets guests, announces them, answers the phone, takes notes—that's all. Because it is the summer, many lawyers are on vacation, and clients rarely walk through the door. She starts to make bets with herself about how long it will take for the phone to ring. The boredom is suffocating.

The lawyers are fine. The older men are too paternal and the younger men are too familiar, but she hasn't lived in this world for twenty-five years without understanding how to both flatter and disarm them. One late night, a young associate follows her most of the way home but even in her heels, she is too fast for him. On the way into the elevator, a senior partner puts his hand on her bottom, and she removes it gently and firmly, smiling all the while. It is not ideal, but it is tolerable.

In the autumn, the office begins to get busier, which she prefers. One morning, one of the lawyers comes in, panting. He has just climbed the stairs from the basement. He has the oddest balding pattern she's ever seen in her life—a circular patch, like a large coin, shining on the side of his head. She wonders if he pulls the hair out when he is feeling anxious. Once, she knew a girl who pulled her own eyebrows out and had to draw them on every day.

The telephone operators—all three of them—went out for shrimp the night before, and are terribly indisposed.

"Come with me, Miss Roback," he says. "You're needed."

She follows him down the stairway.

"I don't know how to work a switchboard," she says. "I've never done it before."

"It's simple enough." he says. "It lights up—that means someone wants to make a call. You pull the cable, you flip the switch, you ask them who they want to connect to. You call that person, you wait until they pick up, you connect them. A monkey could do it."

"How do I know who it is?" she says.

He has already turned his back. "The names are all on the board."

She looks. There are names printed under the little bulbs that light up when a call is being made. Sidney, they say. Walter, Clarence. And also, desk, bellman, and—she looks more closely—yes, it says beer man. She sits on her high-backed stool; it is on wheels, so she can scoot from one end to the other. At least it's cool down here. She should have brought down her purse. Perhaps she will be lucky and it will be a quiet morning. The room smells like mold and damp.

She is sneezing when the first bulb lights up, insistent. She plugs the cable, flips the switch. "Number, please," she says, as instructed, and on the other end, a man with marbles in his mouth calls out incomprehensible instructions. "Could you repeat that, please?" she says, and the message flies at her again, no clearer. "Just a minute, please," she says. Another light has been blinking at her for twenty seconds. This time the voice when she answers is suave and irritated.

"What are you, reading *War and Peace*?" the voice says.

"Just a minute," she says.

Though it is chilly, her hands are already sweating. The board is marked like measles. The cables in front of her are a heap of mixed-up spaghetti. She tries to connect to her first caller again, still can't understand him. "For God's sake," he yells, his voice finally clear, as if something had been obstructing it and was suddenly removed (a cigar, she realizes later, he must have been talking around his cigar). "Don't you speak English, woman?"

The man from upstairs is back down. She could swear that shining bald circle seems a little enlarged. There are two girls from the typing pool behind him. "What have you done?" he says, looking at the tangle of cables, the blinking board. "You've made a real mess. You'd better go."

She starts to follow him back upstairs to the reception desk, and he says, "No. I mean you better go. Scram! You're fired."

These little men are all Napoleons: they like to abuse their power.

As she steps out onto the street, she is surprised to realize it is not even ten in the morning. She doesn't cry: the opposite, she is glad. She doesn't need them. She walks all the way from midtown to the Lower East Side, where she buys a knish and a black and white cookie and decides to keep going, all the way down to the tip of the island, where she gets on the Staten Island Ferry, which she hasn't ridden once, all this time she's been in the city. As she climbs onto the upper deck she feels like a little ship herself, pulling away from the shore. She waves hello and goodbye to the Statue of Liberty, toasting her own freedom, and then takes the boat back to Manhattan, where she decides that's enough of New York and gives her landlady notice.

It is good to have so many brothers and sisters. She writes Harry a letter and it must have been a sad letter because when he writes back he tells her to come to Berlin, there is a room available in his boarding house, and luckily, she still has enough money to book a ticket. She can finish her degree in Germany. She buys a German grammar to study on the boat. So many of the words are familiar from Yiddish, but the patterns are different, the stress falls in a different place, the vowel narrows or opens up. It is like seeing her language in a funhouse mirror, no, in a pool of water, reflected but in shifting waves and ripples that enliven and obscure what is as familiar to her as her own face.

She is not sorry to leave. She never really fell in love with the city. New Yorkers think they live in the centre of the world, but it can be a surprisingly provincial place. She has met dozens of New Yorkers who never leave their own ten square blocks, and because they can purchase spaghetti or a steak for dinner, believe they have sophisticated tastes. New York might have a reputation for fun, but it feels like business, business, business to her, with an icing of desperation—on every corner, someone in terrible distress, and everyone else just walking around them, walking over them, as if nothing is happening at all. The rich are too rich, and the poor are too poor, and the whole city feels like those rickety scaffoldings around the new skyscrapers going up in the middle of town, as if it is about to collapse.

It has been an odd interregnum, an unusual period of drift. Something was missing. She didn't grow roots and she didn't catch fire. She does not want to say that New York has defeated her. She is not defeated. But she does not mind turning her back on it. As the boat pulls away from the harbour, she does not rush to the railings like everyone else to wave goodbye; she looks straight ahead as they leave the port and sail towards the vast and dazzling expanse of the sea.

4.

The streets around the Berlin railway station are full of prostitutes. Her brother meets her there, and it is both good and strange to see him in this unfamiliar place. Her arms barely meet around his waist as she embraces him.

"You look so respectable!" she says, pulling back to take him in.

"You mean I've gotten fat," he says.

On the way from the station she notices clusters of men in brown shirts and armbands, their high boots hammering the sidewalk. Harry points out a red newspaper box, the display window featuring the caricature of a short, fat, slovenly man with a hooked nose, leering over the unconscious blonde woman swooning in his arms.

"I've been seeing these for sale everywhere," Harry says, and he looks pained. "Such trash. Most of the people here, they don't think that way. Still, it's a good idea to be careful." He turns to look at her under the foggy glow of the street light. "I wouldn't have told you to come if it wasn't safe." She can hear a hiccup of doubt in his voice.

His rooming house isn't much, a warren in Mitte near the Charité, where he is studying to be a doctor. When they arrive, there is a problem. The landlady is unconvinced that they are siblings. She keeps looking back and forth between them, sniffing her long narrow nose as if she can smell the lie.

"Your sister?" she keeps saying, and then she rolls her shoulders and says, "Believe me, I've met lots of sisters!"

A mole between her eyebrows twitches every time she speaks. Eventually she says, "Brother and sister like Abraham and Sarah were brother and sister," and Léa looks at Harry in alarm—in Germany, Harry would know better than to mention he is a Jew.

Finally, the landlady concedes. The room has a narrow single bed, a night table, a jug for water, a desk, a lamp, an iron radiator like the ones back home in Montreal. The best part is the window, which is surprisingly large, though the landlady bustles over and draws the curtains, shaking her head, since views are clearly made to be blocked. There is a living room in which she and Harry are not allowed to sit, with a velvet couch and a large collection of china dolls that cover all of the surfaces, and a narrow kitchen which they may use for an hour in the morning and an hour at night as long as they leave it immaculate, *gründlich*, the landlady repeats, which is a word Léa has only ever seen written down. Even though they are brother and sister—having made up her mind to rent the room, she is willing to concede the point—they are not allowed in one another's rooms, so they stand outside to talk, hands in their pockets, on the windy autumn day.

Léa admires Harry's coat, which is mohair and long, and his Homburg hat, which he tells her, unnecessarily, was invented in Germany, and makes him look like all the other burghers of the town.

She starts her classes at the University of Berlin, studying German, linguistics, and sociology. Harry introduces her to wealthy Jewish families, and she begins to teach them English and French. They live in apartments more elaborate than she has ever seen, ten or twelve rooms, with Turkish carpets and gilded mirrors and fresh flowers replaced as soon as they begin to wilt by maids in starched uniforms. These families are nothing like the poor Eastern Jews who landed in Montreal with no more than the clothes on their back and memories of poverty and pogrom. They are cultured and prosperous, with books and pianos, with silver that has been passed on for generations, with someone paid to keep it sparkling. They are more German than the Germans—impeccably correct in speech and action.

But all they can do is talk about leaving.

Soon she realizes that their plans to emigrate are what keep her teaching schedule as full as the dance card of the prettiest girl in the room. Some are planning on moving to Switzerland, England, France. Some are hoping for New York, and they ask her about Canada, but how can she explain it to them? It is hard for her to imagine them finding their feet in the snow and the muck. They call her the Canadian, they pay her well—as much in an hour as she earned back home in a day—and they treat her, not like the help, but like a friend, serving her tea when she comes to deliver her lessons, inviting her to meals or to occupy an extra seat at the opera or the theatre.

Some of the German Jews she knows have already tried to emigrate, but have come back, disenchanted. Frau Salomon, for instance, who hosts a salon every Thursday in her four-bedroom in Mitte and has two maids in aprons to polish the silver and dust the furniture to a golden shine, made a trial trip to Moscow and to Leningrad, and was not impressed.

"They have no culture there," Frau Salomon says. "They are like bears!"

"Tolstoy," Léa says, "Dostoevsky, Pushkin."

"I read *Anna Karenina* in the original German," Frau Salomon says firmly, and because she is German it takes Léa a minute to understand that she is joking.

5.

Now that she is in Europe again, her appetite for travel is voracious. She and Harry decide to go to Rome in the summer, and when they arrive, she is amazed: here is a city to make you drunk on beauty. Unlike Berlin's industrial collage of rust-red brick and greyish skies, the heavens in Rome are bright azure, the buildings glorious marble and stone, the Tiber a tawny, shadowed glitter through the centre. True, Rome is dirty, but everywhere there is a symmetrical grandiosity that broadcasts glories both permanent and ephemeral.

Glorious though not entirely comfortable. Like the statue of Emperor Aurelius on horseback in front of the Capitoline, everything is over-scale. She feels like an ant scurrying in the shade of these enormous monuments. The Colosseum, though massive, is anticlimactic, a cracked crown on the plateau between the hills. It is a kingdom for cats and she spends a woozy afternoon following them through the ruins, not sure which era she is trampling. She loves the flourish of the marble fountains, which are everywhere, their gorgeous waste of water spangling the air. Some of the fountains are ornamented with massive nudes sculpted in poses of languid debauchery, despite the Vatican right down the road. She can't quite figure out how this shining decadence sprawls right beside Saint Peter's and the hundred holy tombs, right next door to Pope Pius himself. Every day she watches the priests in their stuffy black robes walk by these tumescent shrines to beauty and not even turn their heads.

Mussolini's Blackshirts are everywhere, but unobtrusive; they do not seem interested in starting fights, but watch with a flat and implacable gaze. When she sees them, she misses the political energy of Berlin. Their presence is met with impassive resignation. How strange that fascism has won, and yet life continues. In the heat and the haze, the city takes on the enigmatic, dream-like quality of a de Chirico painting: empty squares, long shadows. Beside the Pantheon, two children pick out a cone of gelato each, greedy and oblivious; behind them, a squadron of Blackshirts wait their turn at the counter, preening like a murder of crows. Every day, she walks her feet sore. When she rubs her chest, the dirt rolls off on her fingertips. At night when she bathes, the water is black.

They often go to the opera. The cheapest tickets are in the balconies three stories high, and she can see only the tops of the heads of the singers, but the music soars up.

Like her uncle, she is good at languages. From French, Italian feels reachable, though sometimes she thinks she knows a word and finds it means something very different. In a language class in Grenoble, a teacher had talked about a new concept in linguistics called "false friends," words that sound alike in different languages, but signal differently. So often you think you have encountered something familiar, only to find yourself mistaken. Worse than the opacity of ignorance is the unwitting blindness of false recognition. A traveller makes false friends wherever she goes.

Still, Léa improves quickly. She can fake fluency, and then one day she realizes she is not translating inside her head. She simply understands. It is as if she has been sipping the language through a straw and all of a sudden, she can gulp it down, fill herself with meaning.

She and Harry wander separately and compare notes at the end of the day. Their tastes are opposite. He likes formal buildings, colonnades of arches, statues of military men on horses. She likes the Caravaggios hidden in the niches of churches, where the faces look out in white alarm between deep puddles of blackness, and the statues at the Borghese where it seems marble has been turned into flesh, into something soft enough to pinch, knead, rend. They both get used to drinking coffee strong and black, eating gelato for lunch, eating dinner late at night. When she wakes up, she has nearly missed the morning.

6.

She doesn't want to leave. City of the seven hills, city of longing, city of echoes, city of souls, Rome has her in its thrall. She finds a job as a nanny when Harry heads back to Berlin. Her languages are an advantage; the children she will watch over have already begun to learn English and French. When she comes for the interview only the mother, Laura, is at home. The family lives in a cavernous apartment near the Vatican, in a building painted ochre, and they even have a room for her: a small maid's chamber off the dining room which she loves because she has her own French doors leading to a tiny, geranium-fringed balcony. Their living room is so immense that she feels like she is being interviewed in a courtyard. She answers questions across an abyss of gleaming parquet.

"I am completely exhausted by these children," Laura confides. "They are absolute devils!"

Laura is slim as a girl and seems too young to have three children. She has olive skin and is wearing a white belted dress. She has cut her hair shorter than most Italian women, smooth on top and then flaring out into gentle waves around her face. Nothing about her suggests she is interested in looking after children, even her own.

The absolute devils come in from the park. Their names are Marco, Luca, and Flora, ages six, eight, and ten, and they are also dressed in white, with the same huge dark eyes and black hair. They seem not devilish but cowed. When Marco, who is the smallest, forgets to hold out his hand, Laura looks at Léa, nodding—"You see what I mean?" Léa gets on her knees to greet them at eye level, notices that Luca has trouble meeting her eyes, that Flora, despite her delicate dress, has two scraped knees.

"I mean, I wouldn't ask anyone to look after them!" Laura says. "Unless, of course, you think you're up to it. You did say you have—what—eight siblings? Your mother must have been a saint! But what a shame that you've had no children of your own! I suppose after a childhood like that, you might have had enough forever—are you certain you want to take this on?"

Her mother would have had no patience for any of this: not the fussy outfits, not the forced indoor hush, especially not the mannered fragility. Mama was fiercely loyal to her children. Léa is totally unused to parents speaking of their children in a tone of disparagement, which seems a fashionable pose—she notices that Laura has pulled Marco onto her lap, that she is stroking Flora's hair. She makes a show of her devotion and of her contempt. It's difficult to tell what's real.

"Do they have other clothes to play in?" Léa says, getting up and brushing off her skirt, and Laura raises a listless arm.

"Flora knows where everything is," she says. Which means, Léa supposes, that she is hired.

What Léa has learned from working for the rich at British American Dyeworks and at the theatre is that it is best to be invisible until you are wanted, at which point it is best to appear as if you have always been there, at the ready. What the rich desire is for their immaculate gowns and their immaculate children to appear, silently and on demand, and then to vanish as if they never were. Laura likes to come out at breakfast and exclaim at the beauty of her children, one by one, though that is also a kind of narcissism, since they look exactly like her.

Then she very much likes not to see them except at bedtime, if she is home.

Léa is not expected to do any housework. There is another woman for that, Maria, who has known Laura since she was a child, and is the only person allowed to boss her around. Her job is to keep the children from "being underfoot," to keep them from snacking in excess, to take them outside in the early morning and late afternoon but also to keep them from sunburn, sunstroke, exhaustion, and bad influences, which means, as far as she can tell, most other children.

Luckily, Flora is a little mother, with all the bossiness of an eldest and only daughter. She takes Léa in hand and teaches her that Luca eats only white pasta but that Marco likes red sauce, that there are three parks nearby and that the second has no shade but excellent gelato on the corner. Marco needs to eat every two hours and that's about it, he is basically a happy, feckless child, while Luca is full of fear, he needs his hand held while walking down the street, he needs someone to sit beside his bed until he falls asleep, he needs to be protected from the entire insect kingdom, spiders, bees, and even ants.

Luca is obsessed with enemies, whom he claims are in the treetops at the park and in the shadows of the walls lining the Tiber. Léa tells him he has no enemies a hundred times before she realizes that is a tactical failure. What works is to tell him that she was trained by lumberjacks in Canada to throw axes, that she has an invisible one in her purse, and if anyone ever dares to attack him, she will cut off the attacker's hand, chop, just like that, before he knows anything is coming. Luca smiles and looks at her then—he has a brilliant smile, his whole face lit with the joy of it—and after that she realizes that what calms him down is the promise of imaginary violence, so she tells him stories of heroism and revenge, which she is practised at. After all, she has many little brothers.

It takes her a while to figure out what Flora needs—she is so bossy and so independent that she shakes off affection or help—but once she finds it out, it's simple: Flora needs books. Flora is a reader with a true gift for languages, and her mother reads only Italian *Vogue*, archived by date in the floor-to-ceiling bookcases of her bedroom. Her English reading is already strong, but what she needs is a good story to pull her along. They find a little bookstore near the Spanish Steps that sells books in Italian, English, and French left behind by tourists, and Léa uses some of her salary to buy copies of *Alice in Wonderland*, *The Secret Garden*—books she remembers and has loved since she was a girl. One day, she finds a copy of *Anne of Green Gables* and turns it over in her hands, wondering at the journey this red-haired pigtailed Canadian islander has made to a little bookstore right beside the villa where Keats lived when he was dying of tuberculosis, and thinking of her own journeys and how far she has travelled.

When she gives Flora the book, Flora does not look up from its pages for two full days. When they walk down the street, she holds the book in front of her.

"Léa," she says. "How wonderful it must be! The apple orchards and the funny red roads! I wish I lived there."

"Silly girl," she says, "you live in the most beautiful city in the world."

Flora shrugs her shoulders.

"Too dirty and too many people," she says, mimicking her mother. "It's a disgrace." She starts to call Léa her kindred spirit.

It is in some ways unfortunate to lose Flora's help; when she has a new book, she is much less inclined to assist Marco with the small buttons on his shirts, to play tag with Luca. But it is good to see her competence softened with a little dreaminess. Léa is a strong believer in the rights of children to wander, to daydream, to fool around. She will always be grateful to her parents, even in that workaday world of Beauport, for allowing her to do the real work of growing up through being left alone to play. Maria feeds their bodies with dishes that have a dozen different names but all look like pasta to Léa; their souls must also be fed with fresh air, with the massive canopies of the plane trees that line the Tiber, with words.

She falls into the rhythms of the children's day and of a Roman summer, getting up early before the sun is too strong, resting in the afternoons, and staying up late at night so she can have a little bit of time to herself. Lust is general all over Rome. Every day, she sees beautiful men leaning against doorways, their gazes full of dark intent. In the warm evenings, she leaves the door to her room cracked open as well as the door to the balcony. She turns off her light even before she is ready for bed, since the darkness creates the illusion that it is cooler, and she strips down to her shift. The breeze from the balcony door cools her bare thighs. She wishes she had someone to touch.

7.

It is two weeks before she meets their father, Aldo, who is a banker. He travels frequently on business and this time has been in Milan, Turin, and Florence; she knows he has returned because his beautiful shoes, with the narrow, boxy toe, are left at the door, a habit he picked up when he was working in Asia. It drives Laura crazy—not at all an Italian custom, she says, picking the shoes up and handing them to Maria to polish. When Léa gets up in the morning she is surprised to see him sitting at the kitchen table, already dressed for work, his jacket draped carefully across the back of his chair. Léa has been curious about him. So far, he has been a photo on the mantelpiece, a legend told by the children. When they talk about him, it is as if they are speaking of some mythical creature, rarely glimpsed.

"Good morning," he says. "You must be Léa! I have heard such wonderful things about you from Laura."

This surprises Léa, since Laura speaks to her only to criticize her or to make demands: Léa, why aren't the children ready to leave the house, Léa, come look at this mess that Marco left on the living room floor, you know they are to play only in their rooms, Léa, what on earth is wrong with Luca's face? Can't you tell him to stop it? Poor Luca, for whom just living is an unbearable strain, has developed a set of tics and twitches which help him organize the world, a jerky series of movements with his head, a compulsive rolling shrug, a loud throat-clearing which seems to indicate that he is about to make an important statement even though he rarely follows it with speech.

Aldo seems more German than Italian. He is very formal, and his face is so smooth it is as if he would never allow the impropriety of a feeling to wrinkle the surface. She wonders how he manages with Laura, who is all peaks and valleys. When Laura comes into the kitchen, she realizes that Laura is an entirely different person with her husband at home, subdued and solicitous.

"Léa, good morning," she says. This is the earliest Léa has ever seen her out of bed. "I see that you have met my husband!"

Aldo pulls out a chair for his wife and she sits down as Léa hovers in the doorway.

Everything in Laura now tilts towards her husband—her arms, her crossed legs, her pert and narrow chin. Her hair is already perfect. He, on the other hand, focuses on his coffee and the folded newspaper before him. For the first time, Léa feels a little bit sorry for her.

"Would you mind getting me a cup of coffee before you wake up the children, please?" Laura says, and Léa realizes she is being dismissed.

As she readies the coffee—they have a machine that Maria had to teach her to use, copper with numerous knobs and spouts, she is slightly afraid of it and avoids using it when possible—she hears them speak about a dinner they will hold that night, the list of guests, the menu.

"Oh, Léa," Laura says as she leaves the kitchen, "will you make sure the children are dressed and ready for eight o'clock? And that they are *clean*?" she adds. "We have some very important people coming."

Léa nods. She will feed them at five o'clock, or else Marco will be starving.

The Romanos, as their name declares, have been in Rome for nearly a millennium. They are also Jewish, which is one of the reasons Léa got the job. That seems much less a part of their identity than being Italian, or even more than Italian, being Roman. Léa has noticed the same thing in Berlin: such pride in belonging not only to a nation, but to a metropolis. To be a Roman Jew is to be Roman first. The Romanos's friends belong to the same established caste, the business and political leaders of the community. These are the very important people they expect for dinner.

Because there is so much to do, Léa is sent to the kitchen to help Maria. They will begin with *suppli*, fried rice balls with mozzarella, and *carciofi alla giudía*, which is the strangest dish Léa has ever seen, a giant deep-fried artichoke served alone on a plate, looking like a golden sunflower, or some wild sea creature, all tentacle and spike. They will continue with salted cod, and *cacio e pepe*. For dessert, a loaf cake with dried fruit and pine nuts and almonds, and a tart made with ricotta and wild cherries—by far the most enticing to Léa, though she won't have any of it unless there are leftovers in the morning. Maria displays it to her with maternal pride, the underside of her nails still red with juice from pitting cherries.

They boil the artichokes and then mash them flat with a rolling pin before dropping them into oil. The first time Léa ate an artichoke, she could not believe how much work it was, how much waste it created—the piles of sucked leaves, the spiky choke. She has never quite gotten over the culinary habits of her childhood, when they could not even all fit at the kitchen table, and when you gathered whatever was on offer and ate it as fast as you could before it was all gone, lunchtime a competition, dinnertime a race. In France, she learned to eat artichokes steamed, but she still can't say she thinks they're worth the trouble.

"Why is it called Jewish artichoke?" Léa asks.

Maria says, "This is ghetto food, from back when the Jews were poor and all had to live together, near the synagogue. They could only buy old, wilted vegetables in the market and the cheapest fish, so they put it all in oil and spice to give it a little flavour"—she drops a smashed artichoke into the pot and leans back as it spits oil—"and now it is a delicacy! And we serve it on silver plates!" She shakes her head. "I think it's a crime to fry these nice green artichokes—look at them, they're perfect! And now they will taste like salt and oil. But I don't make the menu, I just cook it."

Like Léa's mother, Maria's hands are covered in old small burns and scars from a lifetime spent in kitchens. She reminds Léa of her mother's friends back in Beauport, country women who worked hard and spoke their minds.

It is past noon before they are done preparing the appetizers, and the children are themselves overcooked. Marco has frightened Luca into hiding in the closet. Every five minutes Laura pops her head out of her own bedroom to scream at Flora, who has finished her book, and is pacing back and forth in the living room. It is not an auspicious beginning to the day.

Léa feels completely coated in oil, desiccated by salt, and would like nothing more than to get in the bath and soak out the smells of the morning, but she is, as ever, at their service: she pulls Luca out of the closet, gets all three out the door although the middle of the day in summer is the wrong time to be outside in Rome.

The streets are at their most vacant at high noon. Everyone is behind closed doors and lowered shutters, trying to keep cool for the next few hours. Shade is scant. The minutes crawl and by the time she brings them home to bathe and dress at five o'clock, she has decided she is not meant for this life, not as a nanny or as a mother, that she would rather the factory floor than the dead tedium of three bored children in a park on a hot afternoon. They are wretched with each other—as she yells at them to take off their clothes, to get in the bath, as Luca screams because she hasn't tested the bathwater and it is just a little too hot, as Flora slams the door and shuts herself in her room, Léa realizes, it's not the children, it's herself she doesn't like when reduced to this state. She sounds like the women she hates, shouting at and threatening their children to make them fall into line. Though every shout diminishes her authority.

As soon as she remembers that, Léa calms down. Marco and Luca settle in the bath, the now-tepid water a soothing distraction. Léa finds Flora and apologizes to her. By the time the guests arrive, they are once again perfect children, ready for display.

Maria is staying to serve. At the last moment, Laura asks Léa to help, with an air of condescension, as if she is doing her a favour. Léa holds the door as the parade of guests files in. The children must come to the table, and it breaks her heart when she hears Laura hissing at Luca to please just be normal, and drags him out of his room. She would love to rescue her sweet, strange little charge, who would like nothing more than to be left alone, eating pasta quietly in the dark. Marco drops his cutlery, and Laura shouts but then makes a fuss of him. Marco is outstanding at avoiding consequence, he need only open his eyes wide and tremble his fat little lower lip and then he is everyone's baby.

After the first course, the children are dismissed. In the morning they will be hungry, tired, dirty, and she will have to be mother and father to them once again. Léa pours the wine, and the tone of conversation changes.

She has barely heard Aldo speak. Just his greetings the morning they met, and occasional barked questions to Laura and Maria about where they have put his trousers, suspenders, wallet, shoes. He seems to believe that the women in the house are in a conspiracy to hide his belongings, which otherwise would have remained exactly where they should be the very moment he desired them. He has been nothing but polite to her, but she can't say she likes him. Now, his voice dominates the conversation. It is deep, and a little syrupy. Waiting with a bottle of wine, leaning against the wall, she listens to the cacophony of guests. As the evening grows late their voices get louder.

They are talking about politics.

"This Lateran Treaty is a very bad sign. Catholic schools? A Catholic state?" a man sitting near the head of the table says. He has round spectacles, and a carefully trimmed beard, and she has heard the guests refer to him as professor. "Believe me, these are the warning bells. We have been here before. A man sent by providence, the pope called Mussolini. He will turn on us soon, just you wait."

"That's absurd," Aldo says. "Nobody has done more for the Jews than Mussolini. You wait, this is all a performance. The pope can have his parades. Mussolini has the power."

"The power!" the professor says. "He would do anything for power. He would shake hands with the devil for power."

Aldo slams his fists on the table, and the room falls quiet.

"You are wrong," he says. "I met him, you know. I told him that we, the Italian Jews, are unshakably loyal to the fatherland. You know, Mussolini looked me straight in the eye and said, 'I have never doubted it.' I carry those words in my heart. I tell you, I wanted to embrace him! I said, Il Duce, may I shake your hand? This very hand! That is the man that providence has given to Italy. Indeed, the pope had it exactly right."

"Exactly right," he repeats, as if the repetition is a proof.

Léa expects shouts, contradictions, arguments, but instead the room falls silent once again. Laura says, "Léa, will you bring out the tart?" For the rest of the night they talk about the weather, and the cherry tart, which is the first of the season, and the children. The women take over the conversation, as if the men might smash it.

In photographs of Mussolini, his head juts forward, his chin is lifted. He wears a perpetual frown. His hair is closely shaved, the transparent dodge of a balding man. With his bowler hat and his lion cub, Léa thinks he looks like a clown, like the priests from her childhood. Everything in Mussolini's stance signals a kind of dominance that she hates. She hadn't thought of it before, but Aldo stands the same way, stomach out, arms folded, head tilted back, mouth tucked in disapproval. Consciously or not, he is imitating his hero.

The next day Aldo leaves for Milan, and the children, as she expected, are out of sorts. It takes a bath, a morning at the park, extra gelato before they seem halfway back to normal. And all the time she is thinking of Aldo thumping the table. There is no dishonour in being a servant, in any honest job— less shame in tending children and in sweeping floors than in making money off the backs of the workers. But she has had enough. She is sorry to leave the children, of whom she has grown fond. Flora is so thoughtful and mature, Marco throws himself into her arms and into the world with robust enthusiasm. Luca will be especially hard to leave; he needs her the most.

"Maria," she says in the kitchen, when the children have gone to bed, "Maria, what do you think about Mussolini?"

Maria says, "I am not paid to think."

"But Maria," she says. "I was told in the last election, there was no other party, no other candidate. And that in the countryside, they are assassinating the opposition."

Maria's hands are shaking. Her eyes are pink. She gestures to Léa to come closer. "My son is also in the countryside," she whispers. "I am very worried for his safety."

Léa did not know she had a son.

Maria's face looks soft and tired. "I need a job," she says to Léa. "I need to send him money."

Then Laura comes in, asking for a cup of tea and complaining that Luca has woken up and Léa should go see what is the matter with him, that Nervous Nellie, that absolute trial of a child, she doesn't know what she did to be so cursed in her children.

8.

As it turns out, Léa does not get a chance to quit.

"We are heading to the seaside for the last two weeks of summer," Laura says. "My mother has a house. We leave in a week. You can make your arrangements now."

"I will book the train," Léa says. She feels a little stung. How casually the rich cast people off, like soiled tablecloths.

"Yes," Laura says. "You should have no trouble."

As a goodbye present, she buys Flora books and Marco candy. Luca's present she thinks about for a long time. In the end, she buys him a watch. It is a little bit expensive, but she decides there is no point in holding onto her lire on these last days, she will only lose money changing them back. As she drops to her knees to strap the watch onto his skinny wrist, she can see how hard he is working not to weep. His nose is dripping—those tears will leak through any egress—and he sniffs loudly as she holds his hand.

"It is the same time in Berlin as it is in Rome," she says. "Imagine! When you are eating your breakfast, I will be eating my breakfast. When you are going to bed, I will be going to bed. You can look at this any time, and know that even though I am far away, I am with you! And one day you'll come visit me in Canada"—she twists the knob back six hours—"and you'll see what it's like to have your nights turned to days and your days turned to nights."

She corrects the time.

By now, he is full-on bawling, his sharp shoulder blades shaking under his thin summer shirt.

"Hush," she says. "You need to be a good big brother to Marco, you need to help him when I'm gone."

Léa has learned there is nothing better for people who feel incapable than taking a little bit of responsibility for someone else, and indeed, Luca is nodding.

"I'm a big boy," he says.

Léa agrees. "You're a big boy."

Even Laura softens, now that Léa is leaving. "However will I manage without you?"

Laura says, but Léa is more worried about Flora, since Laura will rely on her to manage for her—she often does.

After the children go to bed, she takes one last walk around the city to say goodbye to Rome. It is a spectacular evening. The angels on the bridges glow in the moonlight. She walks by the walls of the Vatican, which has just been given the status of a state—a country inside a country, that did not exist a month ago, such is the power of language—and she walks through the ruins of the Forum and all of the glory that has risen and fallen over so many years, and the ruin of history chimes with her own deep sense of transience and homelessness. This too shall pass, she keeps thinking, and it becomes the rhythm of her steps, this too shall pass, of her breath, this too shall pass, until she loses her way and realizes it is prudent to find her way back home.

Rome is a warning. With his beautiful home, and his confident voice, Aldo believes he is invulnerable. He talks about Mussolini like a schoolgirl with a crush. *Chosen-kalah hobn glezerne oygn*, her mother used to say: the bride and the groom have glass eyes. Love makes us blind. Ideology, too, can be a kind of love. A blind spot so large and so deep you can fall right through it.

She leaves before the children are up. Luca has left a note under her pillow. It says, "When I am eighteen, I am coming to live with you. DO NOT FORGET." She puts it in her pocket with her ticket but somehow it is lost on the train, though she spends nearly an hour looking for it under her seat and in the passageways.

9.

Back in Berlin she is suntanned and thinner despite those mounds of noodles, the endless cones of gelato, a Roman miracle indeed. It takes a little while to get used to her new freedom. There are gobs of time, huge armfuls of it, and no small person at her knees demanding her attention. She often goes to the cinema with Harry. They see Vertov's *Man with a Movie Camera*, that fragmented portrait of a Soviet city over the course of a day, and they laugh at the bar scene, when the drunken camera wobbles around a glass of beer, and then itself becomes a character, walking across the screen on the flamingo tripod legs, bowing coyly at the audience. She is most fascinated by an elegant woman in the middle of the film seen cutting and splicing the images together, like a seamstress: as if the movie is her tapestry. She is the wife of the director, and the editor of the film, and as Léa watches her quick fingers she seems the spider at the centre of the web, the woman who weaves the story.

Vertov speaks after the screening. His real name is Kaufman, and he could be a Roback brother or a cousin, with his dark eyebrows and sensual mouth. He looks straight at his audience and recites, "I am an eye. I am a mechanical eye. I, a machine, I am showing you a world, the likes of which only I can see."

Léa is enraptured but Harry is shifting in his chair; he cut into a corpse at the Charité that very morning and knows plenty about making the hidden manifest.

They are at Dovzhenko's *Arsenal* a few months later when the film is interrupted. A banner appears on the screen: *Krach am Wall Street*. Forever she will associate Black Thursday with the scene on the screen right before the movie was stopped, a German soldier driven mad during the Russian Civil War from laughing gas, his eyes covered in goggles, his mouth a dark hole of missing teeth. The projector is turned off, and the cinema-goers mill around on the sidewalk. Wall Street is very far away, and yet the audience seems both excited and dismayed. What happens when millions of dollars melt into the air? Crash is too physical a word: what has vanished is just an idea of wealth. And yet it changes everything. They stand on the sidewalk, talking loudly, asking questions that none of them can answer, until one by one they drift off.

Early in the morning, she wakes up with a sick feeling, a hive of worry buzzing in her brain.

Later that month, Harry gets a letter from Moishe Wolofsky, Léa's movie date from New York City. When Wall Street crashed, he was right in the middle of it, on the market floor. "You've never seen anything like it, Harry," he writes. "Grown men crying and staring in disbelief, their mouths hanging open. In front of the banks, lines that reached all the way down the block, and traders jumping from upper stories as the markets fell. You know when a tree suddenly falls and you can see that all along, it's been decaying, there's a big black hole in the middle of the trunk? It looked like it would stand forever, but it's been rotting from the inside out. Heartrot, they call it. That's capitalism. Decomposing all this time, ready to collapse. There's nothing here for me. I'm leaving the country." He says he's signing up to work on a merchant ship to Denmark with a friend, they're heading to Minsk to work at an ammunition factory. They're passing through Germany. Say hi to Léa, he writes at the end. Maybe he'll see them in Europe, maybe not.

She asks Harry if she can keep the letter. It feels like history.

10.

Her first clients in Berlin hire her to tutor their only son, Werner, in English and in French. The Leaveks are so high-strung they vibrate, so strained with nervous tension they seem decades older than their probable age which, Léa estimates, is no more than forty. It is hard to imagine casual, clever Werner belonging to either of them. He is as relaxed as they are neurotic. She watches his parents looking at him in wonder. He is a handsome boy of seventeen, dark and thin, with clever eyes and eloquent hands, a long patrician nose, his only real oddity a faded spreading birthmark on the side of his face. Once she gets to know him, it becomes part of his charm and gives him a flawed delicacy.

She soon learns that he is good at languages but lazy. She tells his parents they are wasting their money, but he decides he likes to have her around and fails his test deliberately in order to keep her.

"I have nothing to teach you," she says the next time she visits. She rests her bag on the table, unwilling, even, to take out her books. She is frustrated at his obstinacy though she can use the money and it is pleasant to sit there for an hour twice a week eating pound cake and drinking *kirschwasser*, which the Leaveks distill in their own cherry orchards in the Black Forest and which tastes like bitter almond.

"Léa," Werner says, as if she does not already have one foot out the door, "tell me about the polar bears!"

And as she explains that it would take much longer to get to Canada's far north from Montreal than it does, even, to Berlin, that polar bears mean little more to her than they do to him, he is already onto the next question, about reindeer and igloos, and soon the hour has passed with his nonsense questions and her sensible responses so that it is already time to leave when she realizes he has been teasing her the entire time and she bursts into embarrassed laughter.

After that, they are friends, and they talk about whatever he wants: the voyageurs with their long canoes; the beluga whales who haunt the Saint Lawrence River, pale as ghosts in the water; the ziggurat skyscrapers of New York which can reach seventy stories; the new building rising there which will be the tallest in the world.

He reminds her of her little brothers, of Michael, especially, who never stops talking and likes to tell jokes.

Werner has travelled only in Switzerland and Germany.

"My parents," he says in frustration, "believe the only good vacation is one that you have taken many times before, where you are sure of a quiet room and a good hot breakfast. They go skiing in the same resort every winter for a week, go bathing at the same beach for two weeks every summer. Neither of them even much like to ski or swim but it is the thing to do, so. My greatest desire is to see the world."

"Montaigne said if there was one corner in the world where he could not travel then he would not feel free," Léa says, and she sees Werner nod and take out his notebook, where he lists odd facts about the many places he longs to travel. She sees him write it down as an epigraph in the front of the book.

He wants to know about the places she has seen, Paris, London, Rome, New York, Quebec City. He does poorly in school because in his mind he is already far away. She encourages him to focus and he does so mostly to please her, which she discourages.

"Werner, you must learn this for your own sake."

A girl with younger brothers is accustomed to crushes from their friends, but she is ten years older than him. She finds it cute that he blushes when their knees touch by accident under the table, that when she waits for him to answer the door, she can hear him running. His mother hovers in the doorway when they study, she is like a hummingbird and will not sit, will not stay still. He is kind except to his parents, whom he orders around with loose contempt, and she is shocked at his behaviour. Her own mother would have never put up with it—if you asked her to fetch you a glass of water she would ask, why, didn't God give you legs? If you spoke back she'd say—*gey strashe di gens*—go threaten the geese.

"Werner," she says one day—she isn't sure when her job shifted, from teaching language to teaching manners, but maybe those aren't such separate endeavours, each language a code, a map for culture, a way of life—"you should speak more carefully. They have given everything to you, you know. It's disrespectful. More than that. It's cruel. You can do better."

Under his olive skin he grows pale at the rebuke. But she notices that the next time his mother darts in and out of the room, looking for her spectacles or gloves or book, he does not sigh or clear his throat but asks if he can help her.

The truth is, Léa is a natural big sister, totally accustomed to managing the incoherent desires and manners of younger people.

The truth is, a sister is not what he wants.

When she first visits the Leaveks, she cannot believe the amount of silver and bric-a-brac in their living room and cannot imagine the dusting required to keep all of that clutter sparkling. She runs her finger along the mantelpiece as a test and it comes off clean. There are rococo vases with gilded protrusions shaped like shells and leaves. There is a porcelain nude with blushing knees whose golden hair covers her crotch but not her dimpled bottom. There are Baccarat candlesticks and a whole set of Venetian glass, hand-blown and splattered with gold, brought back from their honeymoon—their only time in Italy, Werner says, and all they could say was that the food was too salty and the lagoon smelled like sewage.

Werner claims he is a socialist, and Léa laughs at him. These rich boys, with their fashionable pretensions. She tells him he is too young to join the cause. When she mentions his age, he looks hurt and his lower lip trembles. She was younger than he is now when she started working at the laundry, but she was never young like that.

He has the mannered precocity of an only child, which means he is at once very adult and very sheltered. He likes to read history.

"My hero is Vasily Ivanovitch Chapayev," he says, "the Red Army commander from the Russian Civil War. He was the first to capture an enemy tank, only he didn't know how it worked, so he commandeered ninety horses to drag it back to their encampment. He was illiterate and used to plan strategy on the dirt floors of trenches by candlelight. He modelled the movements of the troops using beets and potatoes."

"Which side were the potatoes on?" Léa asks, and Werner is stumped. She answers herself: "Beets are red."

"Potatoes have eyes everywhere," Werner responds.

11.

Every time a Brownshirt gets on the bus, everyone salutes and says, "*Heil Hitler.*" Léa carries her passport all the time and feels lucky that her eyes are blue. When the policemen stop her, she says, "I am an Ausländer. I don't really speak German very well."

She exaggerates her accent and bats her eyes, and they leave her alone.

Harry is less lucky. At the hospital, some of his colleagues know he is Jewish, and he says they have begun to keep their distance, or perhaps he is imagining it. In response to the change, he seems mostly perplexed, as if this could not possibly be happening to him, as if everyone will soon come to their senses, as if he cannot trust his own reality. In normal times, in a normal place, he would be heading towards a stable, fruitful future, but now everything is darkness and uncertainty. The SA marches in the streets in their uniforms, they storm into union halls, they riot in the bars and nightclubs frequented by the communists and the bohemians of the German left. They copy Mussolini's thugs, with their short haircuts and high boots, and swarm like an occupying army. They have money, they have cigarettes in their front pockets and daggers in their high boots, and they are looking for a fight.

Her classes have the unreal, soap bubble slipperiness of her studies in Grenoble; the ideas seem pretty but ephemeral, disconnected from the urgency of the streets. Half of her teachers are Jewish, including Professor Levy, the head of the Department. She wonders what they think about the growing power of Hitler's party, but they avoid politics as if it were in bad taste to mention it. They are the administrators of a bureaucracy of the imagination, all rule and hierarchy, title and procedure, and they seem oblivious to the poisonous tides lapping at the walls of their ivory tower. At school she is bored and impatient. Professor Levy, swelled and self-important, lecturing on the zeitgeist as dandruff snows the shoulders of his suit: what does he know about history? History is now, and right outside.

The street is littered with pamphlets calling for revolution. Support the rights of the worker! The hope for the future! The equality of all men and women! On one pamphlet, there is an address and a time, and she picks it up, smooths it out, and puts it in her pocket. She dresses carefully that day and walks to the address in the district called Red Wedding after she finishes her classes. The weather has changed, and she shivers in the chilly autumn air. There are men stationed at the door, their hands meaningfully tucked into their pockets. When she comes inside, half the chairs are empty, and the room is drafty and cold. More people shuffle in as different speakers take the stage, and she strains to hear them in the noisy hall. By the time the last speaker takes the podium, the room is full and warm with bodies. She begins to feel flushed.

The man on the podium looks like the clean-cut boys who march in sinister formation down the centre of the street, but how could he be? Instead, he is here, with his military haircut and his Aryan eyes.

"Comrades," he says. The word is swallowed by the large room. He puts his hand on his heart and tries again. "Comrades! I come before you today at a moment of great danger and great opportunity." The room is quiet now, and, gaining confidence, he raises his voice. "There is a man," he says, "who claims he has the solution for all of our problems. He says he will return power to us, the German people, but what he wants is destruction. He says he will bring peace and he carries war. He says he is for the workers, but he is for no one but himself. His criminal thugs march in our streets, our streets!"

Scattered applause in the hall. He's not bad. He could be more confident, but he's getting excited, and his pale cheeks are now red as he stretches out his arms.

"He wants a war? Very well. We will take the battle to him. We will take the battle to the streets!"

As he continues to speak, the hall grows louder with shouts of agreement and rage. The people rise, lifting their hats. As she looks around the room—all these beautiful young faces, glowing with passion—she thinks maybe she has found them, her people, her way inside. She is smiling with eager benevolence, at no one in particular and at everyone there, giddy with expectation, hungry for change.

"To the streets!" they echo, and he calls again, "To the streets!" He jumps off the stage and leads a procession out the door.

Léa follows them, shy and eager. There are more men than women, but she finds a few girls, trailing at the back, and she asks them, in her German which is getting stronger every day, "Where are we going?"

"To look for a fight," the taller one says. She is wearing wide trousers and her thick hair is cut short. "Gerda," she says, and her hand is warm and dry. "And this is Emilia."

Gerda must be close to six feet tall. She has the broad shoulders and big hands of a man, bright brown eyes and a quick smile, and dark hair cut in a bob. Emilia is nearly her opposite. Narrow and short, with straight blonde hair, slanted eyes, and a pointed chin, her lips look like they have been stamped on her face, a dark cupid's bow. Her handshake is limp and cold.

"Will you fight?" Léa asks, excited.

She thinks of Harry, who will certainly disapprove, who might right now be wondering where she has gone tonight. She can picture Gerda rolling up her sleeves and clenching her big hands into strong fists. Less so Emilia, though as she looks at her again, she can imagine her pulling a glittering knife from her full skirts, darting in from behind and fading back into the shadows like smoke.

"Oh no," Gerda says. "They won't find one tonight. We're going dancing, and they'll show up too when they get cold or bored."

"Or thirsty," Emilia adds. "Or lonely."

"Who was the man on the stage?" Léa asks.

"Who, Hans?" Gerda says. "His uncle is a Nazi, so he's always trying to prove himself. Me, I think militarism is a great danger to our movement. Revolutionary means must be aligned with revolutionary aims. We have no place for violence."

"Let the fascists give it up first," Emilia says. Yes, she is the one Léa would be more afraid to meet in a dark alley at night.

Léa is not dressed for dancing, but she has money in her pocket from teaching that day. She rolls up her skirt at the waist to make it shorter and Emilia, sighing, pulls an eyeliner and lipstick out of her pockets and makes her up quickly, under a streetlight, the pencil poking sharply at the corner of her eye. Boys walking by whistle at them as they stand under the yellow spotlight, and Emilia gives them the finger with her free hand while she finishes smearing lipstick on Léa's mouth. The lipstick tastes like chalk. "There," she says, "we just need to blot it," and she presses her lips onto Léa's before she has time to react. She grins, a wide gap between her front teeth. "Now you look like one of us."

Berlin is a night city. In the sunlight the broad boulevards and brick buildings are industrial and bare. When night falls, windows light up with lamps and candles, and small bars and restaurants bloom on every corner. The uncurtained windows are stages for the street, each rendezvous a performance. In the daytime, the police will pull out a ruler and check the length of your skirt. At night, girls lean into doorways and flip up their skirts at potential customers. Emilia is limping in her heels, so she takes them off and walks barefoot. They head to Bühler's Ballhaus on Auguststrasse. The walls are panelled in wood, and the little tables illuminated by candlelight that glitters off every sequined dress. The hard shine of diamonds, the warm glow of pearls.

"That's Clara," Gerda says, and points to a middle-aged woman in a plain black dress sitting in the corner, her back ramrod straight, her eyes scanning the room. "This is her place. She's a legend. After the war, she held balls for the war widows, and the women danced with each other."

"And with the ghosts of their husbands," Emilia adds. Léa is starting to like her now, her cool mischief.

The dance hall is full of women in spectacular dresses, with shining hair and glowing faces. Now Léa wishes she had more than borrowed lipstick. Gerda hands her a glass of something clear and she knocks it back without thinking. It warms her throat, loosens her limbs; she joins the fray in the middle of the dance floor, and tries to remember the moves that Adele taught her a lifetime ago in Montreal, the big leg movements of the Charleston, the rounded bops of the Lindy. She throws out her arms and kicks her feet but then the music changes, it's a waltz, and the riot of the dance floor smooths out as dancers couple up and begin to glide.

Léa is just making her way back to the tables when she feels a pressure on her arm. It's the man from the meeting, Hans, with his jacket open and the top buttons of his shirt undone.

"Care to dance?" he says, and he takes her waist and pulls her towards the centre of the room again.

"I saw you at the meeting," he says, and she nods, she is concentrating on following, which is difficult for her, she always has the impulse to lead. But Hans is good at leading. He holds her firmly, and he moves her so she does not need to think where to place her feet, which direction to face. He asks her all the usual questions, where she's from and where she's staying and why she's here, and he spins her towards him and away while making casual, charming conversation. The candles on the tables are reflected in the mirrors on the walls as the light bounces back off the crystal chandeliers, and the room is more filled with stars than the cloudy night skies of the outdoor city.

Gerda is twirling by herself, careless of the music or of any demand to be paired off, perfectly happy and perfectly out of rhythm. Hans dips Léa and then leads her by the hand to the bar, where he buys her a drink. She swallows in a gulp, feeling reckless. His hand is on her arm and she is not sure what he's doing with her, but she leans in and tips up her face and feels flushed with possibility and happiness. Perhaps, after all, she doesn't have to be alone.

"Excuse me," she says. She feels unsteady on her feet. "I'll be right back." She'll drink a glass of water, splash some on her face. She just needs a moment to recover herself.

She gets lost in the hallways and finds a staircase which she assumes must lead to the toilets, holding the railing to prop herself up. Really, she had not planned on drinking this much. She is wondering if Hans will be there when she gets back downstairs, and she swings open the door at the top of the landing only to find a scene as if from a dream, two men dressed in white duelling in the centre of a packed ballroom, and the polished floors slick with blood.

As she watches, a man skids in the gory puddle, takes a knee, and when he rises his pants are scarlet. The audience is smoking and drinking and laughing, lined up along the walls, there are chairs in a circle close to the duellers and some of the watchers are splattered in blood. A man is looking at her and points, and three men start shouldering through the crowd toward her so she backs off quickly, closing the door, running down the stairs and to the streets outside, forgetting her aching bladder, forgetting Hans at the bar, forgetting even that she is drunk, suddenly sober in the evening air.

She has to stop in an alley to pee on her way home, squatting in the shadows. When she wakes up the next morning it is with a throbbing head, a dry mouth, and a sense of dread, but Harry laughs at her at the café where she meets him for breakfast and says it's only a hangover. She can't bear to tell him about the strange ballroom turned to battle and the way it sounded when the fighting men slid on wood and gore, and how everyone laughed so their mouths were shadowed caverns, so it seemed like they were drinking blood.

It all seems like a sign of more violent times coming, though she does not believe in signs.

Also, she regrets walking out on Hans. That might have been her only chance.

Though she didn't intend it, walking out was a smart move. Léa finds herself pursued, for the first time in her life. Hans shows up at the boarding house the next day. "I missed you last night," he says. "Where did you go?" She doesn't really want to tell him—that surrealist nightmare—but she finds herself recounting the entire story as they walk towards the Leaveks' house, where she has a tutoring appointment. He laughs and she feels stung.

"I'm not laughing at you," he says quickly. "It's just, it's so absurd. A dueling club, that's what you saw. Those clubs are illegal, so they meet by night, in rented halls. Boys playing with swords, that's all. It's harmless—well, obviously not harmless," he amends, and she thinks of the dark slick of blood—"but no harm to anyone else, they weren't interested in you, they were just checking that you weren't a police informer. Though mostly the police don't bother them, and in fact, some of them duel themselves. It's one of those silly German practices, how you prove you are a man. You should look, you'll start to notice the scars. Some of the boys actually have cheated and given themselves scars, you know, to seem heroic. I have a few from when I fenced in high school. I was good at it, in fact, though I gave it up. I am a little embarrassed about them," Hans says, but to Léa it seems he lovingly strokes the faint silver ridges on his own cheek, as if he is proud rather than ashamed.

It has just rained, and the air smells of wet brick and pavement. The first green shoots of spring are emerging from the bare soil and through cracks in the cobblestones, clinging to any bit of dirt for a chance to bloom: snowdrops, crocuses, daffodils. Suddenly, she is wildly homesick for a certain orchard in Beauport where the apple blossoms cluster thick and sweet and the petals shower down like confetti. But spring will not arrive in Quebec for another two months, at least, and she has not been to Beauport in almost ten years. Home is an ocean away. Even so, she is completely there in her mind when Hans takes her hand, which shocks her back to her own time and place so that she pulls away without intending to do so.

"Forgive me," he says, and clasps his hands behind his back as if to conceal them. He is blushing and she feels sorry she has embarrassed him.

"Not at all," she says, and does something bold, lifts up on her toes and kisses his cheek before she can think too much about it. His hand flies up to his cheek, and touches the spot where her lips had been; they are in front of the Leaveks' door, and she says, "Goodbye!" and goes inside to teach her class, a little astonished at her own audacity.

Werner is in a filthy mood for the entire hour, he keeps speaking German and not English to her, and so quickly she can't follow him. He can't seem to sit still and will barely meet her gaze. At the end of the session he says, "So, who is your boyfriend?"

She understands but is also a little surprised. "He's not my boyfriend," she says, but her heart sings a little at the possibility as she lets herself out.

12.

Their first date is on May Day. The early spring light paints every leaf with a stripe of gold, the peonies are blooming, the scent of lilac is everywhere, and she feels drunk with happiness, from the bottom of her feet to the top of her head.

Hans holds her arm and matches her steps as they walk towards Kösliner Strasse. To her disappointment, most of the stores are open rather than closed for the workers' day, business as usual, and people are strolling along the boulevards. Because it is so lovely outside, she and Hans detour along the Spree. They could be any couple going for a stroll on a spring morning.

If they could only continue like that, strolling along the river, looking at the clouds reflected in the water, stopping for a coffee beside the water. If only they could surrender to ordinary happiness.

But then they swerve towards the worker's rally in Wedding.

There is no central location or route, but many of the protestors are meeting here. Even early in the morning it is chaos. There are barricades in the street, the sidewalks smell of sulfur and smoke, people are shouting and running in every direction. Here is Gerda, who hugs her quickly and hands her a banner. Across the road Emilia flashes Léa a gap-toothed smile and raises a fist. Among the counter-protestors she recognizes a group of law students, wearing swastikas, brandishing their dueling swords. They set on the May Day protestors like a pack of dogs.

Léa runs straight towards the fight.

As she watches the slim silver swords streaking in the sun and sees smoke rising from the street behind the barricades, she is confused about which century it is, whose battle she is fighting. The protestors are singing the "Internationale," and Léa is trying to hold onto her banner as a man with three perfectly symmetrical scars on his cheek tries to pull it away.

Hans is shouting for her, no, at her, and she ignores him. She kneels to help a man who has collapsed, his face bleeding. When she stands up, she is knocked over. The cops pull up, flying squads on trucks and motorcycles, brandishing billy clubs and revolvers. Surely to restore the peace?

Then they buckle their helmets and face off against the protestors alongside the fascists. She cannot believe it.

The students have stones and fists but the police have Tanz guns. They are shooting into the crowd, more and more police have arrived, so many she cannot keep track.

Hans has caught up to her. He pulls her back, and as they run away, she is crying. Her tights are torn and her knees are skinned, her palms are raw and bleeding, he leads her down the smaller streets, she is lost. On the main streets they are still shooting, they are arresting protestors who are only trying to get home.

"They are shooting them," she hears people calling on the street. "They are killing them!"

It's a massacre.

The newspapers will report that onlookers were wounded through windows and through doors, bullets fired without warning, women killed, an eighty-year-old man shot in the back. The police will claim they have stopped an armed insurrection and will search house to house for evidence. They will find only old bayonets, a dud grenade, an ancient rifle—souvenirs of an older conflict, not signs of a revolution.

Later on, she will think of this as her baptism by police.

13.

A month later, at the Twelfth Party Congress, the members are infuriated and in mourning.

"This is not social democracy!" one of the speakers cries. "This is social fascism. Capitalism has indisputably entered its third period, the violent death throes before the ultimate collapse. Yes, my comrades, this is the last call, this is the final stage, and we must take up arms, not just take to the streets. This is war."

They are calling it *Blutmai*—Bloody May.

The speakers are enraged. In their speeches the bloodbath is turned to perverse and violent celebration, a provocation to further violence, as if they had intended to be slaughtered in order to prove a point through their own martyrdom. They say they had always expected violence, and that the only solution is now open battle. Their bloodthirsty ardor frightens her. These men in the workers' hall raring to head back to the streets, they are playing right into the hands of the fascists. They are running to their own executions.

And worse: the Nazis, who started the fight, are claiming to be Germany's only chance for law and order. They set the fire, then they say they are the only ones who can put it out. She is staggered at their cynicism.

There are mostly men in the hall, though she sees Gerda in her black beret near the back door. She cannot find Hans, and indeed, he has been elusive over the last few weeks, since the day of the rally. The room is dark and smells of sweat and cigarettes; she keeps getting jostled, men step on her toes in their big boots. They are in such disarray they cannot even figure out what to do with their bodies, how to manage together in a shared space. She feels queasy dismay at the ambient chaos, the voices shouting over one another, the faces red with anger and despair. No one seems to be in charge, and they are like schoolchildren without a monitor, messy fury and posturing bluster.

The lights sputter off, and it is unclear if this is a regular electricity cut or an act of sabotage. A year ago, the courts lifted the ban on Hitler's speeches, but the workers' groups are still not permitted to gather in public. They are no longer fighting an illegal militia: their enemies are also the police and the government.

As the weeks pass, the situation grows more desperate. Their numbers are diminishing. Like dead leaves in late fall, the young men turn from red to brown. She recognizes some of the workers from the hall on the streets and they are wearing SA uniforms. Some of them avoid her eyes and some of them look straight at her, daring her to challenge them. They have the whiskery moustaches of adolescents, and it is hard to take them seriously, with their necks and ears bared in their close-shaved haircuts, but she sees them move in crowds with disciplined and vicious intent, she sees them beat down anyone who catches their attention—a woman in a headscarf, a beggar on the street. There is no code of conduct anymore; she watches old men get punched in the back of the head, men who did not even know they were being followed. She becomes attentive to what is behind her and who is beside her.

She learns to disappear.

14.

At night, she escapes to the theatre, catharsis from the pressure of the streets. She goes to an opera whose name confuses her, *The Rise and Fall of the City of Mahagonny*. It is set in America, she thinks, though an America of the imagination: lumberjacks, frontier towns and bars. Three fugitives end up in a town in the middle of nowhere. They decide to found a city of pleasure, attracting gold miners, gamblers, profiteers.

"Oh, show me the way to the next whisky bar," an actress sings, in an odd, affected English, "for if we don't find the way to the next whisky bar, I tell you we must die! I tell you we must die! I tell you we must die!"

The singer has black bangs, a strong chin, and a crooked smile. She flips up her arm like a salute, cocks her head, more in challenge than flirtation, seems not beautiful but magnetic with her hoarse voice and raw bones. As a performer, her means of seduction is confrontation. Léa has never seen anything like it, and when the woman is on the stage it is hard to look at anyone or anything else.

Léa is having trouble following, or maybe it's that the play doesn't make sense: visitors arrive, visitors leave, no sooner is the town booming than it is falling, there are no laws and then suddenly a trial. Oh, and a hurricane is coming! But the town is spared the hurricane and intoxicated with that miracle they declare Mahagonny a town of no laws.

The second act is all excess.

In the last scene, one of the men is put to death and the town falls apart, burning in the background as the whole company sings, "Nothing will help us now, nothing will help us now."

Léa stands with the rest of the audience and claps. Wonderful, it's wonderful. Art that awakens the world.

Brecht is sitting in the front row, a man with a clever, high forehead and jagged bangs he might have cut himself, black glasses, a clean-shaven chin. He looks as if he is holding something amusing in his mouth and chewing it over. After the show, at the bar near the theatre, he beckons to her with his cigar. His arm is around a young woman, an actress. He is kneading her hip aggressively, as a potter kneads a vase into shape, but he is looking so intently at Léa she almost feels it is her own flesh that is being massaged and stroked. "What brings you here?" he says.

"I am here for university," she says, so excited to meet the playwright that she stumbles over her words. "But I also wanted to come here, to Berlin," she says, gesturing at the room. "To see your workman's theatre. The beauty of what you are building."

His hand has moved up his companion's ribs and now he strokes beneath her breast with his thumb. Léa's eyes follow his wandering hands. Not exactly a handsome man, but everyone is looking at him, and at the ordinary girl upon whom his interest has suddenly fallen. She is in his spotlight.

He leans towards her, his eyes serious, and talks in a low voice. "Nothing is being built here," he says. "Everything is about to fall apart."

Then he pulls his companion onto his lap and it is as if a curtain has dropped between them.

Across the theatre, the woman who was so charismatic on the stage has folded herself across a man wearing a bowtie, who looks like a boy despite his receding hairline. She laughs loudly and strokes his face, kicking her heels up in the air, as if still playing the part in the play, accustomed to always being watched.

According to *Mahagonny*, the four steps to the good life are to eat, to screw, to fight, to drink.

Mahagonny, Léa thinks on the way home, how odd to think of a city named Mahagonny, and then she realizes she has walked right into a pack of Brownshirts, a group of five or six young men. As she walks through their group she feels her breasts grabbed, her ass squeezed, they pass her around and handle her like a piece of meat flung from hand to hand and then she is on the other side of the street and unsure if she has dreamed it, she was so shocked she did not even cry out, and she is both marked and invisible.

Everything to them is permitted, and everything to us is forbidden, and nothing can help us now.

The stage is a mirror. The city is burning.

That night she finds the fingerprint bruises on her thighs and her breasts, and she stays in the cold bath for a long time even though she is shivering, scrubbing at the marks with a washcloth as if she could remove them.

The theatre in Berlin is so far beyond Montreal that she cannot believe that those tawdry spectacles, those red-velvet extravaganzas, ever held her attention. At home, theatre was a luxury, an escape, a fantasia. Here the actors face their audience, point their fingers, have her squirming in her chair. Nothing will help us now. Nothing will help *you* now.

At night, sometimes, she sings that strange song to herself, a tick-tock lullaby—"I tell you we must die, I tell you we must die, I tell you we must die!"

15.

After meetings, Emilia introduces her to the Berlin clubs, and on a foul night in December escorts her to a cabaret where a woman strides onto a dark stage wearing a top hat, a jacket, heels, and very little else, and sings to the audience in a voice of honey and smoke. She has the eyes and profile of a hawk. She looks like the women who are also men, or like a goddess who could change into a falcon and fly. This woman seems like she has the power of metamorphosis. No one could hold her to only one shape. Her voice goes right through Léa, as if she existed just to listen to her.

After that, she goes every night that Marlene is performing, and starts to notice the same faces around her, similarly spellbound.

At the Leaveks', small objects begin to disappear. There are holes in the display cabinets like missing teeth. And then, not just objects. Léa has never been certain of the number of maids in the employ of the Leavek house—it seems at least one is always sitting at the kitchen table, polishing that endless silver—but one day there is no one to bring the tea, there is dust on the once-immaculate table.

Mrs. Leavek goes out every morning with a porcelain shepherdess or set of silver teaspoons in her bag, comes home richer and less encumbered. Though the house is neglected, she seems more confident and driven. She dresses beautifully every day—the prices are better if you don't seem like you need the money—but still, it would have been worth more if she had sold it a year ago, everyone is selling their birthright for a handful of marks, a ticket on a train. She believes mostly in gold, and that she keeps, sewing it into the hems of the dresses she will bring to Switzerland.

Dr. Leavek is doing poorly. The racial laws mean he can no longer work, and his mood is dark. Most of the time he stays in his room with the blinds drawn and the door closed. Day and night mean nothing to him anymore.

When Léa walks into the house for a tutoring session, he is sitting with the light off in the living room, wreathed in pipe smoke.

"What time is it?" he says.

"Ten in the morning," she says.

He nods. "Bedtime, then," he says, and ambles back to his room.

"We are staying until the end of the school year," Werner says. He is angry at this, what does school mean right now when everything has turned to dust? Still, the old conventions hold even as their world falls apart.

What is extraordinary is that even in these end times, people do not change.

When she leaves that day, she finds a folded note in her coat pocket in Werner's careful writing. It is titled, "The Parable of the Frog."

"It happened right here in Germany! In 1869, in Königsberg. A physiologist named Friedrich Goltz put a lobotomized frog in a pot of slowly heating water, and the frog allowed itself to be boiled alive. Of course, the frog with an intact brain jumped out at 25 degrees Celsius. Which means you would have to be an idiot to stay.

"Why, you ask, did Goltz find it necessary to stew a frog whose brain had been cut out?

"He was looking for the soul."

16.

That evening at the cabaret, she sees Werner near the stage. He is wearing a black tuxedo, perhaps his father's. It hangs on him, though the sleeves are too short for his long arms.

"Sit with me, Léa!" he says.

"Aren't you too young to be here?"

He raises his eyebrows and buys her a drink. "I'm here every night," he says, but she's almost certain that's not the case.

She starts to notice him other places she frequents, the café on her corner, the union hall, the Friday market. It could be a coincidence—they move in the same circles, even though he is so much younger. It is a free country. Well, for now, at least. Somewhat free.

She means to ask him about the note, but she forgets to mention it, and as the weeks pass her forgetfulness is so stubborn it begins to feel deliberate. Because they have never spoken about it, it feels like a secret game, and like every secret, creates an unstable complicity.

When she comes to his house for lessons, they never mention their other meetings. She gathers from something his mother says that he has stopped going to school entirely, and when she asks him about it, he shrugs.

"No future, no point," he says, and when she protests he interrupts her. "Don't worry," he says, "I'll show up for exams, and they'll pass me. I don't learn anything there anyway."

From their discussions of his classes, she can't disagree with that.

Werner keeps leaving little notes in her pocket, new parables.

"The water was always warm around here," one reads. "It heats up, it gets cooler, that's as natural as the sunrise and sunset. This water is our home, we have wallowed in this bog for lo these many generations, we have spawned in these pockets of mud. Nobody belongs here more than us frogs."

The next week, the note says, "I have always been ready to leap. For as long as I have lived upon these lily pads my legs have been tensed, my senses alert, at any moment I might heed the call. Only the water is so pleasant today, I think I will linger. Just a little bit longer."

And then, after a night she spots him at the workman's hall.

"If a frog could get out, it would certainly get out. We need to stop blaming the frogs for the temperature of the water. Instead, we should look for those who are lighting fires, who are adding fuel, for those who are fanning the flames."

Like her, he has decided to join the fight.

17.

Léa sells *Die Rote Fahne* on the street in the mornings before she begins her tutoring, and she learns that the street corner is her pulpit. She has a gift for engaging strangers, for the art of the pamphlet and handshake. She likes to be out early, when people are heading to work and the sidewalks shine with possibility in the morning light.

She sells more papers than anyone in her group, and she says it is because she has the best corner. Really, it is that she has the best smile.

Sometimes, the Brownshirts knock her newspapers into the puddles and her hat into the mud, so hard she goes sprawling, holes in her stockings at the knee. When the thugs leave, she turns her stockings around so the holes are not visible, rescues the papers that have not been spoiled, straightens her hair and keeps on selling.

She is moved when Emilia notices the holes and instead of mocking her, brings her new stockings.

"I have dozens," she says, rolling her shoulders, "from my admirers. It's nothing."

But it is something to belong.

Léa is busy all day and every night. She overflows with activities, and is constantly running from one commitment to another, like an errand girl for goodness. Her woman's rights group meets Tuesday nights, and she is often late so she ends up in the same spot near the back door, beside a beautiful older woman. In contrast to Léa's frenetic activity, the woman exudes stillness, so much so that it is calming to be in her presence. Her hair is silver, and she smells of lavender and fresh grass, as if she has always just come from working in a garden.

It is a surprise, some weeks later, to learn that the woman is famous. Her name is Frau Käthe Kollwitz. She teaches art at the Berlin Academy, and lives in Prenzlauer Berg with her husband, who is a doctor. The group plans to organize an exhibit of her work as an anti-war protest. "I'll help," Léa says, her hand up as soon as they ask for volunteers; she goes over to Frau Kollwitz's large apartment on Weissenburgerstrasse to choose the etchings and pick up some posters.

Frau Kollwitz opens the door and ushers Léa to her long dining room table, in a room cluttered with dark heavy furniture. A dozen etchings are spread out and weighted with stones so they do not blow away.

Léa is always self-assured, but something about Frau Kollwitz has her intimidated—no, in awe. Frau Kollwitz moves silently and gracefully through the cluttered room. She has heavy-lidded dark eyes, fine white hair parted in the middle and pulled into a bun at the nape of her neck, the broad downturned mouth of—of a turtle, yes, a turtle is what Frau Kollwitz reminds her of, in her deliberate dignity. In frames on the walls she keeps glimpsing Kollwitz's own face in deeply crosshatched etchings, so that her real face, the hollows under her eyes and the wrinkles in her skin, seems also a copy of those implacable staring images on the wall.

Frau Kollwitz pours tea, careless of the artwork on the table. There are posters spread out, and a series of woodcuts, jagged and resolute in their black-and-white starkness. In one, a series of soldiers are pulled to war, their heads thrown back, their expressions frenzied. Death leads the group, his skeletal arm thrown around the neck of the first volunteer, dragging him out of the frame. Another image shows grieving women in a huddle, their bodies a collective tombstone for their lost sons.

One poster says, "Fight war, not wars." The next shows a group of starving children, their empty bowls held up to a mother's helpless empty hands, and another, perhaps the simplest of all, has a figure throwing up a hand, the other hand to their chest, expression defiant, and says, "Never again war!" The figure could be a man or a woman, it seems deliberately androgynous. Even the race is indeterminate, and the image much rougher than the fine etchings and woodcuts which surround it. Léa is captivated.

Frau Kollwitz says, "This we put by the door, it should be the first thing people see on their way in and the last thing they see as they leave."

She makes the same gesture as the figure in the poster with her own hand, her thumb, middle, and index fingers pointed up, and her palm towards Léa, and says, "It is the *schwurhand*, the gesture for swearing an oath."

That same gesture, made horizontal, is the shape of a pistol, the thumb the hammer, the fingers the barrel. When her brothers pretended to be soldiers, that game her father always hated, they said *pow pow* to their English friends, but *pan pan* when they played in French.

In every country, boys like to play at war, and every language has its own sound for the percussion of a firing weapon.

Léa has barely said two words to Frau Kollwitz but she somehow feels understood. Perhaps it is the gift of an artist who has spent her life looking, really looking, not just at other people but into them. On the way out, she is rewarded with a smile of such brilliance it warms her bones.

18.

There is one picture which stands out from the others. It is a self-portrait, and in it, Frau Kollwitz is young. She is holding a child and laughing. Her cheeks are full, and her eyes are joyful. The boy, two or three years old, grasps at her face, and the picture is so skillfully done that Léa can almost feel the warm, wriggling weight. How many times has she carried a child like that, and felt small probing fingers in a clumsy embrace?

"Käthe," Léa says—it has been several weeks since their first meeting and they are on a first-name basis; indeed, she feels she has known her all her life. "Can you tell me about this picture?"

Frau Kollwitz rises and stands in front of the image, her hands folded in front of her chest.

"That's my son Peter. I was younger than you are now when I drew that picture. I loved to use him as a model. He was so beautiful, I drew him all the time. It is as if I knew he didn't have too long."

She sits down quickly, catching herself on the chair, almost as if she is falling.

"Back then, I wasn't concerned with being an activist, I was an artist and a mother, I helped my husband with his clinic. I saw so many women who would come in to the clinic with black eyes, with broken arms, with battered faces. Always it was the same story—the husband lost his job, and he took it out on her with his fists. All that poverty turned to rage. Or else sometimes—we saw this too—the husband grew melancholy and committed suicide. Either way, these women were left raising five, six children, trying to scrape by with some kind of living on their own. I helped them and I felt for them, but I was nothing like those women. I thought of myself as incredibly lucky. Karl had his work, and I had mine, and we had these two perfect boys. We were very happy. The gods were smiling at us."

She goes over to the bookshelf and pulls an etching out from between two hardcover volumes. She places it in front of Léa, who leans forward to look more closely, and then pulls back when she sees the picture. A woman, nude, cross-legged on the ground, is hunched over the body of a child. He is limp and perfect and dead, his head tipped back like Christ in Michelangelo's Pietà, his head in her lap. She is all dark lines and devouring posture, her face hidden and her breasts concealed by her hair, leaning over his body in a posture that is both hunger and grief. She looks like an ogre or a vampire. It is almost as if she has killed him herself.

"I saw no contradiction between being a mother and being an artist," Käthe says. "I was ruthless in my work. Imagine asking a seven-year-old to pose for this picture. I drew it in front of the mirror, holding him with one arm. He was so heavy, and it was difficult to keep the posture and to draw the pose at the same time. He said, Mother, stop moaning, it will be beautiful when it is finished. I called it *Mother with Dead Child*. Ten years later the war began, and he wanted to enlist. His father said no, but I said let him go, let him defend the fatherland. Back then, I still believed that a country was worth fighting for, and sacrifice was only a word to me. I also thought Karl was trying to control him. He needed to make his own decisions and be allowed his independence. Three weeks later, he was killed."

She takes the picture back and slides it out of sight.

"I kissed him on his forehead and I sent him to die. To lose a child is to outlive your own death," she says. "That is why this exhibition is so important. For all the mothers, and for all the children. For Peter."

19.

"Come to the studio," Käthe says, "I have a few more pieces there." She is the first woman with a studio in the Prussian Art Academy. Léa knows this not from Käthe, who would never brag, but from Emilia, for whom Frau Kollwitz is a hero. Emilia, it turns out, has always wanted to be an artist. She takes a sketchbook to the clubs and cabarets, and from a corner table draws the dancers and the audience, in caricatural tangles of desire.

When Léa arrives Käthe is waiting, wearing a white artist's smock. She looks a little like her husband, whom Léa has often glimpsed passing through the living room in his doctor's coat on his way back to the clinic. Her hands are white and dry with plaster dust.

"Just here," she says, and hands Léa the portfolio, but Léa is looking past her, at the two white giants who dominate the floor.

There they are, Käthe and Karl, larger than life. They are kneeling on rough-hewn blocks, which seem less support or prop than something which binds and constrains them. In the sculpture, Karl's spine is straight, and he looks forward. His arms are tightly crossed and his forehead is furrowed. He holds himself tightly, and Käthe has sculpted the tension in his fingers and the pull on the fabric of his sleeves. In her sculpture, she is cloaked in a cape. Her head is bowed and her hand is at her own throat.

They are like massive chess pieces in an endgame where the first rule is they must not cross each other's paths. What is most powerful is the empty space between them, the way they hold only themselves. Léa is looking at the solitude of their grief.

Käthe watches her, her arms held behind her back.

"They are for the cemetery," she says, "and they are nearly complete. I want them to stand as sentries at the gate, like the angels with flaming swords posted at the entrance of the Garden of Eden, saying here you will not return."

In the statue, she looks like a husk of herself. All the joy has been drained out of her and what remains is a sarcophagus. She is a container for the losses she has sustained.

Léa nods. "My mother lost a child," she says. "At birth. I don't think she ever got over it."

"One does not," Käthe says, and says no more.

She hands Léa the portfolio of her drawings and Léa clutches them like an infant to her chest.

"This is important work," she says, "to be an advocate. To voice the sufferings of all people. To serve a purpose in your time, when so many are confused and in need of help."

She looks at Léa appraisingly. "I would like to draw you sometime," she says, and she opens the door in gentle dismissal.

20.

The exhibition is a great success. There is a line at the door when they open, and Frau Kollwitz moves with grace between the visitors, dressed in black silk, her silver hair pulled back at the nape. Her husband is there, and they are very gentle with each other in the manner of those who have suffered a great loss and understand how easily the entire world could break wide open again.

Hans comes, and Gerda, and Léa spots Emilia in a far corner, drinking wine and laughing, her teeth stained red. Werner comes with his parents, which is surprising—he has told her his father has not left the house for weeks—and he leads them around by the hands as if he is the parent and they are the children.

The fascists do not crash the party, do not storm the room, do not rip the posters from the walls, and that is also a quiet victory. The room does not empty out until one in the morning, but as she cleans up glasses and sweeps the floor Léa feels a little hollow rather than happy, and at first, she can't think why. A pamphlet has been dropped on the floor, a reproduction of the war poster. Someone has used it to hold their cake and then crumpled it up as trash, and she thinks, what happened here, after all?

Frau Kollwitz had told her the exhibition should feel like the end of a war, but it just felt like another event. The same faces, same conversations, solidarity as a closed circle rather than an active intervention. She envies Käthe her talent; even more than that, she envies her faith in the ability of art to change the world. She thinks of a proverb her father used to quote to her. It is not yours to finish the work of healing the world, but neither are you free to abstain from the effort. Thinking of him in his peasant's cap, of his worker's hands and his gentle, bookish mind, she has a wave of missing him and missing home that is so strong she is dizzy with nostalgia. She needs to lean on the wall.

"Léa," she hears a familiar voice say, "have I missed it, is it all over?"

For a second, she thinks it is her father speaking from across an ocean.

But there is Harry at the open door, back from rounds at the hospital, and he is so dear and familiar that she runs into his arms, his bearish hug. He is so much like their father, so kind and so reliable, how had she never realized?

"Easy," he says, and he holds her up. "Did it go well?"

She looks around the room—she has finished cleaning up without realizing it, there is nothing left to do—and she says, "Yes, it did go well, let me show you around," and there it is again, that little spark in her heart.

21.

"We shit on freedom," the Nazi students chant. "*Juden Raus*," their signs say. "*Köpfe warden rollen*," heads will roll. The Nazi student groups recruit from the law faculty, from engineering, from theology and math. The humanities students— philosophers, literary types, artists—are in the union halls, working for the revolution. The campus is a battleground, strewn with propaganda posters and pamphlets, knots of students conspiring in corners and fist fights in the quad. The lecture halls are empty.

The humanities students invite factory workers and the unemployed to the local meetings, trying to win them over to the cause. Freedom for the workers, justice and equality for all: join us, and be on the right side of history. But golden papers rain down from the heavens: Hitler gives work, the papers say. Hitler gives bread. They collect in the gutters and get soggy in the rain, and the factory men who come to the union hall brandish those promises like money. Soon many of them stop coming to the meetings at all. She keeps recognizing her old comrades on the street, in uniform, cigarettes stuck into their armbands—you can buy a man with cigarettes— and they are swollen with power. They walk arm in arm.

Rudolphe is the leader of the local workers' cell. He is a quiet and steady man who prefers to let others take the stage and make the speeches, but he is always there, sitting in the background, with a poised, alert readiness if anyone should need to intervene. He fought at Verdun, Gerda told her. Nine months in that hell. He limps badly and has trouble standing for long periods of time—perhaps another reason he avoids the podium. His stomach was ruined in the war, so he is very thin. One of his hands is bent permanently into a claw, and he is partially deaf.

Rudolphe is the gentlest of revolutionaries: an absolute pacifist, with a soft voice and a softer demeanour. Though she has never had much to do with him, she liked him from the first time they met. He reminds her of her father.

At the workers' meetings on Wednesday nights, they end by singing a new song, "Solidarity."

Whose morning is the morning?
Whose world is the world?

In the world as it is now, a twelve-year-old boy has been beaten nearly to death at school because a classmate said he was a Jew. "*Nein,*" he cried, his face a mask of blood and snot, "*Ich bin kein Jude, ich bin Deutscher.*" He was a Jew, but his father had never told him. So were some of the children who beat him. A friend of Léa's, a teacher in the school where it happened, tells her the story, her face so pale her freckles look like splatters of mud on white paper. Her eyes are like peeled eggs, naked with horror.

So many of her friends want to fight the fascists. They roam the streets at night, every night. That property of the German language where you smash the words together to make a new meaning: one of her friends has coined a new one, a-face-that-asks-for-punching, and every time they pass a pack of the boys in brown she mutters it under her breath. But Léa thinks of Käthe and thinks of her own gentle father, and can't help but feel like their efforts are futile—more than futile, destructive. They remind her of children playing at war. Every act of violence is more fuel for the flames. Or maybe she is wrong; maybe there is no choice but to fight. When she is with Käthe, she feels the virtue of the pacifist position. When she is on the street, she feels full of fury, ready to fight.

At the university, when people ask her what she is she says, "*Ich bin Kanadier.*" If she would say, "*Ich bin Jüdisch,*" they would tell her to get out, fast. They ask how the French and English get along and she says, "Indeed they get along very well. They often marry." The Germans don't believe her. She tells them she is not interested in their politics, she has come to study their language, their literature. She lies. She is red, red, red, she is drunk on those night meetings in the workmen's hall, in love with this new world that is coming, that they are building, or that might already be here: they talk about going to the Soviet Union, where everyone is free.

22.

Hans has reappeared, and she is spending more time with him. He does not explain where he went after May Day, and she does not ask. Those missing weeks are a shadow at the edge of their relationship. Still, she enjoys her time with him. He is like no one she has ever known. He is reflexively chivalrous, will take her arm and walk on the outer edge of the sidewalk so that the passing trams do not splatter her with mud, will open doors before she even realizes she is in front of them. He smooths the world. She is used to her brothers—Harry's prissy stolid loyalty, Leo and Michael's mischief. She is used to dark-eyed boys who pinch and tease, and to the polished men of the theatre, who only want to look at themselves through the mirror of her eyes. She has always shrugged off special treatment as a woman, that controlling paternalism which masquerades as gentlemanly behaviour. Hans treats her with care. He gives her his jacket when she shivers, his arm when she crosses the street. The ease of being with him feels like a betrayal of her own autonomy, and she is sometimes concerned that she feels so comfortable—leaning on him, like any other girl. But she also feels good. Perhaps she no longer wants what she once wanted.

It occurs to her too slowly that despite his revolutionary fervor, Hans comes from money. He brings Léa to meet his mother and introduces her as Léa the Canadian. Even after all this time, she has not told Hans that she is Jewish. She is not sure what the right moment to tell him would have been, but in any case, that moment has long passed. Now it will seem like something that she held back, though she never meant to do so.

Hans's mother seems fragile, sitting on her blue brocade couch beside him, holding his hand with proprietary and performative tenderness. His father died when he was young, and it has been just the two of them at home—more like brother and sister, Hans has told her, than mother and son. Elsa looks years younger than her age, except for her hands, which she tends to hide in the folds of her skirt, and which are spotted and lined, though so soft, Léa had noticed when they were introduced. She talks at great length about the difficulties of the twenties, of all that their family had lost, and as she gestures with her delicate wrists Léa sees only evidence of surfeit. If these are the dregs of a reduced existence, they must have once been obscenely wealthy.

Léa notices that around her the maids anticipate Elsa's needs, bringing coffee in a silver pot, placing a cushion behind her back, a footstool under her narrow feet. Later, Hans tells her his mother has been ill a long time, though he does not specify the nature of the illness, and Léa realizes that this is how he has learned his considerate habits, his way of treating women like convalescents. Which Léa is decidedly not—she resents it, throws off his arm and skips ahead, tries to pay though she has very little money. These efforts seem to both confuse and entice him, since like many men he wants both his mother and her opposite.

It is difficult not to judge Hans after she has seen his marble foyer, the mirrored entrance to his home, the enormous vases of lilies at the door. Hans talks about the workers as if they belong to him and he dresses for meetings as if he is putting on a costume. She can't ask him why or how he can fight this fight and still live this life. She has no right.

But that apartment, and his mother especially, are a stone in her shoe that she cannot shake out. His mother, Hans has confessed, thinks the Nazi goons are not especially nice, does not approve of their brutishness, nonetheless believes if they can just get rid of the Reds and the unions it will be good for business, and what is good for business is good for Germany.

And Hans just keeps his mouth shut. There's no point, he tells Léa. I'm not going to change her mind, anyway, it doesn't matter what she thinks. What matters is the life we make together.

Hans takes her outside the city, to the lakes which surround Berlin—Tegel, Müggelsee, and Schlachtensee, by the edge of Grunewald Forest. The countryside reminds her of the area around Sainte-Agathe, the clear cold lakes surrounded with maple and oak. It is late spring, and the leaves have entered their middle green. Léa and Hans have a drink in the *biergarten* and then rent a boat and drift in the dapple by the shoreline. He reaches over and slides his finger up the inside of her arm; she melts in the light, stretching her sun-warmed limbs towards him. It is a weekday, and no one else is out: gingerly, on the floor of the rowboat, she arranges herself, the bench pressing into her spine.

It is quick, and a little bit uncomfortable—she has leaves in her hair, a splinter in her thigh, and he burns his back— but still, they feel like they have gotten away with something. Her accidental virginity, which she held onto so much longer than she intended, is nothing she will miss. And here in Berlin, where everything is permitted, this seems less consequential than it would have been back home. They keep laughing as they paddle back. He has his camera, which miraculously has stayed dry through their tipsy journey, and he looks at her for a long time through the lens.

In the picture he takes, she seems completely relaxed. Her legs are crossed, her hands clasped on her lap, her hair is loose on her shoulders and wild in the wind, she is wearing what might be called a Mona Lisa smile, one that promises and withholds at the same time.

When she sees the photograph, she thinks he might be in love with her. She does not recognize herself through his eyes—this soft enigmatic woman. She keeps taking the photo out and then putting it away, as if to practise whom she might become if they stay together.

23.

Even after all this time, she is still not a member of the Communist Party. In Germany you need a sponsor, and then you need to be vetted. When her audience with the committee finally arrives, she dresses carefully, in the best clothes that she has, as if going to a job interview: her black dress, her good wool coat with the pale fur collar, her high-heeled shoes, and to top it all off, a cloche hat she bought in Paris.

Gerda is her sponsor and meets her at the workmen's hall. She looks her up and down with open disappointment, and says, "What are you wearing? Oh, never mind, it's too late now."

When she walks into the hall, her heels announcing her on the hard floor, Léa understands what Gerda means. The Party members are lined up behind a long wooden table, facing her. The men and the women both wear short leather jackets, trousers, navy berets and flat shoes. Léa looks like a shopgirl, and if Gerda were not holding her arm, she would have turned right around and exited the room, her cheeks aflame.

None of them greet her or smile. She feels like she is facing a firing line as she stands before them, her hands clasped behind her back. Whenever she is uncomfortable, her first impulse is to laugh, and she can feel that bubble rising in her chest so she pinches herself discreetly and tries to think of things that are sad: the baby elephant in the zoo whose mother would not recognize him, the men sleeping on flat cardboard boxes that she passed on her way to the interview, the way a room looks at the end of a party when all the guests are gone and their remnants are strewn on couches and floors, a mess for someone else to clean up. She has prepared answers to all possible questions in her mind, but to her surprise, the committee doesn't even want to talk to her—they speak to Gerda, as if she cannot speak for herself. As if she is not even a person.

"What is the candidate's name?" a woman sitting in the very centre of the table begins.

She has Léa's application right in front of her, which Léa scratched out at her desk by candlelight the night before, despairing at her own handwriting, at the fragility of the page, at her fountain pen, which kept blotting the words.

"Her name is Léa. Léa Roback."

"What kind of name is that?" a man at the edge of the table shouts, but the woman silences him with a glance, turns her attention back to Gerda.

"Where is she from?"

"Canada," Gerda answers.

"Hmmm," the woman says. She tightens her lips.

Léa had not expected this chilly suspicion. Her feet have started to hurt in her heels so she shifts from side to side, subtly, so she does not look evasive. But it doesn't even seem to matter. No one is looking at her. It is as if, until this process is over, she does not even exist.

"Why does Frau Roback wish to join the Party?" the woman continues.

"To fight fascism," Gerda says. The woman nods, waits. "To participate in the coming revolution," Gerda tries again. "To join the true just cause. To be part of the brotherhood of man."

"And sisterhood!" The man at the end cries out. He must be drunk. Unlike the other men, with their disciplined short

151

haircuts, his hair is long and falls over one eye, giving him an aspect both sinister and charming. They all ignore him.

Léa feels like one of the fat little worms that come out wriggling on the sidewalk after a rainstorm, stranded and exposed.

Gerda says, "Frau Roback has proven her devotion to the cause. Here in Berlin, she has joined in the fight against fascism. She stood with us on *Blutmai*. She has earned the right to membership."

"Earned it?" The woman purrs. Her hand is poised over the page, a talon.

Gerda hesitates. Léa's hands are twitching at her side. She very much does not like being on display.

"She helped organize the exhibit," Gerda adds. "With Frau Kollwitz. She has been distributing pamphlets on the street for us. She attends the meetings. She has demonstrated courage and discretion."

"Let her speak," the man says. "Let her tell us herself. Why do you want to join the cause?"

Léa takes a breath. "To stop the horror," she says, surprising herself. She stands tall, her chin lifted. "To stop the horror."

"And Frau Roback," the man says. "What do you think of the fight for Jewish liberation in Palestine?"

Léa looks at Gerda, who lifts her shoulders. She is not prepared for this question. But she knows what she wants to say.

"I believe in liberation for all," she says.

For the first time, the woman lays down her pen, nods.

"Who else will speak for her?" the woman says, and Hans steps forward. She doesn't understand where he has come from, or how she has missed him in the room. Because of their personal connection, he said he would absent himself from the interview.

They pay lip service to free love, the Communists, but in fact they are a bunch of puritans. Romance—romance is definitely bourgeois.

"I will," he says.

"And what is your relationship to Frau Roback?" the woman says.

"She is my comrade," he says. "Her fight is our fight."

"That is the committee's decision, not yours," the woman says, and waves her hand.

Gerda takes Léa's arm and pulls her out of the room. They stand outside, smoking nervously. In the late afternoon autumn light, everything is copper: the leaves of the oak trees, the brick of the houses. She pulls her collar tightly around her neck. She is not sure whether to be grateful to Hans or angry at him.

Gerda is irritated. "Even here," she says, "it takes a man to vouch for you."

The committee takes longer than she expects. She hadn't even imagined the possibility of getting turned down, and as she stands outside the closed door she wonders what she will do if they reject her. Her feet get cold standing on the sidewalk.

When they call her back in, she cannot spot Hans.

"Welcome, Comrade," the woman says.

Léa flushes with pleasure. "See," Gerda says, "now you are one of us."

On her way home, she buys a blue beret. The cloche—so cute and flirtatious, because you have no choice but to seductively peer out from under it—goes back into her closet, waiting for more frivolous times.

24.

Those frivolous times seem vanishingly distant. The next day, Hans and Léa are walking down the street and they see a group of Brownshirts in a tight circle around an old man who has been forced to his knees. One of them holds up the man's long grey beard—it must hurt, he is pulling his whole head up—and another pulls out a knife and starts sawing at the beard as if he was cutting thick bread.

Léa pulls away from Hans and steps forward. In a clear, strong voice she cries out, "How dare you! How dare you! Are your mothers proud of you for behaving this way?"

She hears Hans muttering behind her. "Léa," he says, "no good will come of this."

They all turn to face her, and dear God, they are young. They are like her little brothers, their faces still florid with adolescent acne, too young, even, to grow a full beard. She shivers though it is warm outside. Hans pulls her hand, but she shakes him off.

"What has he ever done to you?" Léa continues, she can't stop herself. Four of the men rush towards her, and she stands very straight in the face of their rage. The Jewish man stays on his knees, looking up, his eyes wide and unfocused. He is kneeling in a puddle. If she draws their attention, perhaps he can run, but he doesn't seem inclined to move at all. He has collapsed like a puppet whose strings have been cut. His suit jacket is soiled and wet, he sobs into his own collar, and after one of the other men steps behind him and casually kicks him in the back, he folds forward again.

As the Brownshirts start to circle her, Hans steps forward. He speaks quickly and with authority and uses words like fiancée, phrases about how women can be so emotional. She hears him lying with his golden tongue.

She has watched him be persuasive in the workers' halls, and now she sees all of that charm turned to the young men who look like his brothers. He turns to her, and she can see that he is angry—that stiff vein on his forehead, his pinched pale face.

"Your papers," one of the Brownshirts says, and does not say please. She pulls them from her pocket. One of the men looks at them quickly, then looks at Hans, as if his face is her certification.

The man nods, and Hans extends his right arm straight out, palm down, in a Nazi salute. He takes her arm and marches her quickly down the street. He does not slow down until they are many blocks away.

Then he stops. "Do you have a death wish?" he says. "What is wrong with you?"

"You saw what they were doing to that man," Léa says, and then she can say no more. Her eyes sting and her face is red, her hands are hot and her feet are cold, she is out of breath, she will not cry. To her shame, she is crying.

"What do you think they will do to you?" Hans says. He holds her wrists, as if afraid she will run back, though she has been so distressed and confused she would have no idea how to find that street corner.

"You gave him the salute," Léa says. She cannot believe it.

"I did what I had to do," Hans says.

He has recovered himself, and that makes her hate him. You could sculpt his face in marble.

"You need to sit down," he says. "You need to eat something, drink something." She lets herself be led into the coffeeshop, lets him order coffee and cake, lets him spoon whipped cream into her mouth. She is thinking of the man, his eyes two dark pits. She wonders if he is still on that corner. She wonders if he is still alive.

"Léa," Hans says, "are you listening?"

"I don't even know you," Léa says.

How could he raise his hand? That same hand moves to cover her own.

"I love you," Hans says simply. "I want to look after you. I know it is difficult, but we cannot help him."

"But we must," Léa says, except she cannot finish the sentence.

Must what? They said they would make a new world of brotherhood and freedom but it is this other world which is coming, raising a black and red flag.

It is getting late. As they walk home the shadows on the street are long. At her doorway he pauses, and she realizes he expects more.

"I have a headache," she says, and she sees him assume the face he uses with his mother—a slightly aggravated solicitude. She does not have a headache, but she does not feel well. Everything is changing so quickly.

25.

When she closes her eyes at night, she sees the old man from the street kneeling in terror: that could have been her, could have been Harry. She looks for the man and asks about him, hoping for some evidence that he is still alive, but she does not even know his name, and she can find nothing in the papers, no news on the streets. Hans comes to see her, and she will not come to the door. She tries to talk to Harry about her fears, but he says he is too tired to discuss politics. "This isn't about politics," she says, "this is life and death." He closes his eyes and will not respond.

Harry has good reason to be exhausted. He has moved out of the rooming house into an apartment of his own, has married a Jewish girl named Betty who becomes pregnant almost immediately. It is not an easy pregnancy, and she is not an easy girl. He spends long days at the medical school and at night he fusses over his wife, and makes her broth, which is all that she will eat. He rubs her feet and cleans the apartment. Harry looked after their own mother so well when she had a new baby; he is practised in care. Léa comes to help as well, though she is a little impatient with Betty's claims to illness. Having a baby is natural, isn't it the most natural thing in the world? She tries to get Betty outside on walks, claims the fresh air will do her good, and Betty wants to sit down every five paces. After four or five such visits Harry suggests that though it is kind of Léa to come, Betty does not need her help.

In July, a girl is born. They name her Maud, which makes Léa think of mauve, the exact colour of the infant's skin when Léa comes to visit them in the hospital. Harry is, as ever, uxorious, and even Betty seems calmer now, unburdened. As Léa holds the moist, squirming creature she feels full, like the notch under her breastbone was built for that exact weight and warmth.

"My first niece," Léa says as she hands back the baby.

Betty says, "She will grow up to be a strong woman, like her aunt," and Léa smiles. She didn't realize how touching it would be to see her brother become a father. She feels a surge of affection for Betty, who holds the baby with tender confidence. And this baby, Maud, this helpless little bundle of chaotic need: she loves her! The intensity comes as a surprise.

In the July elections, Hitler's party won a third of the votes, more than any other party. She remembers the frog in Werner's parable. When will it be too late to jump? She goes to see Professor Levy. His office is lined with German classics—Heine, Schiller, Goethe, Hölderlin, Mann. He has lithographs of their faces on the wall, and on his desk is a photograph of his family, which she picks up and admires. She has brought a transcript which he needs to sign so she can transfer her credits back home.

"Frau Roback," he says in great astonishment. "What is the problem?"

He listens to her concerns about the worsening violence, the man she saw attacked, the bullies in their brown shirts, the sense that they are—all of them—on the precipice of a great disaster. He leans back in his chair, just a hint of a smile under his curled moustache.

"There is absolutely no need to be hysterical," he says, cutting her off before she can finish. "It is Germany. We are not like the Italians, with Mussolini, that joke. Look at all this," he says, gesturing at the books on his walls. "Maybe Hitler will get elected for a term, but he'll be out in three months. If he tries any of his shenanigans, we will never let him get away with it. The Germans are too intelligent for that! Why, we invented culture."

From his portrait on the wall, Goethe looks down on them with his characteristic expression of perpetual alarm.

"I think perhaps you have misjudged the situation," she says carefully. "They are already letting him get away with it."

Is she overreacting? She goes to see Rudolphe from the Party next, in his home in Prenzlauer Berg. The neighbourhood reminds her of Paris with its wide boulevards and neoclassical buildings. Rudolphe's wife, Mathilde, checks the peephole before unlocking the door: it takes a minute. Unlike Professor Levy, they have already learned to be careful. Their living room is small and tidy, and they sit at a round table as Rudolphe brings tea and cake. Unusual, she thinks, that the wife should sit and the husband should serve, but they are natural about it. She is nearly fifteen years his senior, Hans had told her. They met when he was convalescing. She was a nurse in the hospital. They have never had children—too old, Léa guesses, though she would never ask—and instead look after one another with the kind of complete attention that only childless couples seem able to muster.

Rudolphe rubs his arms and Mathilde fetches him a sweater; she moves to sit, and he rises to pull out her chair; he coughs, and she brings him a glass of water. Once they are finished tending to each other, and the tea is poured, Rudolphe asks her why she has come. He listens carefully, to her concerns and to her report of the professor's dismissal, his right ear cocked towards her—the other side, he tells her, is completely deaf. His wife watches him as he speaks.

"*Es wird krieg geben*, Léa." he says. "There will be war."

Cupping his twisted hand on the table, he lays out his case.

"Krupp-Siemens have expanded their factories, they are working on rearmament. Léa, they are building camps. You are not German—go back to your own country and help build a better land for the working people."

They both accompany her to the door, and their goodbye has an air of finality. She has their blessing to return home. As she hugs Mathilde goodbye her face is wet.

They do not even know she is a Jew.

When she goes back to see Professor Levy, she is determined. "I have decided to leave Germany," she says. "I am well-informed on the situation. I just need you to sign my certificate of studies."

He picks up the piece of paper, coughs, and puts it back down. "I'm afraid that's against school policy, Frau Roback. There is absolutely no reason to transfer."

So there it is, three years of study and she has not made even a mark. As she gets up to leave, she looks back at the photo on the desk.

"Professor," she says, "you need to think of your own family. Think of where you will take them if the time comes when you must escape. Many of my own students are going to Switzerland."

He is shuffling the papers on his desk, and he takes off his spectacles.

"You overstep, Frau Roback," he says. "Indeed, you are a great disappointment to me. I have work to do now, and you, too, should think about getting back to your work instead of distracting yourself with these"—here he looks up and pauses, searching for the words that will wound her most—"these bourgeois fantasies of persecution."

Goethe, Hölderlin, Heine, Schiller, stare from the walls with their blind eyes.

26.

Though she has been avoiding Hans, she still feels compelled to say goodbye. She finds him in his mother's living room, sitting beside a woman she has never met. The woman looks as if she could be his sister—the same upturned nose, light eyes, flat pale hair. Elsa introduces her as Hans's second cousin, from Munich. Heidi. Elsa seems overcome with delight at Heidi's presence.

"You wouldn't believe these two," she says to Léa, in a confiding tone. "When they were children, they insisted they would be married when they grew up. And here they are, all grown up!"

Heidi smiles without teeth, and Hans will not meet her eyes. Elsa has never been interested in telling her about Hans's childhood before.

"Hans," Léa says, "is it possible to speak to you for just a minute?"

"But Heidi has just arrived!" Elsa says. "They haven't seen each other for—can you imagine?—ten years now! They need some time to catch up. Though I look at them, and it seems to me they are five years old and hiding in the bushes playing their little games!"

Her laughter has an edge of hysteria. She also likes playing little games.

"Very well," Léa says. "Adieu, Hans," and then he looks up at her, startled. He starts to rise and his mother pulls him down by the hand.

"Hans!" she says. "No need! I'll show her out!"

Elsa, who never does anything for herself, accompanies Léa to the door and hisses at her to never come back, too quietly for Hans to hear. She closes the door in her face, and she hears not just the lock but the deadbolt and the chain.

Despite herself, in the week before her departure, she expects Hans to show up at the door of her rooming house and beg her to stay. Instead, Werner comes. It has been raining and the rain has stopped but the air is still humid. The raindrops cling to the leaves of the trees and the streetlights glow in puddles. He is wet and bedraggled. His white shirt clings to him and has turned translucent; he holds a bunch of asters in his hand that he has clearly picked on the way over, and they are limp and damp. When he starts to pass them to her they shower the front of her dress so he takes them back, holds them at his side in a loose fist.

"Aren't you cold?" Léa says to Werner. "What are you thinking, coming out in the rain!" She steps out and shuts the door behind her back. It is too late to ask him to come inside, besides she isn't certain that's advisable. She can see the landlady's light turn on behind her lace curtains, and she puts her finger to her mouth so he will speak softly.

"Weren't you going to come to say goodbye?" he says. He looks as if he hasn't slept in days. In the last few months he has grown older, his face is longer, he is even thinner—one of those boys who burns flesh through adolescence, as if he must reduce to bone before he can fill back out again. His ears stick out of his wet hair.

She has been running around trying to wrap up her affairs, pack her things, settle with the school, book a ticket. She had forgotten about him.

"I'm sorry," she says. "It's been so busy!" His mouth twists.

His face is so wet from the rain that it takes her a minute to realize that he is crying. He lifts his hand to wipe his eyes and realizes he is still holding the asters, which he shakes out like an umbrella. Petals litter the ground. He is a chronically ironic boy; seeing him sincere is like seeing him undressed.

"Don't forget me, Léa," he says. He can't keep still and is bouncing from foot to foot. His tone flickers between frivolity and despair.

She wrings her hands. "Could you come with me?" She doesn't know how, but it must, somehow, be possible. Is it possible?

He steps back, shakes his head. "My mother, my father, I can't leave them." And he turns around and steps out of the light.

He has such long legs. He steps over the puddles like an ostrich. That will be her last memory of him, a boy half-transformed into a flightless bird, slick with rain, vanishing into the deep shadows.

Or no, not a boy anymore.

In her pocket—and she doesn't even remember him reaching out—a final note.

"As is well known, warm water is a soporific, even for frogs. The frog drifts in a tepid bath of rubbery contentment. His body is the exact colour and temperature of the liquid which surrounds him, rusty green, dappled in the shade. When the water becomes too hot the frog is past leaping, past thinking words like 'hot,' words like 'ouch,' phrases like 'too late'".

III
Home
Montreal, Soviet Union, Montreal, 1932-1945

1.

When her father sees her, he gathers her into his arms and holds on to her for a long time. He smells like pipe tobacco and sandalwood, exactly as he did when she was a child, and when she closes her eyes she feels small and safe. Her mother's hug is stiffer and more efficient, but later, at the kitchen table, she grabs Léa's hands and her eyes look bright. "He thought you were never coming home," she whispers, gesturing at Papa with her chin.

For the next few weeks, Léa often catches her father watching her, as if he is worried that she might disappear again. There is new grey in his beard and he sometimes stumbles when he walks, though he shakes off her concern and will not take her arm. In her absence, he seems to have gotten older, more frail, and she feels guilty and responsible. Her absence has aged him. Harry's wife and baby are now in Canada, thank God, but Harry insists on staying just a little longer, to get his degree. Léa can tell how bad the news in Europe is by watching how much her father's hands shake as he reads the evening newspaper.

It is strange to be back in Montreal. The city has changed since the Depression: it reminds her more of Berlin than she expected. The mood is tense. She sees families sitting on heaps of their belongings on the sidewalk, evicted to the curb. A trunk, a mattress, a few sticks of furniture, the people so shabby and inert they seem themselves like discarded objects, like they do not have the power to rise on their own accord. The young people seem to have nothing to do and nowhere to go. They gather on street corners. They want to work, there is no work. Aching with guilt as with hunger, they eat their meagre share of the family rations. If you are poor and Catholic you go to Saint-Vincent for potatoes and molasses; if you are Protestant, to the Salvation Army for soup. The Jews have the kitchen at the YMHA, and kiddush after services in synagogue, which has never before been so well-attended. Congregants stuff bread rolls in their pockets for dinner. They steal tuna fish from the kiddush table and sell it to their neighbours.

Her family is lucky to have somewhere to live. Her father is working harder than ever but with little success. He can't collect on debts, he can't strike a deal, he hasn't the least clue of how to work a situation to his advantage. The countryside is ripe for plucking, everyone is in trouble, everything is for sale, and still he fails to make a profit. Her father pays too much and charges far too little, moved by a dirty child, by a ransacked house, by an act of hospitality which his host cannot afford, by the evidence of poverty, which is everywhere. When he is asked how much he will charge for one of his products, his eyes go blank, he looks up at the heavens, and then he says—tell me what you can pay—and he means it! What makes him a good and gentle man also makes him a terrible peddler. His heart is too soft.

Mama says, "It's not his heart, it's his head." She is tired of trying to make ends meet on these dribs and drabs. Leo is still in school, he is still a teenager. He has reached the age of perpetual hunger; she can't keep enough groceries in the house to feed him. But she is back to herself again, practical, loving, competent, aggrieved. The years after the baby died—that ghost of a mother that she became—seem like a half-remembered nightmare. She doesn't like to talk about it.

Léa gets a job at the Young Women's Hebrew Association, in youth programming. There is nothing for young people to do during this terrible Depression, no work and no money to play. She co-ordinates outings to galleries and the cinema, she organizes a little amateur theatre. They have singalongs at night and courses by day. Sometimes the girls watch the boys play softball. The park is the only leisure most people can afford. Fletcher's Field is for Jews, La Fontaine Park for French Canadians. Léa goes where she pleases.

She picks up leftovers from the mansions on the hill, half-eaten birthday cakes and apples lightly bruised, and distributes them to the girls to bring home.

In the spring, she is invited up to Belvedere Road, to meet the president of the YWHA. As she walks up the hill, the houses get bigger, and the city shrinks and unfolds like an opening map; she can see the river, can see the bridges connecting the island, can see the grid of streets mesh and knot. She thinks she can understand how it might feel to live among the rich, to see the city from above and to believe that it belongs to you. The house is right near Summit Woods, and as she walks through, the trilliums are blooming, a thousand rose-tinged blossoms in the shaded paths.

At the Bronfman house, a maid in a starched white collar pours tea from a shining silver pot into china cups. Mrs. Bronfman is a nice woman, well-meaning in her tasteful philanthropy. The rich give away their gilded crumbs as an alibi for excessive wealth. Léa bites her tongue, sips her tea, acts grateful. How do these worlds exist side by side?

The Association provides money for the theatre outings and for plates of cookies at the singalongs, which she quickly replaces with sandwiches, once she realizes that for some of the girls it is their only meal.

2.

Rudolphe has given her a name, and as soon as she can, she tracks him down. Fred Rose—né Fischel Rosenberg—is five foot four, a little man in tailored suits, with a small moustache and a high intelligent forehead. His eyes are kind and his ears stick out. He looks like an accountant but talks like a revolutionary. Like her, he has worked in factories, though as a supervisor, not on the floor. He tells her that at his factory there was no ventilation, and they kept the windows shut to protect the equipment. Sometimes the girls would faint from the heat, right there at the tables. Once he found a girl passed out while holding a glass bulb, her hand a spiderweb of blood and shards.

Fred is at every demonstration, and for such a small man has an enormous voice. You can hear him shouting for blocks. He has been arrested twice, and the second time sentenced to a year at Bordeaux jail for making seditious utterances. That was in 1931, the year everything changed. Before that, the government mostly left the Communists alone. The Party wasn't legal, exactly. It was grey. But that January, the Ontario Provincial Police raided the head office of the Party in Toronto and the houses of the Party leaders and arrested eight key members. A death blow for the Communist Party, the commissioner called it. Seven of the men were sentenced to prison. Even worse: the Party itself declared unlawful under Article 98, and any participant, supporter, or proponent subject to up to twenty years in prison.

"The Red Squad came and testified at my trial," he tells her, "with their little books of lies. They used to follow me everywhere, even into the steam bath on Saint Lawrence. You should have seen them, sitting naked with their legs crossed tight on the bench, stumbling through the fog like three blind mice."

He laughs. "They said I claimed I would die for the movement. I told the judge, why would I do that? I love life! I would never say something so stupid."

The judge sent him to jail anyway. At first, he was afraid of prison, but then he realized that those boys behind bars were just like the men he knew back home, just trying to get by. They wanted the same things, a place to live and something to eat. A little dignity. He got along just fine in prison, and now he is back on the streets, unbowed. If anything, emboldened.

"I'm fighting for them too," he says, "so they can go home. Léa," he tells her, "you have returned just in time for the revolution."

In March, a man is shot in the back during an eviction. His name is Nick Zynchuk, and he is a Ukrainian, a recent immigrant, who came to Canada for a better life. Some of the papers call him a foreign agitator but he was nothing of the sort. Just a worker without a job, who was climbing the stairs to retrieve his suitcase, his coat, his hat, when they gunned him down. The constable who shot him is named Joseph Zappa. He claims he thought that Zynchuk had a gun, but there are witnesses who say there was no evidence that he posed any threat at all. Just a poor man shot in the back. Just another man dead.

Léa goes to the funeral, and there are thousands of people there, marching in the sleet and rain. She catches up to Fred and he says, "Here you are!" his cheeks red and his eyes delighted. He offers his arm and they take the lead, together at the head of the procession, walking in synchrony. When the police arrive on horseback, they charge the march as if the mourners are rioters. Running down the street, shivering and wet, she thinks of the police in Berlin, the flying squads which rushed to the scene only to help the bloodshed unfold. Neither in Germany nor in Montreal can they be trusted.

When the girls at the YWHA seem like-minded, she quietly tells them about a Marxist study group that meets in the evenings. Though secrecy is not in her nature, she teaches them discretion. There are new protocols to keep the members safe and to keep their activities hidden. To Léa, it sometimes seems like a game of sardines from her childhood, packing into a dark closet and holding your breath.

It often feels like a double life, going back and forth between the Communist Party and the wealthy women of the board of the YWHA, who have perhaps cut back on a maid here, a subscription there, but have largely kept afloat on a bubble of prosperity through this difficult period. She collects bags of castaway items, barely used, and distributes them among the needy. They have clothing giveaways which feel like fashion shows, and the girls model the dresses for each other.

What she wants is to keep busy, to keep hopeful. For now, she feels less desperate than she did in Berlin. She has been spinning like a top, from city to city, following the restless, searching agitation of her youth. She is surprised at how content she feels to be at home.

3.

In May the newspaper reports book burnings in every major city in Germany. In Berlin, the Nazi Student Association holds a bonfire in Opera Square. They march with torches and armfuls of library books to feed to the hungry flames.

Léa had spent many hours in the library on Dorotheenstrasse, with its high vaulted ceilings and niches of books. The news hits her like a blow. A library, that sacred place of journey and of refuge. That temple. She holds a lonely vigil in her room in Montreal that night, reading forbidden books by candlelight.

The newspaper reports that the Nazis distributed "fire oaths" to read as the books were consigned to the flames.

As they burned the books of Erich Maria Remarque, who was wounded in the trenches and wrote the greatest German novel of the last war, they cried: "Against literary betrayal of the soldiers of the World War! For the education of the nation in the spirit of battle!"

As they burned Freud and his disciples: "Against soul-shredding evaluation of sexual activity! For the nobility of the human soul!"

As they burned Marx and Karl Kautsky: "Against class struggle and materialism! For national community and an idealistic lifestyle!"

As they burned the poems and essays of the pacifist Ossietzky and the satirist Tucholsky: "Against impudence and presumption! For veneration and reverence for the immortal German national spirit!"

She reads that they are burning Brecht's plays, and wonders if he is still in Germany.

Goebbels himself was at the rally, that skeletal, rat-faced aesthete. In the photographs, men throw books like footballs into a burning pyre, and the flames rival the height of the opera house behind them.

She is so afraid for her brother. She is so, so afraid.

With reason. That month, Harry is stopped on the street and beaten badly. He is the frog in the fable and has stayed in the pot too long; he gets out, but no medical degree. He is lucky to escape, but he will have to find somewhere to start again.

Though they are grateful to have him home, the mood in the house is sombre. Harry has always seemed a little older than his age, too burdened with responsibility. Now he seems crushed, despite his beautiful new baby, despite his escape.

"We are safe now, safe!" he keeps saying, as if trying to convince himself.

But they do not feel safe. In Toronto, a group that calls themselves "The Swastika Club" hangs the flag of the twisted cross on the Beaches to keep the Jews away. They say they have nothing to do with Hitler; they just want to keep the beaches *clean*. At the baseball game in Christie Pits, there is a knock-down, drag-out riot after the Pit Gang unfurls a blanket with a giant swastika on it and the crowd howls "*Heil Hitler*" from the stands. On both sides, some have come to the game prepared to rumble; they are armed and itching for a fight. They fight with knives and baseball bats under the blinding electric lights of the stadium until the early hours of the morning.

Harry is undone. "Here, too," he keeps saying, shaking his head.

"Here, too," Léa says. "But look what happens when we fight back."

They gained control of the swastika banner that night and ripped it to shreds. A small victory, but a significant one. The mayor of Toronto has now announced that future displays of the swastika are prohibited. In Berlin, she'd see the swastika occasionally, and then, one day, it was ubiquitous, those harsh banners desecrating the sky. She knew then it was time to get out. Symbols change, and reality succumbs. If she sees the flag here, she will tear it down.

McGill lets Harry in, despite the quota, and he decides that what he wants most is to study the mind: how people could succumb to this irrational moment. Madness is a storm in the brain. The clouds are moving over Europe, lightning flashes from field to field, and faster than anyone could have imagined.

Léa wishes she could bring herself to hate Berlin, but it was one of the most wonderful periods of her life, and mostly she is sorry to see the city fall under this dark spell. Those were terrible, beautiful times.

And what she saw there has changed her life. She no longer plans to teach literature, to speak from a podium about Goethe, Schiller, Heine, who from their silent portraits watch with flat eyes the conflagration of the great disaster. No, she will devote herself to the living, to teaching them about their social and economic conditions, about the possibility to make change, not to live in the past but to create a better future. Which she believes in, despite the events of the last few months.

She believes, she believes, she must believe in the possibility of a better future.

4.

The girls lucky enough to have jobs work in the dress factories. Conditions are very bad. "They treat us like slaves," her neighbour Estie says. "I'm there at seven in the morning, and if I'm even a minute late the foreman docks my pay. I'm standing at the table, there's not even a stool for me to lean on, Léa, by the end of the day my feet are killing me. There's no air in the room, and no daylight, I ruin my eyes on the stitches, my throat hurts and my head hurts all the time. When I go home on the bus I can't sit down because I'll be too stiff to get back up again." Her husband has tuberculosis and is too sick to hold down a job; Estie brings home piecework and gets her daughters and her mother-in-law to sew in the evening and on Saturdays.

"It's a scandal," Léa says. But how can it be a scandal if everyone knows that's just the way it is?

Estie shrugs. "There are ten girls who would take my job if I walked away from it."

On Saturday afternoon, strolling near the angel on Mount Royal, Fred introduces Léa to Josh Gershman, who has come over from Toronto to help organize the garment workers. Josh has full cheeks and a shy smile; his high forehead and arched eyebrows give him a curious expression, as if he is always about to ask a question. He fumbles with his pipe as he tries to shake her hand, and finally gives up, aiming a funny little old-world bow in her direction.

"Charmed to meet you, Léa," Josh says, his accent strong. He comes from the Ukraine, where he started work as a dyer in a factory at the age of ten. At sixteen, he helped form a Jewish defence group, guarding his town against pogroms.

His father had already left for Winnipeg; after years of trying, Josh was finally able to obtain a passport and ticket to Canada to join him. While he was on the long boat trip across the Atlantic his father passed away. He was only a few days too late to see him one last time. "I left the Ukraine as a son, Léa," he says. "I arrived in Canada as an orphan."

Josh started off in furs and now works as an organizer for the International Union of Needle Trade Workers. In Winnipeg and in Toronto he had some success, but the Montreal girls are difficult.

"Léa," he says, "they are so backward, you can't imagine. Last year, in one factory, we had a strike. A short strike. Léa, it was beautiful. We started on Sunday, it ended on Thursday. You know Diana Dresses? They make a nice product and the boss, turns out, not such a bad guy. He agreed to a raise, three-fifty a week, nothing to sneeze at. They had the money for the girls by Sunday. And the next week these five girls are waiting for me at the office, at seven in the morning. Mr. Gershman, they say, we have to give it back. The chairlady, this beautiful girl, she hands me an envelope. It's the money, the increase, for each of the workers. All of it. Please, she says, we can't keep it. They went to church on Sunday and the priest told them it was dirty money; it was a sin to take it. I tried to explain to them that the sin was exploiting the workers, they earned that money, but they wouldn't even hear it. Those lovely, stupid girls." He shrugs his round shoulders. "These are the kinds of backward people I'm dealing with."

He is organizing another strike now, a bigger one.

"You should come by the picket line, say hello," he says. "Give the girls a little support."

She has the afternoon off at the YWHA. She heads downtown, and there he is in the middle of the picket line, but his face is bandaged. He looks like the invisible man from the story, you can barely even see his eyes. His arm is in a sling.

"My God, Josh," she says and he shushes her.

"It's OK, Léa," he says, "keep your damn voice down."

She sidles into the line beside him, and he talks to her in a low voice. "You ever heard of George the Peyos?"

She nods. It's hard to miss him, a young man with long white forelocks. The story is that when he was in Russia and the Cossacks came to his village, his hair turned white from terror overnight. Now he terrorizes other people; he collects for the mob, he roughs up the uncooperative. He offers costly protection.

"He came to see me," Josh says. "After the town hall meeting Saturday night. You know how he speaks, very polite. 'I'm sorry I got to beat you up,' he said, 'what can I do? I need the work.' I thought fast, I said, listen, you don't have to do this. I'll get the girls to call up their bosses crying that you attacked me. It'll look like you did the job, they won't know any better. I could see he was considering it but he said, 'That's not good enough, they have to see that I beat you.' So, this morning, Marie-Claude she comes over and she wraps me up like a present," he gestures at Marie-Claude down the line with his sling and she smiles at them. Then he looks around, and in case he's made anyone suspicious, he hunches over and groans in pain.

His charade works but the strike does not. Over the next few weeks there are scabs, rumours, arrest. The labour minister gets involved; the bosses accept his proposal of third-person arbitration, but the union doesn't trust it. Some of the shops offer a raise of 20 percent; others threaten to close their doors and leave the city.

Lots of the Jewish girls are fired. Everyone knows they're the troublemakers. To get new jobs they need to wear little crosses around their necks. Those who are still employed drift back to work under a cloud of rumours and threats. Gershman claims they won, but it doesn't look like victory. The gains are no sooner announced than they dissipate, and anyway, what does a raise mean when the next day you get fired? He is losing his members to Bernard Shane at the International Ladies Garment Workers Union, whose strategies are more conservative and who blames him for the job losses, for the blacklist of the Jewish girls, for all the fallout of the strike.

Léa walks around with a sick feeling in her stomach. It was not her fight and yet she feels diminished by the loss.

5.

At domesticity, her sisters have long outpaced her. They are getting married and starting families. She goes to visit their new babies and witness their novice efforts at housekeeping and motherhood, a flowered cloth on the table and a pot of soup on the stove. She likes to hold the babies and to marvel at their floppy damp newborn warmth, their tensile toddler strength. For the hours of her visits her arms and heart are full.

"Léa," her sisters tell her, "you're a natural. Don't you want a child?" They are envious of her boundless energy, her cheerful calm. "I used to have that kind of energy!" they say. "But just you wait until you have a little one of your own!" It sounds like a threat.

She is nearly thirty and she will get on the floor with her nieces and nephews and enter into their play as if childhood was a world from which she had never been exiled.

And then she will walk home alone, swinging her empty arms, glorying in her freedom.

Léa still goes to the theatre, the concert, the cinema. She likes quality, but occasionally indulges in more popular entertainments. The midget's palace is on Rachel Street. Léa has often thought about going inside and when her little sister Annie invites her, she cannot resist.

"Listen to this," Annie says, reading the pamphlet. "The palace was founded by a man named Philippe Sr., the seventh son of a seventh son. His father stood six foot three but he was only thirty-six inches tall. That's what, Léa, three feet? He ran away to join the circus at the age of twelve, and worked for Barnum and Bailey, then decided to return to Montreal, to be his own impresario. He brought his wife Rose Dufresne with him and turned their home into a living museum—and here we are now—with elaborate furniture built to order. He has named them the king and queen of all midgets, and their child, the little prince, Philippe Jr."

"He has seized the means of production," Léa says.

"Yes," says Annie. "Admirable."

"Why mimic this bourgeois fantasy of royalty?" Léa adds. "And is it ethical, really, to make yourself a spectacle? The poor child."

"But nonetheless," Annie says, "I would like to see it."

The proud parents have hired a full-sized nursemaid who walks through the dollhouse like one of Swift's giants. There are stone lions couchant on the steps. Admission costs a nickel.

The boy's bedroom is called the chamber of the prince and has elaborate Louis XIV furniture, silken drapery, a miniature piano, gilded mirrors, the feet of the table carved into lion's paws as if it might stride across the floor. The boy is wearing a top hat and tails on an ordinary afternoon, sitting on the floor and playing with a wooden train. He seems uncomfortable in his formal wear, though not especially conscious of being on display. He glances at the open door when they appear but looks away almost immediately and returns to his play.

He is tiny, but all children are tiny. Despite the grandeur of the room, it feels stuffy and even a little shabby. The gilt is peeling, the silver brocade stained. The nursemaid is sitting on the couch, looking bored and reading through a woman's magazine. The king and queen of midgets are nowhere to be found.

Annie is delighted by the small piano keys, the elegant, delicate chairs, the yellow silk tassels on the curtains. Léa is less entertained.

"To the capitalist, we are all midgets," Léa says as they leave the house. "But even the midget capitalist is a king." She hears the sound of her own voice, the old rigidity, and she laughs to soften it. Lighten up, Léa, her family is always telling her. Lighten up.

Annie seizes her arm.

"Did you see his tiny hands?" she says. "Do you think he can play that piano?"

"Do you think we should buy a croissant?" Léa says, and Annie laughs and drags her forward, skipping towards the boulangerie.

Even after the dime for admission, they still have money to burn.

"Let us eat cake," Léa announces, swinging open the door with her hip into the good warm caramel smell of burnt butter and sugar.

She chooses a *pain au chocolat*, still warm, and they divide it between them on the sidewalk. Chocolate in the corners of her mouth and crumbs raining down to the cooing acclaim of the pigeons. Life is a crowded shop window of delights.

6.

Some friends and comrades have already made their move to the promised land of the Soviet Union, and at Party meetings they share the dazzled accounts that arrive in letters. "We are more greenhorn than the greenhorns," one emigrant writes. "Everything is different here. A palace courtyard is a playground for the people. The prisons—can you imagine?—are left unlocked, and prisoners can come and go as they please."

Moishe Wolofsky, her long-ago New York movie date, is one of their correspondents.

Léa starts writing to Moishe again and likes the lazy pace of transatlantic mail. He seems to have no hard feelings about New York, and she thinks he is brave to have made the journey east. He is casually flirtatious and friendly, and she can spend weeks anticipating his response. She feels more free writing to him than she once did speaking with him face-to-face, and she likes his letters more than she liked him in person. It is like having a boyfriend without the burden of having a boyfriend.

The Wolofskys were always well-off, and Moishe was born to the good life. But he has the ardour of a convert now. He writes letters about the lectures in the factory, about the satisfaction of working for a cause, about the readings and theatre and music every night of the week, about trips to Moscow and dachas in the countryside.

"This has to be the Yiddish capital of the world," he writes to Léa, "It's intoxicating. So much life."

In his fourth letter he says, "Léa, you need to see it for yourself."

Why not, she thinks. She has grown restless and tired of planning theatrical revues and sweet-talking the ladies of the board so that they keep their pocketbooks open. When she tells her father that she is going to the Soviet Union he looks appalled. It is worse, even, than when she went to Germany.

"But you understand," he says, "what they did to us. Why we fled."

She does not. He has never spoken of that part of his life. Looking at his gentle face, she feels the pull of untold stories. Would he tell her now? But he does not elaborate. A lifetime of keeping silence is too much to break.

"It's different now, Pa," she says. "Haven't you read the news?"

He offers no further resistance, but she avoids being alone with him, and sometimes she catches him staring at her with a hurt and frightened expression on his face.

An organization called Intourist organizes missions and promotes travel to the Soviet Union. She buys their guidebook. The first page boasts that "each year brings more and more industrial enterprises, power plants, metallurgical works, factories, combinates."

"How glamorous," Annie says, "a veritable Paris of the East! Imagine, more and more combinates! What on earth is a combinate?"

"A socialist enterprise that produces primary farm commodities and also processes the product," Léa says automatically, as if answering a test question, and Annie throws a sweater at her.

"When are you going to settle down, Léa?" she says. "Why are you running away?"

"Away?" she says, confused. "No." How to explain to Annie, that she is running towards something? Some breadth, some greater possibility, some kind of redemption, right here on earth? The line from Shelley's poem flashes into her mind—the power is there.

She books passage on the Gydnia line and sails to the worker's paradise.

7.

The most direct route is through Germany, but it is impossible to return, much as she misses her friends. It is a black hole— no letters have arrived for many months, and she has no idea how her comrades in the movement are doing, no news of Emilia, Gerda, Rudolphe, Käthe. She thinks if Werner had made it out, she would have heard from him by now. And she suspects that Hans may have switched sides and decided to make his mother proud.

She is sick with the memories of the people she has left behind. She dreams about them every night in her narrow bunk on the ship, and often they are so angry at her for leaving, but when she tries to hold onto them, they drift into the air like smoke.

When she arrives in Minsk, Moishe is waiting at the train station with his friend. He looks as awkward as he ever did: she thought she would feel something when she saw him, but her heart is hollow. The first surprise is that he has changed his name as part of his project of reinvention: new name, new life. Call me Bill, he says. Bill Walsh. His friend, the other Moses, has also taken a new name, Dick Steele, which sounds like the name of a comic book private eye. "Why not something Russian?" she asks, and they look at one another, surprised. There is a long pause. "I guess we didn't even think of it," Bill says.

They are an odd pair. Bill has Groucho eyebrows and a high, already receding hairline, a long face, a long nose, big ears, a sombre aspect. Even when he smiles, he seems shy about it, as if it is not a natural expression for him. Dick, by contrast, is playful and handsome. The girls back home used to say he looked like Clark Gable.

Bill and Dick take her back to their cramped apartment. There is newspaper spread over the table instead of a cloth, and their hands are black with ink and red with juice as they eat pickled beets, rye bread, and hard-boiled eggs. The table is so small that their knees touch and suddenly all she wants is to lie down. Where will she sleep? She is tired from her journey and her stomach is upside down. Travel is a kind of vertigo. She is nauseous and feels at odds with time and space.

The dinner shows no signs of ending. A bottle of vodka comes out. She coughs at the burn and puts her glass down. Moses—she needs to remember to call him Dick—drinks his vodka and then her own and becomes rosy and lively. Bill with his big hands keeps knocking forks and knives off their makeshift table. Her eyelids get heavy, it has been a long day of travel, they won't stop talking, mostly to one another, as if they have forgotten she is there.

These two bachelors in this small space with no idea of housekeeping, they didn't even have three cups to drink out of when they sat together. Bill drinks out of a bowl, like a dog. At last Dick stands up, brushing crumbs off his lap onto the floor, and announces that he will spend the night at a friend's. He nods at Bill—so they had planned it—and slams the door because, as she has already learned, it always slams unless you hold it very carefully as you close it.

Once Dick is gone, they fall into silence. The candle has guttered down and casts haunted shadows. Bill cleans without really knowing how to clean, piling plates rather than washing up, creating little piles of crumbs and then abandoning them. Despite her exhaustion she helps him because she is impatient with his incompetence.

He moves the table and pulls out two narrow mattresses, side by side, and she lies down. She thinks about why she has come. She believes in equality; she believes in freedom. In her traveller's melancholy, she believes she has made a terrible mistake. Bill has gone to the washroom in the corridor, and he has been there a long time. She covers herself with the sheet—too thin, too worn. Here she is, freezing in a narrow bed, uncertain if she should take off her skirt. Is this freedom? She puts on her sweater and coat, shrouds herself in the sheet, and falls fast asleep.

8.

When she wakes up in the morning, she has slept twelve hours, and Bill has gone to the factory. He has left her a note and coffee and a roll on the table. The coffee is cold and bitter. She is embarrassed, but she also feels much better. She opens a window though it is cold outside—she can see snow, pinprick flakes though it is already March—and eats quickly, then goes into the hall to find the toilet, washing with water in the absence of soap, the towel rough as cardboard. She comes back to the room and makes order as best she can, scrubbing the windows and surfaces with an old shirt which is, she hopes, something she can use as a rag. She ventures out on the street and feels surprisingly at home, mostly because she is surrounded by Yiddish. She picks up snatches of phrases, and notices faces that look just like some of her relatives back home. She wishes her father could be there with her, and see this confident, crowded city of Jews.

Other, less welcome surprises. She passes the broken window of a cellar and glimpses bodies stretched out on wooden pallets, as abject a scene as any she has witnessed in Berlin or Montreal. Women are begging near the entrance to the market. Children sleep on benches, the bottoms of their feet black, shoeless in the cold. A worker's paradise, they said. An end to homelessness, an end to poverty. The streets here give the lie to that.

Though at least she does not see that grotesque juxtaposition which was so everyday back home—the ultra-wealthy stepping over the poor on their way into their lavish homes or luxurious restaurants. Everyone looks more or less the same, dressed in drab greys and browns, with occasional dashes of color, the women with shawls wrapped around their heads, the men in caps and jackets.

The other thing she notices is lines everywhere, lines so long and immobile that it seems waiting itself is the activity. In some places, it is clear what the crowd waits for—bread or milk. But sometimes she can't tell, it is just a long line of people waiting at a doorway, gossiping, rubbing their hands together, and stamping their feet to keep warm. Waiting for a door that might not open, for something that may never arrive.

She comes back to the apartment when she is too cold to keep walking. There is no sign of Bill. The water from the tap tastes a little like egg. There is barely any food in the house, so she dips the stale end of bread into water to soften it and chews slowly. There are a few books, but all are doctrine: she is not in the mood for Engels, she is in the mood for Dickens, and for the first time she feels a sharp pang of homesickness. She tries to stay awake, but she drifts off again, the candle melting into a wet wax puddle and the room so grey in the dusk.

They come in around ten, talking loudly, still together. "A lecture at the factory, Léa," Bill says. "About industrial agriculture. It was fascinating. The efficiency!"

She grew up around farms, he grew up around printing presses. What does he have to do with agriculture?

They have brought back food for dinner—herring, black bread, potatoes, sliced onions—and she realizes she is so starving she feels faint. Like the previous night, Dick and Bill talk through the meal, their mouths open as they eat, gesticulating with knives. She chews through her sleepy nausea, and all she wants is to lie down again.

This time, when Dick leaves, Bill sits across from her and takes her hands. "It is good that you've come," he says. "I have a friend in Moscow with an extra bed. They need help in the crèche where she works, and she has put in a word. When I have a vacation, I can come visit you."

She can see he is trying to let her down easily. She pulls her hands away and he looks at her with a killing kindness, his full lower lip trembling.

It is a risible misunderstanding, and she wants to explain herself to him, but she doesn't want to hurt his feelings. She feels about as much attraction to him as to the half-finished cold potato on the table. Mostly, she feels relieved.

She takes Dick's bed one last time and sleeps as chaste as a sister beside Bill, rolled up in all the blankets she can find to keep warm. In the morning, he walks her to the station and hands her a ticket, three hard rolls, an apple, and a twist of salt in paper. It is another week before she realizes what that apple must have cost him.

In his own way, he was trying to be kind.

9.

When she gets off the train in Moscow it is early morning, and the thin light pours like milk over the platform. She stays on the bench beside the ticket agent, as Bill had instructed, for nearly an hour, sitting on her feet to keep them warm, until a young woman in a bright red shawl comes running down the platform calling her name. When Léa stands up the woman embraces her and to her own surprise she finds herself tearing up at the woman's warmth. It feels good to be welcomed.

"I'm Anna," the woman says, "and I'm so glad you're here! We're going to have a wonderful time!" It is a relief to hear English. Léa has so many languages, but Russian is a wall for her, and since her arrival she has missed her usual fluency.

Anna takes her hand as they walk down the street. Her room is small, which is no surprise, but it is tidy, and all kinds of small gestures have been made to beautify it. There are lace curtains at the window, an embroidered shawl over the table, a few flowering weeds picked and arranged in a tiny glass vase. There is a silver samovar in a corner, and Anna tells her to sit down, arranges a pillow behind her back, tucks an extra shawl around her and gives her a sweet cup of tea, talking all the while. She is all superlatives: it is *wonderful* that Léa has come to stay and she must come see the most *extraordinary* park and the children at the crèche are *exquisitely* darling and she has to try this *gorgeous* honey cake from a bakery down the street, they just happened to have it this morning but it's not often available. It tastes just like sunshine.

Léa takes a mouthful. It tastes just like…honey.

Anna is from New York, but she has family in Russia who never left. The silver samovar belonged to her grandmother.

She has been there only six months—"But I *love* it, you'll love it too, so much is going on all the time in Moscow, and I feel so *useful*, really, even the most ordinary things are meaningful here because *together we are building a new world.*"

She looks so solemn when she says that, like a schoolgirl repeating a memorized lesson, that Léa starts laughing. Anna looks startled for a minute, then laughs along with her. Anna is a pretty girl, with black curls and shining eyes, rosy and plump. Léa is all elbows and angles; this girl is soft everywhere. She seems very young to Léa—Léa, who is barely past thirty—but that is part of her charm, and despite her youth she is maternal, bustling around the pretty little room with clucking attentiveness.

"I need to go to work," she says, "is there anything else you need?"

"A book?" Léa says, and Anna laughs. "I have a whole pile, I can't resist collecting them, though I never seem to have time to read!"

She points Léa to a small tower near the armchair and leaves her with a hug.

The books are the only dusty objects in the room. No one has touched this pile for a long time. Léa finds a volume of Chekhov stories, falls asleep, and dreams of silly women in pink silk dresses with small, fashionable dogs, a Russia which seems as far away as home.

In the morning, Anna takes her to the daycare. Léa cannot help but notice that in this world of liberated women, all the childcare still seems to fall to them. The exception is the man who runs the crèche and spends most of the day behind the closed door of his office. When Anna introduces Léa to him—his name is Alexander, but she calls him Sasha—she blushes all the way down her neck, and later on goes into his office and closes the door, so there is something else that is just the same as back home.

Very well. You cannot change all of society overnight. There is so much else to celebrate, all the people on the street, and everyone busy, and so much culture. The workers get cheap front seats at the opera, and every night the theatre is full, except instead of the furs and silks of His Majesty's back home they have come straight from work and are dressed in coarse wool and burlap. The hall smells like onion and tobacco and everyone has dirt under their nails, but it is a wonderful performance, and at the end they get up and applaud and talk with appreciation and expertise that rivals any audience Léa has ever seen. That is wonderful. Even though she is tired after a day of working with children, she goes out almost every night. Sunday to the ballet, Monday to the symphony, Tuesday to the theatre, and there is a Yiddish reading group she likes on Wednesday nights.

She goes folk dancing every Thursday afternoon, in the Great Park of Culture and Rest. The dances remind her of a hora at a Jewish wedding. She joins hands with strangers, weaves her feet in a circle. One day, she is dancing, and the sky is suddenly black with small planes, there must be a hundred of them, darkening the sky like a plague of locusts. She drops her partner's hands and looks up. People are pointing and laughing, and the sound of the planes drowns out the music of the accordion and the cries of children. She blocks her ears with her fingers as from the heavens dozens of parachutes descend, opening like chrysanthemums over the river and the grass of the park. Men tumble to the earth, untangle themselves from silk and rope; bystanders rush over to fish them from the water, to stroke the silk of the parachutes. It might be the strangest thing she's ever seen in her life.

"Incredible," the woman beside her says in Yiddish—she is one of the more experienced dancers, and during the breaks she leads singalongs of workers' songs, holding a long scroll so the audience can follow the words and participate.

"What is it?" Léa asks. "Some kind of sport?"

"Of course not," the woman says, with the haughtiness of the Moscow born-and-bred. "This is no game. They are preparing for war."

Léa looks at the crowd. One of the parachutists is necking on the grass with a folk dancer she knows; they are rolling around in the ropes, knotting their limbs together. She thinks of Hans and wonders if he will be caught in a more lethal embrace with one of these very soldiers when the war comes, as it must soon come.

She hears that back in Minsk, Hirsch Wolofsky has paid his son a visit, and Bill has agreed to follow him home. She is also supposed to go back, but she keeps delaying her return.

Often, she has the apartment to herself—Anna is with Sasha, she assumes—and she continues to develop her taste for the solitary life. She likes to know that the only mess to clean up is one she has made herself. It is a consequence of growing up in a large family; her space has never been her own, and neither has her mind, really, because she was always so likely to be interrupted.

She is just settling down with a book and a pot of tea when Anna comes in and brings the weather with her, cold air and a storm brewing. Anna knocks over a little pile of papers, and when she kneels to straighten them, she bumps into the table near the door and spills the whole pot of tea. "I can't bear it," she says, and sinks to the floor. She starts crying as Léa fusses around her with a dish towel, a glass of water, futile gestures of comfort, covering Anna's cold cheeks with her warm hands.

"Whatever is the matter?" Léa says.

Sasha is married. Sasha believes in free love. Sasha is not free to love. Sasha cannot have a child. The Party, in fact, has started to turn back to a more traditional model of the family. They prefer that members in positions of leadership not be divorced. The rhetoric has changed: from freedom to family. The Soviet woman is being urged to go to work, yes, but to put on lipstick and an apron once back at home. There are not enough babies being born.

That doesn't include Anna's baby, of course. This one is not wanted.

Sasha has told her that the abortion clinics in the Soviet Union are the most hygienic, the most advanced in the world. He has told her that he needs to go see his grandmother in the countryside and he doesn't know when he will be back. He has told her that he knows she will do the right thing. Sasha has already made an appointment for her to see the local panel so the procedure will be approved.

"And then he said," she says, crying so hard the words are barely audible, "are you certain it is mine?"

Léa brings Anna toast and lukewarm tea sweetened with jam. She rubs her back and her head the way she used to do for her mother, and she sings her to sleep.

Anna later tells her about the abortion panel, which consisted of a group of three women: a doctor, a representative of the Commissariat of Health, and a secretary. They sat across the table from Anna and did not offer comfort as she cried. The policy was not to abort a first pregnancy, they told her, but exceptions can be made if childbirth will endanger the mother's life. She told them that if they made her have this child, she would throw herself off a bridge, and they looked at her with contempt. Moscow has thirteen abortion clinics,

195

and more abortions each year than babies born. It will cost forty rubles, money that Sasha had failed to provide or even mention. She has to go back to the clinic, and a surgeon will dilate and scrape her uterus. The operation is done without anesthetic. She must stay in the hospital three days, and her work must give her a full two weeks off. In the interview, no one mentioned a father. Anna wept and hiccupped through the interrogation and when she got up at the end the woman doctor said, "Next time maybe you will think about the consequences." Léa wants to track down that doctor and slap her consequences off her face.

It is not this alone that makes her decide it is time to leave. But day by day, the shine is fading off the city. She hears about more people like Sasha, the old bad behaviours dressed in new clothes, and she wonders how much has really changed. Moscow feels to her like a mean, hard city, with cold winds and unfriendly people. It is nearly impossible to get anything done—every enterprise is a chain of obstacles—and she hates being unable to master Russian. She thinks of the way that sometimes at sunset, the clouds seem to form imaginary cities, spectral towers and phantasmagoric castles. And then the dark falls, and it all vanishes. She's not sure what she can trust.

That year, spring takes forever to arrive. Every day there is a rime of frost on the branches, her feet are always cold, and she finds herself suddenly, wildly missing home. Her siblings are all growing their families. Annie's daughter is four years old. Harry is in Kansas, of all places, where he is doing a residency in psychiatry, and he has just had another baby, a little boy this time. In his letters, he tells her about a plague of grasshoppers on the Plains, writes of sleeping on the screened-in porch with the children so they can get some air in the hot desolate nights. Her arms ache for them, her family. She is a full-grown woman, and she misses them so much.

Whatever she's looking for, it's not here.

10.

In her absence, Fred has run for Parliament downtown. He lost by ten thousand votes to Sammy Jacobs, but his three thousand ballots are double the number of registered Party members. The Liberals have repealed Article 98. For the moment, the Party is not illegal and their membership is growing. All this is good news. The public is finally catching up with them.

On the other hand, Arcand's fascists have ten members for every one of their own.

She needs a job again, and this time gets lucky. The Party needs a gathering place, and what better than a bookstore? With Fred's help, she rents a storefront on Bleury near Dorchester. She will be the manager. She knows a great deal about books and nothing about business.

They call it the Modern Book Shop.

Though he is no communist, Papa is so proud; in his opinion, books are the most respectable commodity. She has moved back in with her parents. All the other children are now out of the house, and Léa, who travelled the farthest of all of them, is living in her childhood bedroom. She is worried it will feel like a loss of freedom, but something has shifted. They have learned to be adults together. They play cards on Friday nights, and otherwise keep different hours. She has the comforts of home, and all the space she needs; it is an ideal situation. This time, she thinks she is home for good.

Their first week the bookstore windows are smashed. Léa sweeps glass off the floor, shakes shards out of the books, and sets up the window display once again.

At the bookstore they sell novels, journals, pamphlets, newspapers, and of course the holy trinity: Lenin, Engels, Marx. *The Daily Clarion* comes from Toronto, wrapped in brown paper, and is boldly displayed in the window. They host book clubs, member meetings, open classes about the labour union movement and tenants' rights, even classes in French and English for immigrants. Some of the books are impossible to find in Canada, so Léa takes the bus into New York State on buying trips and sits demurely in her seat as the border officials check passports and look for contraband. She puts the books under her skirts, thinking of a story from the Bible about the matriarch Rachel, who stole her father Laban's idols and hid them in the saddle on her camel, sitting above them as he searched the caravan. No one has ever stopped her; she has the gift of an innocent face, a wide-open smile.

The best books are published by Victor Gollancz, from London. She buys them in Plattsburgh and reads on the way home, folding the books inside magazines to hide them. She loves John Reed's account of the October Revolution, *Ten Days that Shook the World*. Lenin wrote the introduction. She sits in her seat by the bus window, in her prudish skirt and sweater vest, legs modestly crossed at the ankle, and her mind full of wild visions of Red Guards at night lit by torch fire, rallies that fill the square.

Being a girl is good camouflage for the revolution.

The police come by the shop frequently. She buys cheap books with red dustjackets for them to confiscate—they might as well be illiterate; she's just waving a flag at a bull—and she keeps the good stuff behind the desk.

The bookstore is a gathering place, but also a recruitment opportunity. She is skilled at knowing whom to approach and whom to ignore. Spies come by often; she has a nose for them. They loiter at the counter and pick up books without reading them. Once a boy who barely seemed old enough to shave, let alone join the Red Squad, stood by the shelf with a book held upside down for a good ten minutes before he corrected it. Lionel Groulx, the anti-Semitic priest, sends spies to buy books that he can use in his attack on the Judeo-Bolsheviks who are destroying the province. She jokes that he must have the best Marxist library in the entire country.

She knows many of the faces from the workers' hall and from demonstrations, and new people come in every day. The bookstore keeps getting vandalized, so they organize their own defense league, a shock brigade to stand outside overnight, holding baseball bats.

In Berlin, they burned books. Here is a cause she would guard with her life.

11.

On a wet spring Thursday, a slim, middle-aged man with a pencil moustache spends a long time browsing the shelves, and they get to talking. He looks-—the word teases at the edge of her memory—he looks, yes, debonair in his French beret and long scarf, like a writer or an artist. He tells her he is a surgeon and works in thoracic surgery at Sacred Heart. He is planning to visit the Soviet Union later that year. He is interested—very interested—in public health for the people, he has seen the devastation the Depression has wrought on the working poor, he has a working group called the Montreal Group for the Security of People's Health, he has a flyer and can he leave it right there? He would very much like to see how Soviet hospitals and doctors operate, to examine a system of socialist care. To look, you understand, not to listen to the propaganda or to meet the bureaucrats but to see the patients with his own eyes. He talks so quickly the sentences spill into one another.

"I'm not convinced," he says, "that your socialism is not merely a modern religion. I'm not certain that it is the solution to the problem. But I have seen the problem with my own eyes. Good Lord, you would have to be blind not to see it."

He gestures towards a vibrant yellow car badly parked too near the corner. "I'm selling my old steed," he says, hand over his heart. "To pay for the boat. Oh well, sacrifices must be made."

He is intense, and a little nervous. Up close, his charm seems compulsive. She can't tell if he is flirting. He pulls books off the shelf carelessly, weighs them in his hand like fruit, puts them down on any near surface. She will have to clean all that up once he leaves.

"Tell me what I should be reading to prepare for my trip," he says.

"What kind of thing do you like to read?"

"Medical literature," he says immediately, and then pauses. "And also, poetry. Blake and Whitman, the visionaries. Stories. The great Dostoevsky! The immortal Tolstoy! Something in that line."

She tells him Chekhov was a doctor and finds a volume of Constance Garnett's translation. "And this," she says, "is quite new. It was published in 1933—we have only the one copy."

"Red Medicine," he reads. "Socialized Health in Soviet Russia." He flips through. "When a Russian becomes ill the government does something about it," he reads. "Well, exactly as it should be."

She tells him that she has only recently come back from the Soviet Union.

"Really?" he says, looking startled. "And what did you think?"

"It's hard to find the words for it." She hasn't yet resolved the contradictions of her visit, the moments of cultural abundance and the contrast of familiar hypocrisy. "You'll have to see for yourself. You'll learn more in two days than in two years of reading!"

"Not much of an advertisement for your bookstore," he says, and holds out his hand. "I'm Norman." His handshake is brisk and firm.

"Léa," she says, "and it's the other way around. All this"— she gestures at the shelves—"is an advertisement for the land of socialism."

"Very good!" he says. "I will come back when I return and tell you all about my trip."

He pays with a handful of coins from his pocket. He doesn't bother to count the change, just sweeps the rest back in as if money doesn't matter to him and puts the books under his arm.

"Dasvidanya," she calls out as he opens the door, and as he looks back, he touches his fingers to his beret in a military salute.

"*À la prochaine*," he says, and gets in the little yellow car, pulling out so fast he provokes a riot of honks, his scarf flying behind him.

"How on earth," she asks Fred when he comes by the bookstore, "did that man get involved with the movement? He looks like such a dandy! And he must come from money."

"It's a crazy story," Fred says. "He was driving through the protest last week—just by chance, he knew nothing about it. The policemen charged the protestors on horses and he stopped his car in the middle of the street to give first aid to the injured, right there in his back seat."

"I was at that protest!" Léa says. "On Saint Lawrence Boulevard. I was holding a banner. Milk for our children, bread for our wives, jobs, not breadlines."

She shakes her head, remembering the policemen on horseback, looking like rampaging centaurs.

"It was damn murder that day."

"Wait until you hear the next part," Fred says. "The following day, he just burst into the Montreal Unemployed Association and handed them his card. He said," and Fred deepens his voice. "'I am Dr. Norman Bethune. Any man, woman, or child you send me will receive medical treatment free of charge. By next week, I hope to have another ten doctors doing the same.' It was quite an entrance." Fred sounds envious.

Dr. Bethune does not have ten doctors, but he seems to have the strength of ten men. Since the day of the rally, Fred says he's been showing up everywhere. Holding the lines against evictions, at block committee meetings, at speeches about unemployment.

After that, Léa looks for him. She keeps her eyes peeled for his jaunty cap, his narrow moustache. But he is more rumour than body. He is seen so many places it is almost as if he is more than one man.

12.

At Stan's study group the next week she hears less flattering stories about Dr. Bethune. Stan comes from Toronto and became radicalized, like Léa, while studying in Europe. He went to the Sorbonne, where he fell in with a group of left-wing students and happened to attend the funeral of the last survivor of the Paris Commune of 1871. "Two hundred thousand of us, marching to Père Lachaise," he told Léa the first time they met. "On the way to the funeral, you could say I had an awakening. Capitalism, that was a living death. But those of us who marched together were at the beginning of a creative renaissance the likes of which the world had never seen." He is new in town and came to teach at the new working man's college, Sir George Williams. His Marxist reading group runs every Wednesday night.

Stan looks exactly like what he is: a middle-class intellectual from a good family, with large round glasses and dark suits. His role is to provide the Party with intellectual credibility, and to connect them with a middle-class membership. Section Thirteen, a new bourgeois corps: about a hundred members who don't carry membership cards or show up in public. Their job is to work behind the scenes, and their identities are top secret. Léa is one of the only members allowed to know their names.

Irene Kon, who recruited the new members, is looking like the cat who has swallowed the cream, her slim legs wrapped around each other at knee and ankle. She is the only one Léa recognizes, except for the artist Fred Taylor. With his Westmount duplex and his buttoned suit jackets, Fred Taylor is about as bourgeois as they come. His brother is an honest-to-goodness plutocrat, with silk top hats and racehorses.

They are gossiping about Bethune before the study session.

"Beth, they call him." Taylor says. "He's a cad. We used to play poker together, in 1930, during the early years of the Depression. We would go to all the blind pigs—you know, the bars in basements and back rooms where you could gamble and drink moonshine all night. Beth was a bad drunk. Some guys know how to hold their liquor and some guys don't and that's just the way it is. When he drank he was a different person, and that wasn't someone I wanted to know. He would insult people, pick fights. Mind you, he knew better than to pick a fight with me. But I got tired of cleaning up his messes."

"Well, he's on our side now," Irene says.

"Beth a socialist? I don't believe it. Always looking for something to save him. If not a skirt, then a cause. He'll move on soon."

As they walk home together, Irene tells her what Taylor really has against Beth. Beth once took a prostitute as a dinner date to Taylor's Westmount house, and at the end of the night drunkenly announced that he would now return her to the streets "from whence she came." Taylor was insulted. Not for the woman's dignity, but for his own.

Irene says, "You know, Taylor once told me that he could never respect a woman who did not save herself for marriage. But then again, he had no reservations about marrying his own first cousin!"

They have a child now, and it all seems to have worked out. His wife, with her open heart and natural bent towards justice, got him involved in the Party in the first place, though now that they have a child she is rarely at the meetings.

The Party is full of these characters. For every idealist there's someone with an entirely different agenda, rebelling against their background, or trying to impress a girl, or proving themselves to a nemesis from the past who has long since forgotten all about them. She wonders, sometimes, what she is trying to prove. If she could have been like her sisters—married, a mother, happy or at least content on that well-travelled road—perhaps she would have done so. She doesn't have much choice, though at every step she has been making choices. This life, her life, it feels inevitable.

How strange that all of her hard-fought decisions add up to something like fate.

13.

She does not expect to see Beth again, but a few months later he is back. He has spent two months in the Soviet Union, which took him to the limit of his visa; he wishes he could have stayed longer. He was supposed to attend a medical conference in Leningrad, but he tells her, unashamed, that he just went to the first session, then decided he could read the papers for himself, that he would learn far more by visiting the hospitals and sanatoria and interviewing doctors and patients. Also, there was a world to be discovered, outside the doors of the auditorium. He couldn't stand the idea of coming all that way and staying inside looking at the same four walls, talking to the same forty people. He walked the streets, swam in the Neva, visited the museums.

"It's marvellous, Léa," he says, "the sun doesn't set, even at ten o'clock at night, and people stroll along the river arm in arm. As if sleep has been conquered by the revolution!"

What he found in the sanatoria was even more astonishing.

"They have reduced tuberculosis by fifty percent, Léa, and this in just eighteen years—years which were challenging in every respect, and yet, to have made such progress against the white plague, the captain of death! Treatment is free and considered a human right: imagine that. They test children as a preventative measure."

Beth can barely keep still for excitement; he has advocated this strategy for years. He is not a believer, but here is a miracle.

Beth had a bad case of tuberculosis in his thirties. He was put on bedrest for an entire year. "Léa," he tells her, "I have had enough lying down for a lifetime."

Never mind lying down, he cannot stand still. He has a reputation—and not entirely a positive one—for doing the very fastest surgeries, to minimize shock and time under anaesthesia. He has re-introduced controversial old methods of treatment, has thrown a handful of maggots into an open wound, has again and again practised the art of medicine as resurrection. He will operate on even the most advanced cases of tuberculosis, because what do they have to lose? Without the operation, they are certain to die. His goal, he says, is not to treat tuberculosis but to eliminate it. Which is to be done by eliminating poverty.

He now has a plan for public health care, modelled on the Soviet Union, and he has presented his manifesto to the premier of Quebec and the mayor of Montreal. So far, no luck. He keeps trying.

She comes to a speech he gives about the Soviet Union to a confused audience of surgeons and general practitioners.

"This is a looking-glass land," he says. "The Russians, like the White Queen in Alice, are accustomed to believe many impossible things before breakfast. They believe," he says, waving his cigar, which he has forgotten to light, "in the unlimited and heroic future of man."

He catches her at the reception afterwards.

"Comrade," he says, dipping his head. "I finished all the books you gave me! Do you have anything else for me to read?"

"I have something for you," she says, "but not to read." And the next day she brings two women to his clinic in the YMCA in Point Saint-Charles. The first has been coughing for weeks. Her body is racked when the fits come upon her, as if she is possessed. Her lips purse and strain like she is convulsing into labour.

"They call this the strangler," he says, looking at the telltale white film at the back of her throat. "She needs to be isolated, especially from children."

Léa knows the girl, who shares a room with four siblings in Verdun, taking turns sleeping on the beds and on the floor. Isolated how?

The second patient is four months pregnant. Twenty-four years old, with five children already.

Bethune shakes his head. "I can't do much for her," he says. He sends her home with a gallon of milk, a bag of bread and fresh fruit. He tells her to come back and he'll check on the progress of the pregnancy.

She remembers Taylor's warnings, but Beth seems like a different man than the one who drank all night and could not end an evening without picking a fight.

She has heard that he had his heart broken by a girl from Edinburgh; they have been married twice, divorced twice. She divorced him the first time; he divorced her the second time, to even the score.

"When we married," he says, "she wore black. She broke a mirror that morning. There was nothing but signs."

He still calls her his wife.

It is lucky for Léa that she never liked a flirt, because Beth is the kind of man who sets himself the challenge of making every woman fall in love with him, though in the most eccentric fashion.

"What a magnificent set of hips you have, Léa," he says to her, "what a pelvis for childbearing. Are you certain, then, that you want to waste the gifts that God bequeathed you?"

She laughs him off. "I have dozens of children," she says, "my nieces and nephews, the children of the workers. Besides, you know very well I am too old."

"Nonsense," he says, "you still look like a maid, I am certain that your ovaries are no older than twenty-one." Then he gets very serious and says, "Léa, you and I are alike, we can't have children of our own because the whole world is our family. We are like monks with a holy purpose."

Léa snorts. "Some monk you are."

His affairs are an open secret. Though it is also true that when he speaks about his work, it is with a kind of reverential and flamboyant austerity which makes her think of the priests in Rome.

Despite his flirtatious behaviour, he speaks to women with respect; he has no patience for the old hypocrisies, bunkum about the feminine mystique. No male mind or female mind, he says, only human beings. But he is also one of the biggest snobs she has ever met, in his turtlenecks and tailored flannel pants, with an eye for beauty that goes along with a desire for control. More than once he has threatened to buy her a dress.

It is possible Beth might regret his childlessness. In his apartment on Beaver Hall Square, there is an enormous doll in the corner named Alice. He says it is the only issue of his marriage, and he gets custody for half the year. He loves children, and with Fritz Brandtner opens up an Art Centre for them in his apartment where Fritz teaches them to draw and paint. When they come over for class, he sometimes lets them play with Alice, but Léa can see the concern in his eyes as he watches them, so she tends to hide the doll behind a screen before the students arrive.

And does Léa feel a twinge, as she sits with the children and watches them lean over the paper Brandtner has provided, gripping their crayons in their fists with such heartbreaking seriousness?

But if she had a child the life she has built for herself would be impossible.

Beth lives like a millionaire, with a view of the city from high windows covered in red velvet drapes, furniture he has designed himself and rich rugs on the floor, the walls hung with paintings, including his own, and his diplomas framed in the toilet, which is exactly, he claims, where they belong. He earns a lot of money and spends it as freely, handing it to friends and strangers alike, shrugging off the objections of the horrified and prudent. "Money," he likes to say, "is just a medium of exchange," as he hands it away. She could spend hours in his library, where every book carries a bookplate of his own design that reads, "This Book Belongs to Norman Bethune and His Friends." He can't stand liars or hypocrites or people who want to schmooze but if Léa tells him about a little girl who isn't well, he will immediately say, "What's the matter with you, bring her right here."

He signs petitions. He sees children whose parents can't afford to pay a doctor. He speaks terrible French. "What kind of French is that, Beth?" she asks the first time she hears him.

"The kind," he says, "they speak in Edinburgh."

Even the nuns cross themselves when he passes. *C'est un Protestant mais c'est un homme de coeur,* they say. She can forgive him his romances and his sudden moods and the fact that he's a bad gambler and a worse drunk and his dilettantish careless display of wealth—she's never seen anyone use their money more foolishly—because at every sickbed he is suddenly a saint. She sees the spirit possess him.

"Once, Léa, I was treating a girl with tuberculosis. I was leaning over and listening to her chest and she rose up on the bed like a ghost—she was that pale—and said, I've never been kissed, I don't want to die without ever being kissed."

"What did you do?" Léa says, though she already knows the story.

"I kissed her, of course," he says. "It was her deathbed request."

"Could have been your death, too," she says.

He looks serious and says, "It comes for all of us."

He likes that Keats poem a little too much, about being half in love with easeful death. He likes the idea of a good-looking corpse.

"And who said you're good-looking?" Léa says.

"We're alike, Léa, you and me, we burn fast and bright."

"Not me," Léa says, "I'm a stayer."

"What?" he says. "So sorry, I wasn't listening."

Most people find him exhausting, but Léa gets a kick out of his exuberance.

That Christmas, he sends her a greeting card. She opens it up, her mother hovering over her shoulder. It is a copy of his Compressionist's Creed—a parody of the apostle's creed, in tribute to collapse therapy, a controversial treatment which forces air into the chest of the tubercular patient until the lung collapses, allowing it to rest. In his time as a patient at the Trudeau sanatorium he read about the therapy and insisted on trying it, against the advice of his doctors. He believes the procedure saved his life. He has now designed his own version of the machine, which he sketched on the back of the card, along with a seasonal greeting: "Wishing you a happy pneumothorax!"

"Is it a joke?" Mama asks, confused.

"It's just Beth."

14.

Disaster. While making a delivery, Papa collapses on the street and dies. He is sixty-three years old. Léa is so consumed by the practical details of the first twenty-four hours, the Jewish imperative to get the body in the ground, that she can scarcely believe he is gone.

Such a meek man, such a gentle man. Such a good man.

He never should have been on that corner, should not have had to schlep and hustle into his senior years. He was not cut out for it, not even when he was young. He should have been left to his books, which he loved, to his learning, which he loved, to his grandchildren, whom he should have had more years to love.

She covers the mirrors in the house, puts cushions on the floor and leaves the door unlocked, an open invitation for mourners. The confinement of the seven days of mourning is excruciating. She is itching to do something, to walk around the block, at least. She feels smothered by the dark room, the stuffy air, the constant burden of the grief of other people. The bagels, the babka, the herring, all the herring.

But at least her brothers and sisters are there, so many that even this sombre gathering feels festive, and they bring their children. It is extraordinary how magnetic children are in a house of mourning. Every eye is on Annie's new baby Berel, every hand outstretched to catch him in his unsteady toddler trot, like a drunken sailor on a rolling deck.

When she lies down at night Léa feels suffocated. She cannot even think of the world outside. It is as if death has shrunk her into these four walls.

She is worried for Mama, but Mama seems have settled into her role as primary mourner. She drinks tea, drinks in stories, hears new things about the man she married when she was only sixteen years old and he was already twenty-nine. For instance, did she know he had trained to be a physician? But never got the chance to practise, unclear if that was because of anti-Semitism or just the reality of a new wife, of many children, of the need to provide for the house. To be a provider: how many other lives sacrificed to that one, how many possibilities? But he had never seemed resentful, never seemed to feel—as Léa now feels on his behalf—cheated of a life that would be more his own.

She gathers cushions from around the house and surrounds herself as she sleeps in order to soften the ache of missing him. On the fourth day she is so restless, she has polished every window and wiped down every surface until she sees her own pale face, that her mother says, "Léa, just go outside." After four days inside, the streets seem saturated with early October light, and the leaves have begun to change.

The world on fire calls to her as she walks across the mountain and looks out at the city spread beneath her feet.

When she comes back her sisters and brothers are playing a new game called Monopoly. The house is all family and no strangers, and she recognizes her emptiness as hunger. She heads over to the table and has an open-faced sandwich of rye bread, butter, and herring, then another.

"Léa," her brother Michael says, "help me, save me from the monopolists," and she looks at the board. Rose has taken over Boardwalk and Park Place. No surprise. She's always been ruthless.

"You chose to play the game," Léa says, and she goes to her room and sleeps for twelve hours on her narrow single bed. When she wakes up, even though it is only the fifth day, she decides she has had enough of mourning, the bookstore needs her, and she needs—she needs the world.

15.

The next time Fred runs for office, he tries for the provincial election, and he asks Léa to help him. She turns her shoulder to the wheel. Every minute she is not at the bookstore she is at his office on Sainte-Catherine Street, or she is on the sidewalk, going door to door. She will knock on every door in Montreal if she has to; her knuckles are raw with the effort. The French-language Communist newspaper *Clarté* is published from the office that serves as election headquarters and the rooms smell of newsprint and tobacco. Sometimes men who have nowhere else to go sleep on the floor. At night, it is a sea of bodies, and in the morning, the bedrolls are tucked under tables and desktops.

There is always something to do, which is how she likes it. Supporters come by with donations. Most of them are European, recent arrivals: Czechs, Italians, Hungarians, Poles. Her favourite is a Finn named Eino. He is so tall, he needs to duck to get under the door frame, a goyish giant in this room of clever little Jews. When he comes to see her, he blushes from the tips of his ears to his collar. His hands are as big as baseball gloves. He brings his daily gleanings in a twist of newspaper, pennies and nickels mostly, with the occasional triumphant dollar bill. "Not much, comrade," he says each time, and shrugs as he spills the change on the table. "More tomorrow."

The week before the election, fascists break into the office. They smash the windows, they throw the leaflets on the floor and stomp on them, and when she protests, one of them, a redhead with a Hitler moustache, hits her in the face. The police stand by the door, idly swinging their batons. Blood drips into her eyes. She wipes her faces and gestures at the cop, accusing him with her red hands.

"Aren't you going to do something?" she says, and he shrugs.

"You better go see a doctor, lady," he says.

She is so mad so she can barely keep her languages straight. She spits at him in Yiddish, "*Finstere leyd zol nor di mama oyf im zen*—may your mother see you suffer in darkness"—and then in French, "*osti de câlisse de ciboire de tabarnak!*"

Then she backs away, because even though she is angry she has never been stupid, and she saw his knuckles whiten on his baton when she shouted at him. She heads not to the clinic but home, where her mother washes her forehead and calls her a careless child even though she never has felt more adult, more righteous or clear on her role in this mad world.

16.

Election day is a farce. The Liberals have paid the street ladies of Saint-Louis two dollars each to vote for their incumbent. The girls sashay in wearing elaborate hats to cast their votes, and an hour later they are back, different hat, same vote. Léa is seething, wringing her hands on the street, why won't anyone do something?

She calls one of the girls over. She's seen her before. She came to visit Léa with a specific and private and all-too-common problem, and Léa took her to the doctor of last resort, and that is why she can parade down Park Avenue with her twenty-inch waist and three-inch heels, as she casts vote after vote for the enemy.

Léa grabs her by the wrist, "Do you even know who you are voting for?"

The girl shrugs. "A politician," she says.

Léa drops her hand. After all, it is good to see her walking down the street, even if she is cocky and foolish. The last time she saw her, Evelyn Walker—her name comes back as she strides away—was lying in bed and the sheets were stiff with blood.

Léa rubs her eyes. It is a long day to live through knowing they have already lost. In the end, Fred gets only 538 votes.

"But just wait until we find those guys who voted for us!" Léa says, having already recovered. In her mind, she is at the next vote, the next fight. In her mind she has already won.

17.

From Spain, there are reports of riots, executions, even death squads. It makes Léa think of the street fighting in Berlin. Beth says, my God they will make the world a slaughterhouse; he is already preparing to travel there to support the Republicans, and he has an idea for a transfusion unit that moves like an ambulance to where it is most needed.

The Quebec papers have taken the side of the fascists. They are fighting Franco's war for him. Every day, there is a new story about the Republican outrage, the churches desecrated, priests attacked, nuns assaulted.

"Come on," Léa says, throwing the paper down, "they should be ashamed to publish such lies." She writes a strongly worded letter to the editor, which they do not print.

Fred tells her that a delegation is coming from Spain to seek their support and is scheduled to speak at Mount Royal Arena. Among them is Father Sasarola, whom the church has denounced; it drives them blind with rage that one of their own has joined the Republican cause. Pro-Franco protestors show up at the arena carrying sticks, bats, and canes, and it is after eight when they realize they have been shouting at an empty building. Anticipating trouble, Fred had moved the meeting to a nearby hotel.

And there is Léa, chilly in her autumn jacket, sitting near the doors and straining to hear the speeches from the stage. Behind her, the staff have gotten a phone call warning that there is a mob now heading in their direction. The manager pushes past the crowd to tell Fred to shut it down, and she can see Fred—who is looking professorial in his tweed coat—shaking his head.

When the lights go out, she is not surprised; since they would not shut down the meeting, some enterprising hotel employee has shut down the power. They shuffle into the street, ahead of the mob, and make their own ways home. Léa is disappointed; it is an anticlimactic end to the evening. Together, they can fill a room with righteous, joyful fury; on their own, they unravel in separate directions, pulling their coats closed and bowing their heads against the wind, all of the warmth and excitement of the gathering lost.

Yesterday felt like summer, but today she feels the chill in the air. The newspaper says there will be frost later in the week. No matter how late it comes, she never does feel ready for winter.

18.

On a Sunday in late October, one hundred thousand men gather at Champ-de-Mars, the site of the Montreal citadel, named for the Roman god of war because of its old role as a military parade ground. They have come together to celebrate the Fête du Christ-Roi, a recent addition to the liturgical calendar. La Fête du Christ-Roi commemorates Christ's sovereignty, his power and dominion over all nations and all laws.

"There is no church-state problem in Quebec," Fred says, in a version of the old Yiddish joke. "The church rules over the state, no problem!"

This year, participants in the Fête du Christ-Roi would like to make clear that Christ truly hates communists. Indeed, the parade has two purposes: to acclaim the royalty of Christ and to protest against the communists, "*dans notre pays*."

"*Vive le Christ-Roi!*" they cry. Also, "Down with the communists! Down with the Jews!"

Fred puts on a hat, goes to watch the demonstrations, and comes back shaken.

"We live in a fascist province," he says.

In Quebec City, Duplessis leads the celebrations. He announces that the government is going to take "necessary measures." Necessary: that vague and chilling word.

All of the hate is perversely good for recruitment. Each meeting, there are a few new faces in the halls.

"They're waking up," Fred says, and he walks to the podium with a bantam strut.

He introduces a speaker from Kiev, who has come to talk about the new Jewish Renaissance.

"We have entered a new golden age," the speaker tells the audience. "In Kiev, we see an extraordinary flowering of Yiddish theatre and literature. There is no gap between the working class and the world of culture. Every working man is a Shakespeare."

He looks like a peasant himself, in his heavy coat and baggy trousers, a dusting of dandruff on his shoulders. His white beard is streaked with sulfur at the corners of his mouth, he must be a smoker. Léa accompanied him at lunch; he ate five bread rolls, heavily buttered, belched loudly, and left crumbs all over the table. She was embarrassed for him, and then ashamed of herself for noticing. A golden age.

A voice from the audience cries out: "*Et les seize? Et Zinoviev?*"

Fred takes the stage and looks for the dissenter with an air of exasperation.

"You do recall the confessions," he says. "Espionage, poisoning, sabotage. They were guilty. They admitted they were guilty."

He turns to apologize to the speaker, who is smiling dumbly, his eyes wrinkled depths in his round face. He does not know French and has understood nothing. For the audience, though, the question hangs over the rest of the meeting, which winds up quickly.

Léa tries to remember what she knows about the trials and the August executions, the sixteen Party members accused of conspiring to kill Stalin. She is an inveterate reader of newspapers, a clipper of articles, but even when she goes home and looks through her files, she can find nothing.

Later on, she attempts to capture what had happened in the room. What made it feel so disconcerting? She feels as if something is being kept from her, but she's not sure why or for what purpose.

She asks about it the next day—"Who was that man?"—but is immediately dismissed.

"A spy, of course," one says.

Another says, "A provocateur."

"They will make up any lie to discredit us," Fred says.

"But wait, the sixteen—were they guilty?"

"Of course, they were guilty. Zinoviev, Kamenev, the rest of them, they admitted it, the whole thing," he replies, a little gruffly. Léa is his favourite, he is not accustomed to her questioning him. "They had to execute them. What else could they have done? You see, they had no choice."

Lev Kamenev, Trotsky's brother-in-law. Grigory Zinoviev, former head of the Comintern. And fourteen others, almost all Jews. Shot in the cellars of Lubyanka prison after confessing to a plot to kill Joseph Stalin. If they confessed, it must be true. Must it be true? "In the Soviet Union," Fred tells their mostly Jewish membership, "there is no anti-Semitism." Léa feels a vague unease at his confidence. She remembers her father's terror when she first told him she was travelling to the Soviet Union, and thinks of the speaker from Kiev shoving bread rolls into his mouth like a man who was starving.

But Fred—Fred has a direct line to Moscow, he would know. Fred would not lie to her.

At the bookstore, they are feeling the strain of being constantly under siege. A letter is slipped under their door, all jagged letters and aggressive, erratic capitalization. "Last Warning. We give you three days to close everything or else we put dynamite around the Modern Book Shop. The police are with us and you know it. We will be there this week. We are and will remain Fascists." The bookstore increases security and starts a twenty-four-hour guard, all volunteer, but Léa can tell that people are getting tired—the air of excitement, of like-minded ease that prevailed in the first months that the bookstore was open, is gone.

In its place, suspicion and dread.

19.

Rumour has it that the garment workers are going to try to unionize again. The International Ladies Garment Workers Union is sending Rose Pesotta from New York City. The ILGWU have been successful in organizing unions in New York, LA, and Toronto, but as long as Montreal stays unaffiliated, the bosses will just pack up shop and move their manufacturing to Quebec, where the mayor and the premier and the bosses and the church conspire to break the worker's spine.

Montreal, the armpit of North America. Come for the cheap wages, stay for the graft.

Rose Pesotta is famous. She sounds and looks Italian, but everyone knows she is Jewish: born Rakhel Peisoty, to Yitzhak and Masya of the Ukraine. Apparently, she fled to America when her parents tried to marry her off to a good village boy from Derazhnya. She changed her name and found her feet in New York City. Léa has been following Rose's last campaign, the Flint sit-down strike, very closely. In Flint, the struggle for the auto workers' union often looked like war: police with guns and tear gas, strikers with broken bottles and hammers. When the workers occupied the factory, General Motors turned off the heat and electricity. Rose bought out a department store's worth of wool socks and pyjamas, turned flannel blankets into ponchos for the men to wear, brought even more blankets to line the automobile seats which served as makeshift beds. The leaders of the labour movement got death threats. A warrant was issued for her arrest, and the threatening letters she received often spelled her name wrong: Rose Pertola better keep away from Chevy 9.

"I changed my name at Ellis Island to accommodate the Americans," she said in an interview, "and even in their death threats, the Americans can't be bothered to get it right."

When the workers won, Rose Pesotta climbed in through the window and hugged men who had not showered for forty days. The men painted their fingernails red in protest and to show through their immaculate polish that they had not broken the strike with work. They marched out waving American flags to the music of a brass band.

Rose Pesotta looks like she eats trouble. Her cheeks are rosy with it. She has the sharp nose and black eyes of a fox; she has an ebullient figure that she belts into a waist. She wears black dresses with white collars that make her look like a nun, she believes in free love, and when she gets to Montreal, she walks all the steps of the oratory in her high heels and then turns around to proclaim the view all too wonderful. She is a *farbrente maydel*—a fiery girl. That Rose Pesotta is a force of nature.

She is looking for someone who speaks Yiddish and French, who can move between the Catholic girls and the Jews in the factory, someone with a track record in the movement, with a passion for their cause and the ability to communicate it. She is looking for Léa.

The timing is good—the bookstore is about to close, and Léa needs a job. She will work on the floor, but really, her work is to organize the union.

When Léa arrives at the factory, she should not be shocked. But it is worse, even, than she had imagined. The pressing rooms are so hot that pregnant women and new mothers lactate as they work, wet blooming circles on the fronts of their dresses, milk dripping onto the dirty floors. The bathrooms are filthy—there is no paper in the stalls, no soap at the sink. When they are behind on the line their lunch breaks are cancelled, and they bolt dry sandwiches in the hallway. The smell of the starch in the air makes their eyes water and their throats hurt. The windows are so dirty it is constant dusk, even in the middle of the day; when they open them up, cold drafts race across the room, and the windowsills fill with snow. Roaches skitter across the floor and rats run under the sewing tables. Even when the girls are not at work, they can feel their skin crawling. It is impossible to make enough money working regular hours, so everyone takes home piecework and sews at night and on the weekends, their apartments extensions of the sweatshop, their mothers, aunts, children, all extra hands to finish the labour.

But you only get piecework if you're nice—some women go home with big piles, some women with nothing at all. Everyone knows what a closed door means. Everyone knows you are not being *asked*.

It is no better than cannibalism, they are being cooked alive in there. They are being eaten. Léa walks around with a quiet fury burning in her chest.

Their first action is a radio broadcast, and that is also their first mistake. Walter Schevenels, the bespectacled general secretary of the International Federation of Trade Unions, is visiting from Paris and sits in as a guest speaker on their program. To their focus on the need for a trade union among the dressmakers of Montreal, he adds a heartfelt plea for the loyalists in Spain, fighting Franco's fascism.

The next day, all that is reported in the newspaper is outrage at the audacity of supporting the Spanish Republicans. Beware these dangerous Communist agitators, these greedy outsiders, hostile to our workers and our faith.

Rose Pesotta is taken aback: who are these Catholics who take the side of the fascists, not the side of the poor?

"Welcome to Quebec," Léa says.

Rose decides not to distribute the movement's journal, *Justice*, because they have been publishing so many articles on fighting fascism in Spain. Here, this must not distract from their mission. Instead, she focuses on building the movement among the dressmakers: hiring a secretary, setting up the union office, furnishing it with a library, a kitchen, a piano, a radio, a gramophone, even a stage.

She believes, with Emma Goldman, in everybody's right to beautiful, radiant things.

They have an open house on Sainte-Catherine's day, the holiday for old maids. The office is full of women in yellow and green hats, yellow for faith and green for wisdom, many decorated with the emblem of the garment worker's badge, pierced through with the flourish of a needle. Léa is now in charge of the educational programs. She is resplendent in her green beret, handing out pamphlets, shaking hands, dispensing hugs.

She has long passed twenty-five, the official age of spinsterdom for the Catherinettes, when their prayer shifts from *"Donnez-moi, Seigneur, un mari de bon lieu! Qu'il soit doux, opulent, libéral et agréable!"* to *"Seigneur, un qui soit supportable, ou qui, parmi le monde, au moins puisse passer!"* Indeed, as a woman over thirty her prayer is supposed to be, *"Un tel qu'il te plaira Seigneur, je m'en contente!"*

But after all, she is no Catherinette, she is a midinette, the term for the factory girls who break for lunch at midday at the local diners. She is content to make her own living at her own pleasure. She has no patience for what is only bearable.

Poor Saint Catherine, who was strapped to a torture machine meant to tear her apart, as punishment for refusing the advances of a man. She survived, only to be later beheaded. She should have fought harder for her freedom. Others should have helped her fight.

They go into the park and shoot off Catherine wheel fireworks after dark. When Saint Catherine was bound on the execution wheel, an angel came and freed her, splitting the wheel with tongues of fire. A coven of women in wild hats laughs as the sky spits flame.

Montreal, just you wait.

20.

In January, they inaugurate their union branch: Local 262. Second mistake. At the open meeting, a photographer takes a picture of the officers. The next day, their faces and names are in *L'Illustration nouvelle*. Some girls are fired that very night; the next day, even more are let go, seven from the Queen City Dress Company. Some of the girls are locked out of their houses by their own mothers. This is beginning to feel like the failed strike of 1934, when they took to the streets and one thousand women lost their jobs.

"Just don't let them lose their nerve," Rose says. Léa canvasses the girls, dispensing courage as if she was handing out Aspirin. She goes house to house that evening, sitting with the girls on their beds and at their kitchen tables, asking them what they really have to lose. For the girls who've been locked out, she finds temporary homes; she brings envelopes of cash to the girls who have been fired and promises them she'll help get their jobs back.

"But how do you know?" a girl named Claudette asks, clasping her hands so hard her fingers turn white.

"I have faith," Léa says, and instantly feels awful about her answer. Faith is for priests and grifters; Léa believes in hard work, in protest, and in the power of the strike. She starts to backtrack, but Claudette, who grew up with the nuns, releases her hands and rolls her eyes to the heavens.

"I also have faith," she says. "I have faith in you, Léa."

On her way home, Léa offers a just-in-case prayer to Saint Jude, the saint of lost causes, whom she does not believe in. But what a good mandate for a saint.

In the churches, the Sunday sermons all warn the girls away from the Jewish union, as they like to call the International Ladies Garment Workers Union. But this time, the French girls are on their side. Together, they fill the halls and walk in pairs, like the animals of Noah's Ark, arm in arm to the registration tables.

In April, they hold a general meeting in the largest auditorium they can find, and the crowds spill into the streets and listen through loudspeakers. They sing "Solidarity Forever" to the weak April sun. The crocuses are blooming.

Spring is a good time for a strike.

In Detroit, a single factory held all of the dies used to stamp the automobile parts for the Buicks, Pontiacs, and Oldsmobiles made all across the country. Occupying just one building meant paralyzing the entire industry. "Listen," Léa says to Rose as they plan the strike. "We can do the same thing here. We just took home the piecework for the summer season. The girls have all the belts and loops and cuffs and collars to finish the dresses in their apartments. We have some leverage." Rose nods. "You tell them to hold onto those pieces. If the factories want to make the summer season, they'll have to negotiate." Léa flies around the floor, making sure everyone got the message. Those frilly bits of fabric are their hostages now.

In late-night meetings, they brainstorm a list of demands. They want a forty-four-hour workweek. They want a wage increase and time-and-a-half for overtime. They want their Saturday afternoons. They want clean toilets and towels in the bathroom. They want to open a window. They want the bosses to stop pinching them in the hallways.

The week of their first general meeting, *The Gazette* reports that a contract has been signed between the Catholic League of Needle Workers and the garment industry. The surprise announcement is meant to kneecap their efforts. The Catholic League is a rival union but does not deserve the name: they serve the church of business first and the workers can go hang. Léa stands on the street reading about the contract, her hands cold. The conditions are worse, if anything, than what they already have. A minimum wage lower than the law provides for men. No overtime. And even less money for those employees "infirm" or "not normal," which means an extra license to exploit those already most disadvantaged. Léa is incandescent with fury.

On the contract, the names of Jewish factory owners are listed alongside the Catholic ones. At Local 262, Léa mimeographs the evidence of their betrayal. She shares it with rabbis, with community leaders, with anyone who can exert pressure and make the bosses feel some shame.

It does not take long. By the end of the day, a letter appears in the *Keneder Adler*, signed by four Jewish factory owners: "We wish to make a declaration to the community... we never authorized anyone to sign our names." They call the agreement a "so-called contract," and wash their hands of it. "We want nothing to do with this Jew-baiting Catholic syndicate," they declare. Léa has bought some time.

The union men from Toronto arrive on the train, in their sack suits and trench coats. They take the stage and pound the podium in English, confused when they garner no applause, illuminated when the French translation raises the roof. The girls fill Sainte-Catherine Street in their Sunday dresses, sing *Alouette* and *The Victory Song*, sing *O Canada* in French and the ILGWU anthem in English, sing *for the union, bom bom, nous gagnerons, bom bom*.

It is clear that the police do not know what to do with these midinettes, in their hats and ribbons, looking like anyone's sister, anyone's mother. In Oshawa, the General Motors workers are on the picket line, and the premier, Mitch Hepburn, has hired his own militia to suppress them: Hepburn's Hussars, those sons of mitches, twirling billy clubs and menacing the line. Duplessis is no better, but these girls have tied his hands. He can't figure out how to appear like the protector of Quebec's beloved daughters if his police force strikes them down on the streets.

For the moment, he holds back.

They are having a marvellous time. Rose Pesotta orders ice cream and pastry for the commissary, hires bands and clears the chairs off the floor at the worker's hall so the girls whirl off the picket line and onto the dance floor, kicking up their heels.

Léa gains five pounds in a week. She has been eating nothing but croissants. It looks good on her, she is always on the edge of too thin, her nervous energy burns more than she can consume. She can't sleep, she stays up late helping staff the commissary and raising spirits on the dance floor. She gets up early to hand out pamphlets and hold the line.

Pesotta pauses to watch her, her arms folded across her broad chest.

"Five of you, and we'd take all of North America," she says.

The men in Oshawa have won; the girls listen to the news on the radio together and cheer. It was Passover only a month ago, the ground still covered in snow. They told the old stories of slavery and redemption.

What better time than May Day to celebrate their freedom?

21.

On Friday afternoon, Hirsch Wolofsky, the editor of the *Eagle*, gets a tip. Hirsch always liked Léa, even though he does not approve of her politics; he wouldn't have minded if his son had ended up with her. He can't let her walk into this trap. He sends her a message. Duplessis has issued a warrant for the arrests of Shane, Trepanier, Pesotta. Shane and Pesotta are to be deported as foreign agitators. They need to hide, and quick.

Léa finds Rose in the office, and her lips are pale.

"Here's what I think," Léa says. "If you get arrested, you won't be able to find a judge to release you on bail until Monday. On Sunday, the girls will go to church and at mass, the priests will order them back to work. You need to keep your head down."

"My head," Pesotta says, and touches her hair.

Léa books her a room across town under a false name. Rose spends the entire morning in a local beauty salon. She has a facial, a manicure, a haircut, sits under the hood dryer. She stays inside and out of sight as long as she can. When she is done, she can barely recognize herself.

Because they can't find her, the arrest warrant is not served, and at the National Assembly on Monday, Duplessis backs down. This is no longer looking like a fight that he can win.

The meetings with the manufacturers begin on Monday evening, and go all through the night. It is two in the morning on Wednesday when they finally reach a settlement.

All week, Léa has felt like a full glass of champagne was balanced in her chest, bubbles bursting into the air. She has brimmed over with excitement. But something strange happens: they win and she feels flat. She is sorry it had to end so soon. She had never felt so alive.

The girls come back to work, collecting their union cards, but when the ones who sat out the strike begin to show up, shamefaced and eager, there is a problem. The hall is full of true believers; they won't work with scabs. Rose goes back to the stage and recalls Christ's words of forgiveness on the cross: "Father, forgive them, they know not what they do."

Rose has learned something about working in Quebec.

Rose Pesotta's arrival at the union conference in Atlantic City is triumphant. She is Victory leading the people, a French-Canadian delegation behind her. They will sing her down the aisle to the *Marseillaise*.

Léa stays home. She would have liked to go, but she has work to do.

22.

Thérèse Casgrain: high heels, silk dress, fur stole and a pearl necklace. When she walks into Léa's office she looks like a Westmount matron who has wandered into the wrong place. "So you have your union," Thérèse says, "but what about the vote?" Her hair is perfect. Her posture is extraordinary. Here is a woman who has never had to slump over a sewing machine, who has an invisible golden thread that runs through her spine and connects her straight to heaven above. Léa has heard of her, of course, but until now, they haven't exactly moved in the same circles. She's a millionaire's daughter, a politician's wife. And the unlikely leader of the suffrage movement in Quebec.

"I never intended to be a public figure," Thérèse says over a cup of coffee that morning. "It was something of an accident. My husband was about to give a campaign speech, and he suddenly fell ill. So, I went up to the podium and spoke for him. I'm not even sure what I said! But it was well enough received that some women came to see me afterwards and convinced me to get involved with the cause of women's rights. And here I am."

The Party claims to have at its heart the problem of inequality, including the inequality of women. For that reason, Léa has held off on getting involved with the feminist movement: bourgeois, the Party leadership says, divisive, and in any case, unnecessary. But it's true that neither here nor in Moscow do women seem a Party priority. "We could use your help," says Thérèse, and Léa smiles. She doesn't have to choose between the Party and the women's movement—she has two hands, doesn't she? And she doesn't need anyone's damn permission.

Each year, Thérèse finds a member of Parliament to sponsor a suffrage bill, and each year, the bill is rejected. "We will wear them down," Thérèse says, "but the vote is just the beginning. We need equal pay for equal work, we need to educate our children, we need to end this curse of the slums, this blight on our society, and to advocate for dignity for all." She clasps Léa's calloused hands with her smooth kid gloves. "I have a feeling," she says, "that we will be friends for a very long time."

At the League for Women's Rights Thérèse sounds passionate and confident. "We have had enough," she says, "of second-class citizenship. We have had enough of closed doors and false promises. We have had enough of being put on a pedestal. We demand a podium. We demand our voices be heard." Her silver hair shines like a crown and her cheeks are flushed with emotion. She looks like the statue of Athena Léa once saw in Rome; she looks like she was born for victory.

They campaign door-to-door to talk to women about the vote. The first time they go, Thérèse picks her up in a Cadillac, with a driver. "Next time, we go by bus," Léa says, and makes the driver park in the alley.

Is it helpful or just confusing that Thérèse dresses so elegantly, with little satin hats perched on top of her beautiful silver hair? The women of Verdun and Saint-Henri seem dazzled by the vision on their doorstep, Madame Casgrain in her splendour. But Thérèse is remarkably down-to-earth, even in her high-heeled shoes. Like Léa, she can talk to anyone. They quickly learn to do the rounds during the day because in the evenings, the husbands just slam the door on them. They bring pamphlets and drink endless cups of tea. They ask the women about their children and their husbands and their work, and they circle deftly to the vote. Don't they deserve, after all, to have a voice in their own affairs, in the households they run and the lives that they live? Don't they deserve to be treated as citizens, as full people?

Thérèse and Léa. In their unassuming way, they become notorious.

23.

Two months ago, Duplessis passed the Padlock Law. He declared, "The world is in a crisis more dangerous and evil than the most grave and destructive of diseases. Nowhere else but in Quebec is there a law protecting people against the vile cocaine of communism." The attorney general is given the right to lock the door of any building used to propagate or support communism or Bolshevism for up to a year. "It is unlawful," the law says, "to print, to publish ... or to distribute in the province any newspaper, periodical, pamphlet, circular, document or writing whatsoever propagating or tending to propagate Communism or Bolshevism." Individuals accused of doing so will be imprisoned from three to twelve months.

The terms—so broad, deliberately undefined—capture anything the province wants to call subversive. You are a communist if you are accused of communism by those in authority. If you are accused, that means you are already guilty.

It reminds Léa of a strange little story that she read in Berlin, the gift of a friend from her boarding house. She thinks the writer died young of tuberculosis. The story was about an execution machine which kills the condemned by inscribing their sentence on their body. Guilt, she remembers the story claiming, is never to be doubted.

Just so with the Padlock Law: it is a reversal, a perversion of everything the justice system once claimed to uphold.

She finds herself, and not for the first time, illegal. Her work in the trade union is illegal. Her mother's house, where she stores pamphlets and has built a library, is illegal. It feels as if the very space inside her skull is illegal.

She trains her nephew, who is the youngest and fastest and most unobtrusive member of the household, to sweep up any offending literature as soon as they hear the Red Squad is approaching, and to throw it out the window into the back alley. A paper riot, a snow of subversion. It is also his job, when the squad has passed, to go into the alleyway and gather up the offending, offended books, their spines jarred and their papers aflutter, and bring them back into the house until the next raid.

It is a cat and mouse game. In this case, the mice are smart and the cat is dumb, slow-moving, a lazy predator more likely to do damage by a stray clumsy swipe of a paw than by a targeted strike. Léa likes staying a step or two ahead of those fat cats in uniform, though not as much as her little nephew, who becomes expert at his task of running through the house and sweeping up anything that might come under suspicion.

But the stress is not good for her mother, who has chest pains and feels faint every time there is a knock at the door, even if it is only the milkman. It's not a heart attack, just a panic attack, they've checked with the doctor. Still unpleasant, still frightening.

The Red Squad raids the Artistic Print Shop and Old Rose Printing. They raid the Jewish Cultural Centre and confiscate the portrait of the Yiddish writer I. L. Peretz because his bushy moustache leads them to mistake it for a portrait of Stalin. They raid Fred's house, and Irene's house, and Stanley's. At Léa's house they take her copy of Huxley's *Brave New World*, though she tries in vain to explain that the book is literature, not propaganda, and anyways is satire, and furthermore, has nothing to do with the Soviet Union. They take her souvenir case from Grenoble, they take her address book, with all of the names and contacts of her friends in Europe, and who is to say if they are even still at those addresses, or in hiding, or in prison, or worse?

The letters she has recently posted to Europe have all come back, marked return to sender. Those are under a floorboard, and they do not find them.

"Take this," Mama cries, pressing a bible into the indifferent hands of a policeman. "It's communist! Take it!"

The policeman—Léa has seen worse, some are just doing their jobs and some of them are sadists—puts the bible down on a coffee table.

"You can keep your prayerbook, lady," he says, and Léa sends her mother to her bed to lie down before Mama can argue with him anymore. She likes the feistiness of her mother's old age.

"The older I get the less I care," Mama says, but it is the opposite, she cares too much, but is no longer afraid to show it. As Léa gets older they are more like friends or roommates than like mother and daughter. They have begun to resemble one another.

It is worse at work. The trade unionists are pedalling away as hard as they can from their socialist beginnings. They are so afraid of being labelled communists that they are fleeing right back into the arms of the bosses. Léa's boss at the union, Shane—she doesn't trust him. He's looking out for himself.

24.

Beth comes back from Spain in June, on a speaking tour to raise money for his cause. Despite the Padlock Law, despite the risk, people come out to the Forum to hear his testimony. There are thousands there, maybe tens of thousands. Léa wants to say hello but she can't even get close.

Nonetheless, she hears him as if he is speaking to her alone.

"I saw the refugees walking along the road with all that is left of their earthly possessions," he says. "I saw the bombing of the cities, and the bloody evacuations. I saw"—and his voice catches here—"the bombardment of Almería."

He is overdoing it, she thinks; a little too moved by himself. He is too busy to see her before he leaves again, and she pretends not to mind his breezy telephone goodbye.

She is a little surprised at how much she does mind, hanging up the phone and staring at the cracked plaster on the wall.

Some of the business of the union is not official. When the girls get pregnant, they come to her for help. The spring is a busy time for unplanned pregnancies; first Ida from reception, then Edna from the sewing room, both crying their eyes out in the office.

"I have money," Ida says, "I want to take care of it."

She isn't showing at all.

"I have some names," Léa says, and tells her about a doctor on Sainte-Catherine Street who will see the girls after hours. "It'll cost two hundred dollars."

"That's too much," Ida says. "He gave me fifty."

"Then tell him to give you more," Léa says. She points at Ida's stomach. "He gave you that, didn't he?"

But Ida shakes her head.

The next day, she knocks again. Her face is determined.

"I found a woman," she says. "I need you to come with me."

"I can lend you some money for the doctor," Léa says, wishing Beth was in town again, but Ida says, "It's all set up, I'm going in the morning."

Léa takes the day off work and meets her on Parthenais Street. The woman who opens the door is wearing a stained apron and has a kerchief on her head. She looks at Léa with suspicion, and says, "You can't be here. You come back at noon, she'll be ready."

Léa protests but Ida says, "Please. I'll be all right."

Léa walks down to the river to watch the boats. She has a book, but she can't concentrate on it well enough to read. She thinks about that poor girl, all alone. When she comes back at noon, she knocks and knocks. The woman blocks her and curses at her to be quiet. She won't open the door all the way, so Léa pushes past her, and rushes down the grimy hallway.

It is an abattoir; so much blood on the floor it looks black, and the outline of a body under a soiled sheet on the bed.

"She hemorrhaged," the woman says. "It happens sometimes."

She does not sound sorry.

As she slams the door, Léa says, "You ought to be in jail."

But she can't go to the police. She rests her forehead on the closed door. If Beth had been there. If she had raised the money. If she had told Ida to wait. If an unplanned pregnancy was not a death sentence. She is supposed to go back to work, but she can't sit still. She walks all day, back down to the river and then up the mountain, helpless with fury. She walks until her feet are blistered and her brain is quiet, and then she goes home and sleeps for a long time. In the morning she is alive and Ida is not, and that is a travesty. All day, girls keep coming to her office and breaking into tears, and she comforts them. She is calm again now, but she cups a seed of righteous fury in her chest. She is no longer angry at the woman on Parthenais Street, who was the instrument and not the cause. But the men and their laws, she would set it all on fire.

After Ida, Edna is afraid of back-alley abortions, but she is even more afraid of going to hell. She hides her belly as long as she can, and because it is her first pregnancy it is seven months and summer before she abandons her layers of camouflage and her father realizes it is not winter weight that swells her stomach, it is sin and shame. Edna's mother smuggles some clothes through the back door and Léa loans her a suitcase and helps her take the tram to the Hôpital de la Miséricorde, on Saint-Hubert Street.

As if it has happened overnight, Edna looks suddenly, enormously pregnant. She holds the rail as she climbs the grey stone steps, and at reception is met by a nun who takes the suitcase and says, "You won't be needing this." The nun adds, "Your name is now Humiliation. Please follow me to your quarters."

Edna looks over her shoulder at Léa. The nun has her by the hand and pulls Edna—now Humiliation—towards the stairwell where Léa cannot follow.

Two weeks later, she gets a hysterical phone call. "I can't stay here," Edna says, "it's awful. They're have us working every minute of the day, Léa, they treat us no better than animals."

She has snuck down to the reception desk, and the call is cut off without warning.

But how to get her out? They lock the doors at night, and by day the nuns guard the entrance. The girls are prisoners.

Léa has a friend, François, who works for the police. She met him when she was marching at a protest; he was there to keep the peace. At first, he was taciturn, but Léa could talk to a rock. It turned out his mother used to work in the garment industry.

"I need your help," she says, "come meet me on your lunch break." With François behind her, she marches up to the entrance of the hospital, wearing her best suit.

"I'd like to see Edna, please."

The nun at reception says, "No Edna here."

François puts his hands on his hips, and Léa says, "It's official business. I'm not leaving until I see her."

The nun looks over at François, unsmiling in his uniform, and turns without a word. When Edna appears she looks awful, dark circles like bruises under her eyes. She is wearing a shapeless grey smock and stumbling in shoes that do not fit.

"Now, what is your business with Humiliation?" the nun says and Léa would like to spit in her face.

"She needs to come with us," Léa says, and François nods, God bless him. There is a tug of war when Léa takes Edna by the hand and the nun still has her arm, and then they are free, moving as fast as they can down the sidewalk past the blooming linden trees, Edna surprisingly agile for a woman in her condition. They collapse on a bench across from the statue of the angel on the mountain, and François says, "I'd better get back to work."

The abduction has taken less time than standing in line for a sandwich.

"Do you have a cigarette?" Edna says, and brings it to her lips. "God, I missed this. They had us working in the laundry, some of the girls would faint from the heat. But the worst of it is they wouldn't let us smoke. What an awful place! Oh, Léa, your suitcase, we'll never get it back."

"It doesn't matter."

"The look on her face when she saw the cop! Léa, you're a miracle." She sinks into the bench, her stomach a bubble in front of her. "But now where do I go?"

The Salvation Army also has a maternity hospital, in Notre Dame de Grace. They are less strict with the girls and, despite the name, less focused on salvation. Edna can stand it. The birth comes early, and there are two babies, both with Edna's red hair, each weighing less than a small bag of flour.

Edna's father has agreed to let her go home but not, he says, with the fruits of her sin. There are places for unwanted children. She sobs as she tells Léa that she has no choice.

Once again, Léa helps her. They bring the twins to an orphanage in the east end of the city. Léa carries one of the babies and Edna carries the other, and they bring cans of formula, blankets, hand-finished swaddling clothes, hopeful offerings to start them in their new life.

Edna is resolute. She has painted courage onto her face, blue on her eyelids and pink on her lips and cheeks. Still, her mouth trembles. She looks exhausted and slack.

"It's for the best," Léa says, but she is shocked when they arrive. There are so many children, and though the nurses seem nicer than the nuns, they still look distracted and overwhelmed.

"Where should I leave the formula?" Léa asks, and the nurse says, "Oh, wherever you like." She lifts the baby from Léa's arms and sends them out of the room. Edna sobs all the way home. It has only been a week; her belly is empty, but she still looks pregnant.

Edna is allowed to visit on Sundays. On her first visit, the babies are sleepy and lethargic. They feel even lighter than they were at birth.

"Are they alright?" Edna asks.

The nurse says, "Babies need their rest."

On their second visit, the babies seem a little more alert and Edna thinks they recognize her. "Is it possible they know me already?" she says. Léa looks into the small, crumpled faces. How strange that the eyes of brand-new babies seem to hold the wisdom of generations. They have the cloudy luminance of opals.

On their third visit, she cannot find the twins. "Where are my babies?" Edna says, frantic, spinning from cradle to cradle.

She finds a nurse she recognizes, who says, "Oh dear. I thought they told you. Those poor girls are in heaven."

Léa grabs her by the waist as Edna buckles. Getting her to the tram is an ordeal, but neither of them has the money for a cab ride home.

"Oh, God," Edna moans, and weeps so loudly that other passengers take one look and do not board, though the driver, bless him, pretends not to notice and keeps them moving smoothly down the road.

Those poor girls are in heaven.

Edna goes home and later that week, jumps off the Jacques Cartier Bridge and into the river.

25.

At work, Shane is still head of the local. Léa hadn't expected to be asked, she doesn't even want to be the boss, but it's a shame that even in a girl's shop, a woman is never in charge. Shane from Toronto—he still hasn't learned French. He treats her like his secretary, not like his comrade.

The gains they have been promised are vanishing into air. Shane is friendly with the bosses—too friendly. His wife comes to the factory and says to the manager, "You give me wholesale." She leaves with armfuls of clothes. Whose side, then, is Shane on? He goes out for long lunches, and when the boss comes to visit, he closes the door.

"Mr. Shane," she says. "It's not the factory that pays you, it's the union." She has never known how to keep her mouth shut.

Shane says they're having trouble finalizing their contracts because of the communists in the union. Most of the workers want to co-operate, but those troublemakers are splitting the ranks. It's their fault negotiations have stalled. He starts pulling union cards for the girls who have been speaking up.

On the floor, conditions are deteriorating again. When he talks about it, he is all excuses. He sounds like one of them, an apologist and a reactionary. His union is not communist, he insists, not at all: they are fighting for the worker but as patriots, not traitors.

To prove it, he sells out their own members.

So Léa quits.

"Come and visit us, Léa," Shane says sentimentally, affectionate now that he knows she is leaving.

"*Gay kaken afen yam,*" she fires back over her shoulder, go shit in the ocean, and she really does wish she had a picture of the way his face looked so she could gaze at it on her bedside table before going to sleep and laugh and laugh.

She is unemployed but she is busy. There is the Women's League and the Party and so many other causes. At the Civil Rights League she meets a girl named Madeleine, a student at McGill. She has a round face, surprised, expressive eyebrows, and dark curly hair. She looks like a schoolgirl, and is so excited to meet Léa, she can barely speak.

"I admire your work so much," she says, and Léa isn't sure where to look.

"There are many of us," Léa says, her whole face a blush. "There's nothing special about me." Her dimple winks in and out as she smiles at the girl.

In the spring the king and queen come to visit, and Léa cannot believe the excitement. Her neighbour Jean-Claude swathes his balcony in Union Jack bunting, and the French-Canadian boys have all bought themselves little British flags and tied them to the handlebars of their bicycles.

"*Mais pourquoi?*" she calls out to Jean-Claude, who is tying even more flags to his balcony.

He shrugs and says, "*Mais pourquoi pas?*"

Montreal loves a parade. The police close off the streets, down Park Avenue to Saint Hubert, down De Lorimier to the Jacques Cartier Bridge, from Sainte-Catherine to Saint-Denis and finally around city hall, where the mayor goes onto the balcony with the king in front of the cheering throngs, and says, "You know, Your Majesty, some of those cheers are also for you!"

On the main route, people are selling spaces in their windows and their balconies. Indeed, they have been warned of the danger of balconies collapsing from overcrowding. That night, Montreal's aristocracy will eat turtle soup and squab with the royal couple at the Windsor Hotel. The next day, there are two full pages of coverage of the outfits worn at the banquet. Léa is disgusted.

"I could have taken them on a tour," she says. "Down by the docks. Where the children don't even have clean water to drink. Let alone turtle soup and sequined dresses!"

It is the season of silly events. At the end of July, the *Jeunesse Ouvrière Catholique* organizes a mass wedding. There are over a hundred Roman Catholic couples, over a hundred priests, and like the cherry on a multi-tiered and inedible cake, the archbishop himself.

"Space for one more couple," her sister Lottie says, and Léa is too distracted to be sour. Mostly, her family gave up teasing her about marriage long ago, but every so often Lottie hauls it out, like the dusty cardboard box of Passover dishes that must appear on schedule once a year.

In the newspaper, there is a photograph of the baseball stadium full of people. The grooms in navy suits, the brides in white gowns and veils, and six bishops. Twenty-five thousand guests throng the stands.

"It's a home run," Lottie remarks, reading over Léa's shoulder. "A hundred home runs tonight!"

"Don't be crude," Annie says. "Look, the chaplain told them to postpone their honeymoons. He said they should get to know each other first before gallivanting around in hotel rooms. But I've heard all the rooms in Sainte-Agathe have been booked for months."

"Marry or burn," Lottie says.

"Burn, no question," Léa answers, flipping the page and skimming the type. "This is not news," she says. "What about Europe? What about the war?"

"There may not be a war," Annie says, and Léa rolls her eyes.

"These men can save their honeymoons for a trip to Europe," she says. "In uniform."

She has been in a dark mood all summer. Still no news from friends in Germany. And all around her, Montreal is giddy with summer, but Léa sees the madness coming. The August air is so heavy that every day feels like swimming through a warm weight, and the evening brings no relief.

At the end of the month, when the newspaper announces the Stalin-Hitler pact, it feels like the very thing she has been dreading, and still she cannot believe it. It is not possible. She stays in bed, she who is never tired and never sick, and her mother brings her chicken soup. Doubt takes her like an illness; her head hurts, her stomach hurts, she cannot finish a sentence or even a thought. Four days later, she drags herself to her Party meeting and it feels like a funeral. Each time someone starts to speak they stop again. It is as if they are stepping on each other's throats.

When the war begins on the first day of September, she does not know how she feels or where she stands.

Léa goes to visit Fred, who has been to the national meeting of the Party, and she sees him looking defeated for the first time.

"I spoke up," he says, "me and Salsberg. No one else. The Party has voted against the imperialist war. They need to stand with Stalin. Be patient," he says, so softly it is as if he is speaking to himself, "the Soviet Union needs to build its strength. Don't worry, Hitler's time will come."

But he looks thin, he has dark circles under his eyes.

"What's happening there, Léa," he says, "is a nightmare. They're persecuting them. They're killing them. You know—you remember. They're not going to stop."

"Us," Léa says. "They're persecuting us." In her mind's eye, a man is on his knees in a puddle. He looks at her without seeing her and in his terrified gaze is a premonition of the years to come, broken glass and devouring flame. Could she have saved him then? And can she help them now?

"You know," Fred says, "it's a damn shame the communists and socialists never could get along." The Communist Party has lined up behind the Soviet Union, the worker's nation, which can never be wrong. And the socialist parties who want to fight Hitler have already begun to agitate about the new imperial autocracy radiating out of Moscow.

It is a deep betrayal. And it makes her sick to see Stalin and Hitler shaking hands in the newsreels, looking like the best of friends. She cannot find her feet.

26.

Annie, of all people, tries to rescue her. She comes to visit with her children and insists Léa accompany them to the park.

"For goodness sakes, you're walking like an old lady," Annie says. She is looking very smart, in her round white sunglasses and a belted summer dress. When they get to the park, Léa sits down on a bench. She has been indoors nearly a week; the world is too loud for her, the trees too green, the sun too hot. Her stomach is acid and her eyes are smoked with grief.

"Wake up, Léa," Annie says. "Look around. It isn't like you to sulk."

Léa opens her mouth, shuts it again, like a dumb frog.

"Ha!" Annie says. "The last person I ever expected to run out of opinions. Listen, Léa," and her gaze wanders over the park, distracted, until she finds her daughter on the swing, her son in the sandpit. "You're not helping yourself. You were always the first to get to work. So, get to work."

"I feel like I've hit bottom," Léa says.

"Then there's nowhere to go but up!"

Oh, but she's wrong. In the next weeks, the news will be worse and worse. Poland crumbles. Michael and then Leo announce they are joining up. In America, Harry has joined the army Medical Corps, though he is already forty years old and could skip the draft.

And Beth. Poor Beth is dead. His final mission took him to the Communists in China, performing surgeries at the battlefront. He cut himself while operating on a soldier and died of the blood poisoning he contracted. It is hard to imagine him gone. She had never known anyone so alive.

"I support you," she says to her brothers in their brand-new uniforms, "but I hate this goddamn war."

The Party is changing. The cells, already secretive, become smaller and more constrained. They meet at night, they keep the lights down, they lower the shades and lower their voices. All public action is put on hold, no marches, no protests, no posters, no lectures. Léa, who blooms on the street, wilts in the shadows. Some of the members—some of her friends—drop out. The Jewish members leave in droves, and when Léa is asked to explain or justify the Party's stance on this terrible war she finds herself without words. She still goes to her meetings, but they now feel like walking into a depressing miasma. The members no longer talk about politics—how strange, when they once never ran out of things to say. It used to be Italy, Chamberlain, Hitler, the Padlock Law, Spain, talk talk talk until the small hours of the morning. They used to have spaghetti dinners and red wine, and they would each chip in a dollar which went towards expenses and anything left over to the Party, and they would sing Russian folk songs and play records by Paul Robeson and Dinah Shore. Now there are long silences, there are minutes that pass as slowly as hours, there is a palpable sense of unease and an anxious, inertial apathy.

They go through their agenda items: the sale of subscriptions to *Clarté*, which is steady but slow, the raising of funds, which is not too difficult, because there are a few supporters with deep pockets—mostly from Section Thirteen, the Party's hidden wallet. They discuss recruitment, which is nearly impossible, although the French-Canadian cells are having more luck. The anti-conscription movement, resistance to another English war, has contributed to their popularity among the Québécois.

And finally, they arrive at self-criticism and denunciation. This member has been hubristic. This member has been sectarian. This member has been tribal and regressive. They sit in a circle of rapturous contempt and take turns flogging one another with words.

After these sessions, she is so agitated and troubled that she cannot sleep, and she tosses and turns all night, dreaming of nonsensical trials and random accusations. She tries to defend herself only to find soap bubbles rather than words rising from her mouth and bursting into air. She wakes up exhausted.

Members begin to beg off early, and the group becomes smaller and smaller, until, without even a real decision or discussion, they stop meeting weekly, even monthly. Léa continues her work; she is helping Fred Rose, and still co-ordinating with Section Thirteen. Fred has decided she will work in one of the new war factories and will once again build a union.

She believes, yes, is a believer. In the workers. But the movement, well. It is very difficult.

Fred is bitter and pale, puffy even though he claims he cannot eat.

It is dangerous to be seen together in public, so those occasions where they would once meet up, the rallies against fascism and for workers' rights, dry up. Without gatherings and protests, can you even have a movement? She feels like they have been treading water for a long time. The water is getting murkier, and her body is getting heavier, and they have lost sight of the shore. She is not sure how long they can go on.

Clarté keeps getting printed, on mimeograph machines hidden in cabins in the Laurentians and basements near

McGill, but their newspaper, full of propaganda about Stalin's war, seems barely worth the effort of distribution.

When the War Measures Act is invoked, it is no surprise. It makes little difference in Quebec. They have already gone underground.

"It just means we need to watch out for the RCMP as well as the Red Squad," Fred says. "Beware of men on horses. And the smell of manure."

He speaks lightly, as always, but his face is grim. He is going into hiding and will live in safe houses, spare bedrooms and hastily converted offices, moldy basements and living rooms with a sheet flung over the couch and curtains tightly drawn. He comes out after dark, his hat low on his forehead.

He has a baby daughter and sometimes after the meetings are over, he visits his wife so he can watch his little girl sleeping.

Other members have also gone into hiding. The Red Squad find them at their safe houses and arrest them while they are playing cards, eating breakfast, bathing their children. Once during a marriage ceremony which was being conducted in secret, in a living room, with a chuppah made out of a tablecloth and broomsticks.

The head of the Red Squad has announced, "I will find them all, and I will hang them all." Often Léa learns that her acquaintances are members of the Party only after they are arrested. They have become so very isolated. Those bastards at the head office in Toronto have fled to the United States, where they swan around, sending orders from the south where they can breathe like free men. Tim Buck, the leader of the Party, she never had the time of day for him; she cannot but blame him for his freedom.

She is worried about Fred. He looks broken. He has become conspiratorial. He has a sore molar, and they can't figure out how to get him to a dentist. He tries to joke that the stress has made him lose his hair, poor Fred, who has been prematurely bald as long as she has known him. But there are other ways that this confinement makes him old. He paces the rooms like a caged lynx, and when he sits down can't stop shaking his leg, tapping his knee. It is as if all of his drive for action has turned into an anxious restlessness that is eating him alive.

Fred is fixated on Duplessis, even though he is no longer in office. Maurice Duplicity, the sawdust Caesar—"Our Mussolini," he calls him, "waiting in the wings, he'll be back. Do you know he was born on the same day as Hitler?" Léa is concerned about Fred's blood pressure and his health. When he is in hiding, she is his default wife, fussing over him and reminding him to eat, bringing him cups of tea when he asks for something stronger.

"It's bad for you to think about Duplessis so much," she says.

"You know, to love the workers you also have to be able to learn how to hate."

Sometimes she finds him writing, sitting on the sofa which is also desk and bed with a pad of paper propped on his knees, in the dark because he is afraid that turning on the light might make him visible from the street. His pipe smolders at his elbow, propped in an ashtray or in an empty bowl. She is afraid he will burn down the apartment and she is afraid that he will burn himself out. Even his bravado rings hollow, as if he is imitating the man he used to be.

Then one day, something changes. The anger goes right out of him; he is like a stocking that has lost its stretch. She finds him puddled on the couch, drinking Scotch.

"I have decided, Léa," he says, with the deliberate enunciation of a man who knows he is drunk, "that I am on vacation. You know, I've never had a vacation! I need a pack of cards."

She brings him detective novels and boxes of candy. He plays endless games of solitaire when he is alone and poker when in company, calls her sweetheart and asks her for refills, or worse, just lifts his glass. Again, she feels like a wife, and it is exactly as irritating as she imagined. But she also feels sorry for him. Sometimes, when she comes to visit, he has fallen asleep in the middle of the day and when he wakes up his eyes without their glasses are so confused and naked, he doesn't know where he is.

"Is that you, Léa?" he'll ask, like a child afraid of the dark.

One of the worst things you can do to a person is to rob them of productive work, she firmly believes that. Despite his constraints, Fred tries to run the Party, but he can't do much. He comes up with grandiose plans, scribbled in his black notebooks, tries to explain them and then collapses in exhaustion. "It's no use, Léa," he says, ripping out the pages and throwing them on the floor.

She would not for the world tell him how much of a relief it is to step back out onto the street after she visits him in his various hiding places, how she tilts back her head to feel the sun hit right between her eyes and breathe the unstale air, how, as she heads home, she walks so fast, dear God, she is almost running away from him.

Those weeks and then months are the worst, even more difficult than when her father died. She feels like she is fighting a double war, first against Hitler, and then against imperial capitalism, and in each battle, she is also her own enemy. She has noticed that when her friends in the movement talk about the Jewish situation in Europe they are dismissed. She has watched that active repression create a dead silence and it puts a cold splinter in her heart.

But she is not built for despair. She takes her doubts and fears and puts them in a box at the very back of her head. As is her habit, she drowns her worries in activity. There is more to do, right here in Montreal.

Work has always been her tonic. She gets a job at RCA and learns the line, gets to know the workers, co-ordinates with Gilles, who has also embedded from the Party but as a manager. They are making radios and radar for the war effort. Though she still does not support the war she likes the idea that this assemblage of metal and glass and wire, which she has helped put together with her own hands, will sail across the ocean and maybe save a life. Her brothers are in training so at least she does not have to worry about them yet. Her mother is busy, going to sisterhood meetings for her synagogue and knitting socks for the soldiers. Léa often arrives home so late at night that she only sees her mother when they pass each other in the kitchen, making morning tea and toast.

She lives day by day. Right now, it is hard to think about the future.

27.

What goes almost unnoticed because of the war is the passage of Bill 18 at the National Assembly. Unbelievable that Quebec women are the last to have the vote, in 1940, more than twenty years after the rest of the country, and such a long time coming. How the politicians fought against it! Henri Bourassa, who warned of the creation of veritable women-men. Louis-Arthur Giroux, who said that were the bill to pass, women would be like stars who have lost their orbits.

Thérèse, glowing with success, holds a subdued celebration. Still, this feels like a paper right, not a revolution. They are years from the next election, and who knows if by then they will even still have a country? Would Hitler stop at Europe? Just like men, to finally give women the right to vote during a period in which so many rights are being suspended.

"Not like you to be a cynic," Thérèse says. She is already planning to run for office. She is wearing her pearls and looks more than ever like a political wife, her marcelled hair immaculate, her nails gleaming half-moons. Léa knows she is tenacious underneath her brittle, glittering façade; she has watched her walk into the offices of politicians in Quebec City as if she owned them, has seen the men in suits stammer in the face of her certainty. Thérèse wears her wealth and charm like polished armour, in part to intimidate, in part to dazzle them with splendour.

Léa has other gifts, but she does not have the birthright of wealth: the feeling that you always belong at the table. When Thérèse was a little girl, her father was elected to Parliament. She played hide and seek in the House of Commons between sittings, crouching behind the benches as her father looked for her, trying not to sneeze in case the sound echoed against the high ceilings of the empty chamber. She has always been an insider. And now, her husband is speaker in that same house; here is another magic key she has to open the door for her own political career.

Her husband Pierre is basking in her success. "I will retire now," he announces, pouring glasses of claret and handing them out. "I will become Thérèse's campaign manager, and when she wins, I will stay home and look after my grandchildren."

Thérèse smiles as he speaks and places her long fingers on his arm. It is a wonder how she manages him; and four children, now grown; and the politicians, and the protests, and all of the rest of it.

Léa sips her wine and sits on the edge of the chair. In rooms as grand as this one she never feels quite settled.

The next day the paper announces that Pierre Casgrain is the new Secretary of State for Canada, responsible, among other duties, for the RCMP, who are in turn responsible for ending the Communist threat in Canada. So much for staying home and looking after the grandchildren. Yes, Thérèse is her friend, they have marched side by side, they agree on the rights of women and to some degree on the rights of workers but thank God they never spoke about the Party. She thinks of the distance between Thérèse's well-appointed living room and the series of modest apartments that Fred squats in like a nocturnal toad, and she resents her for the life she lives in the open, under crystal chandeliers and in rooms in tall buildings with windows as large as doors that open up to the very heavens.

28.

In June, when Hitler invades the Soviet Union, all she feels is relief. They are saved; they will all be saved. Léa has not taken a deep breath for two years.

Churchill will not use the word alliance, but the newspaper reports that he has offered aid to Russia and has announced they now have common cause. Any enemy of Hitler is my friend. "We will fight him by land," Churchill writes, "we will fight him by sea, we will fight him in the air until with God's help we have rid the earth of his shadow." He calls Hitler a "bloodthirsty guttersnipe." He also says—always unwilling to miss a chance to insist he was right—that none of this was a surprise to him, that he had warned Stalin.

Léa is no fan of the British Bulldog, and he is no supporter of the worker. Still, she thrills to his bombastic eloquence. He is a good man to lead the fight. In the Soviet Union, the Red Army is in action; Moscow claims to have shot down sixty-five Nazi planes already.

The Montreal newspapers seem whiplashed by the rapidity with which an enemy has turned ally. "No hats went into the air here today," the front page of *The Gazette* reports, and mentions that there will be glad hearts "when it is realized that thousands of Germans are killing thousands of Russians and vice versa." The paper is more afraid of being red than they are of Hitler. But in any case, *The Gazette* is wrong. On the Plateau, they have been dancing in the streets all night, they have been singing songs of revolution and songs of peace. Léa is high on happiness.

The next day is a workday like any other. She almost never calls in sick, but this once she walks downtown in the sunshine to meet Annie. It feels like a holiday; the sidewalks are packed and the cafés full of women in summer dresses and straw hats.

"You have to see this, Léa," Annie says, breathless. She pulls her by the arm down to Eaton's, where the Hammer and Sickle is flying over the department store's elegant façade. The red flag is bright as a cardinal against the clear blue sky.

So this is the end of working in secret, of living a double life. It is possible now to be a patriot and to be a communist. It is possible, now, to win this war.

She stands there, her head thrown back, jostled by passersby on the sidewalk who walk down the street without looking up, who have not yet realized that the world has changed.

29.

After two months of secret negotiations, Fred and the other leaders of the movement come out of hiding. They are interned, forty-two of them, and spend eleven days in jail—a token. The premier of Ontario comes to visit them with boxes of chocolates and congratulations. They are on the same side now.

They change their name to the Labour Progressive Party, but what's in a name? Same members, same values, in all meaningful ways the same.

Some of the Jewish members come back now that their souls are no longer split between fighting for the worker and fighting against Hitler. The French-Canadian membership, on the other hand, suffers. There is more talk of conscription, which the Party still opposes, though less avidly now that Stalin is in the war. The Québécois members feel abandoned. Fred was always good with his French constituents; he recruited them in part on the grounds of their own inequality in Canada, talked about the higher wages in the English provinces, talked about the injustice of their position. They called him a *bon gars*, and even though they disagreed about the national question, he was good at deflecting their frustration and just refused to fight. "Aw, you guys," he'd say, and then he'd change the subject, his pudgy cheeks red, a childish softness in his face which made it difficult to keep arguing with him. "We're on the same side." But now they are not. The closer they come to conscription, the more French members drop out, and the ones who stay—Henri, Rémy, Gilles—are the real stalwarts. And even they are having doubts.

"You know I'd do anything for the Party," Henri says. "But I'm tired of being treated like a second-class citizen. Why does Toronto get to set the policies? Why isn't there a single Québécois in the leadership? Why can't they even pretend to care about our membership?" He was fired at the garment factory right around the time Léa quit, but the Party hasn't yet found him a new position. He is working as a waiter in a café and has a five o'clock shadow on his chin and three-a.m. circles under his eyes. The money he earns now wouldn't support a dog.

Poor, beautiful Henri. With his long dark hair and expressive brows, he looks like a poet. He is the type who falls in love hard and often, with ideas as well as people. He is built for heartbreak.

"It's not right," Léa says, "but it'll change soon, just wait."

"Oh, Léa," he says. "You're a true believer." His voice sounds wistful. She can't tell if it's a compliment or an insult.

Paul Robeson is coming back to Montreal, and this time he plays the Forum. The concert is sponsored by the Quebec Committee for Allied Victory, and behind him on the stage hangs a giant poster reading, "Every Canadian Must Fight," which depicts a worker in overalls right behind a soldier in uniform, handing him ammunition as he loads his rifle. In the poster, the worker and the soldier look like lovers; the worker embraces the soldier from behind.

The Forum is as full as it gets for hockey games. There must be fifteen thousand people, and just about everyone Léa knows is there. Henri is there too, and when he hugs her he lifts her off her feet. The stadium is a garden in full bloom, every lifted face an open flower.

Paul dedicates the evening to victory and to peace, and to all the workers of the world—the applause for that last statement is a little more muted, this is a mixed crowd, bullish on victory, hopeful for peace, but not particularly interested in the revolution. This is not a night for the "*Internationale*." Instead, he wins them over with folk songs in French, and then transitions to blues and spirituals, a local choir as his robust backup.

Listening to his voice is like being rocked in strong warm arms; she closes her eyes and sways along to "Water Boy," and the whole crowd sings along to "Go Down Moses." He finishes the night with "Old Man River," and his own version of the final lines: "I must keep fighting until I'm dying." His voice is so low she can feel it in the bottom of her spine, which she was once told is the seat of the soul. Music is the most powerful way to turn a group of individuals into a collective. She sings as loud as she can and still cannot hear herself in the voice of the crowd. What a perfect night.

When they disperse on the sidewalk after the final encore, it is as if they are coming back to their singular selves, each heading in their separate directions, shaking off the net of music that just a moment ago had gathered them close and made them feel, yes, something like universal love.

It is a pity that it must end.

She bumps into Fred on her way home, and he says, "I'm running for office again. There's a by-election, and this time I'm certain we will win. What do you say, kid?"

She says, "I say we must keep fighting until we're dying."

He seizes her hand and lifts it to his lips, an oddly chivalrous gesture. "That's the spirit!"

30.

When she is back in the office, it feels familiar, but everything has changed. In the winter, Stalin was on the cover of *Time* magazine—the Man of the Year!—and Fred rips it out and hangs it on the office wall. Léa is swallowed up in the madness of campaigning, mimeographing posters and putting them up on every lamppost and brick wall, knocking on doors with an indefatigable energy that can feel like mania. They print in English and Yiddish and French, Fred's face in three-quarter profile, his cheeks full, his ears sticking out, his balding head disheveled—but still, his eyes look kind. "They're not electing me for my good looks," he cracks. No Slums, the posters read. Social Security. National Unity. Free Speech.

"How about free love?" Henri says.

Léa says, "You wish, buddy." Victory over fascism, rights for French Canadians, outlaw anti-Semitism. They hold meetings in living rooms and backyards, rallies in workers' halls and open squares, they fill Fletcher's Field and paste posters all over Saint Lawrence, Saint-Denis, Colonial, so many posters it's a mosaic of faces. You don't get an answer, you keep on knocking, you don't convince them the first time, you keep on trying, Léa and the other members throw themselves into the six-week campaign as if it is the Eastern Front.

"You're going to have to slow down, Léa," her sister Annie says, "learn to enjoy your life." But this is what she loves, standing on a street corner handing out pamphlets, starting conversations. She loves to look at people's faces. Every interaction is an opportunity for a vote. Her neighbours throw up their hands when they see her. "Léa, we already know!"

To everyone's surprise, her sister Rose has turned religious. She runs the sisterhood at her synagogue and organizes bake sales, where she brings her famous brownies, her light-as-a-cloud sponge cake. Her house has satin curtains and a cleaner who comes twice a week to vacuum the wall-to-wall carpet. Rose's eldest delivers copies of the *Daily Worker* for Léa, pedalling over the mountain on his bicycle to pick them up after school and before piano lessons.

"I love you, Edgar," Léa says when he arrives, "but when the revolution comes, we're going to have to shoot you down like a dog. Tell your mother we're coming over for dinner Friday night." It is a family joke, the distance between her politics and their own. Still, she does sometimes wonder how their lives would change when the revolution happens. Even in her imagination, she cannot get farther than the struggle. Cannot quite picture the peace.

The Liberals are up to their old tricks, but this time the Party knows the drill. On election day, the aircraft workers surround Fred's headquarters to protect them. The neighbourhood is full of reporters watching out for election fraud, and four of them are beaten up by the Liberals' goons, but the goons get caught. At the back of the Liberal office, a reporter spots lead pipes and wooden clubs, intended to be used to drive voters away from the polls. There are just too many people in the street and too many watchful eyes in the crowd for them to get away with it. The polling lines spill out on the sidewalks.

It is a beautiful day to vote. Léa pamphlets up until the very last minute, she walks old women to the ballot box if they are unsteady on their feet, she knocks on doors and tells the lie-a-beds to get up and out, it's time. At ten o'clock at night, the office is packed like a can of green beans, and the street outside is full of members listening on the radios perched on the windowsills.

It's close. The Liberals are lagging well behind, Fred Rose's people are taking their votes, but Paul Masse of the Bloc is showing strong. Masse is running on an anti-conscription platform, which has given the nationalists quite a boost. He's ahead, then Fred pulls up, and falls back again; the crowd boos, cheers, sings, it is the longest horserace any of them has ever watched, and at eleven o'clock when the winner is announced the streets explode.

"He won, I can't even believe it," Henri says. "By a Jewish nose!"

The street is so wild with joy you would think they had just won the war.

Léa scarcely knows whom she is embracing. She is crushed in the general good will and struggles to get outside and breathe in the fresh night air, where thousands of people swarm the Main and follow Fred's car in a victory parade. It is a humid, heavy night; the air is crackling with electricity, and she has heard it's going to storm the next day. Good; if it had rained just a day earlier, people would have stayed home instead of going to vote. Amazing how precarious it all can be, a hundred and fifty votes the difference between loss and victory.

"I haven't seen anything like it," she overhears a passerby in a bowler hat say, "since we won the Stanley Cup!" Then he gets into a very serious discussion about the odds this year, they're coming back, he thinks—the Rocket's leg is all healed up, he should be ready to play—he's feeling pretty good about their chances.

The next day, *The Gazette* is snippy about Rose, noting his razor-thin margin and writing, "His victory shed no glory either on him personally nor the views he is credited with holding." The pipes and bats have mostly gone unused; the police report it was the quietest election in years. A few of the newspapermen were attacked by the Liberal goons, and their photos are in the papers, showing black eyes and split lips. "Pretty stupid," the Liberal candidate Lazarus Phillips says, who despite his name has failed to resurrect the chances of his party. "Pretty dumb of them to mix it up with newspaper men." He promises to return the journalists' confiscated cameras.

"Sour grapes," Fred says.

This morning he is untouchable, his thinning frill of hair a halo in the sun. "We've arrived, Léa," he says. "What do we do now that we've arrived?"

As if on cue, the thunder cracks outside, and the skies open.

"It's good," he says, switching topics mid-stream. "It'll clear the humidity, it'll clean the streets. And now I don't have to wash my car"—his car, which was touched by a thousand hands the night before as if he is the new pope.

31.

Is it possible, now that her heart is no longer divided, that Léa thrives on war? There is plenty of work now, and a spirit of solidarity that Léa recognizes from the picket lines.

And the women! They are finally wanted. A quarter-million in the war industry and a million on the farms. The paper has dozens of ads for jobs for women. At the movies, the newsreel shows women at work and announces that "Joan Canuck has forsaken *Vogue* and *Vanity Fair* for blueprints and construction plants... when victory is won, a great share of the credit will be due to our fair Amazons in overalls." Half of the registrants in the training programs for the war industry are women. They are learning to manufacture and to fill ammunition, to carve wood and weld metal, to wire radios and electronics, to be chemists and laboratory technicians. They are learning that their skills extend beyond the nursery and kitchen. The paper reports that the war plants have started day nurseries in Montreal and Toronto for working mothers, and have installed beauty salons in the factories, open late and in the early morning. A girl can work the night shift and get her hair done before heading home.

Léa closes the paper, touches her own hair incredulously. Imagine wanting to bother with that after a night at work. She is still at RCA, working the assembly line, and they don't have any beauty salons there, nor any beauty queens either.

The papers also emphasize thrift and solidarity. Ads urge citizens to hold back from unnecessary long-distance calls, to stretch their meat rations with Bovril, to make no more coffee than needed. There are wartime nutrition tips every Tuesday. Class C meats lend themselves to broiling, make a ration-thrifty mixed grill with calf liver and lamb's kidney or sliced sweetbreads, a coupon's worth of chopped lamb with a pinch of herbs and onion fried as flat cakes is a delicious meal. Most advertisements double down on patriotism—drink Pepsi because it's good for morale, smoke Players because the Navy does—and some of the articles are also advertisements, like the one for the little girl who helps her mama deliver fabric to be sewed for uniforms, but also eats Kellogg's because cereal is quick, and leaves no pots to wash, and therefore leaves more time for the war effort.

Her mother has bought a copy of the *Victory Cook Book*, and she is following their meal plans religiously. It is a Thursday, so they are having liver and baked potatoes, and the liver is a little greyish and overcooked. Mama is a frugal cook, but not a talented one. Along with the liver, she has brought a *Maclean's* article to the table, and in the summer evening light, she reads it out loud.

"Listen to this, Léa," she says, in an upholstered, mock-heroic voice. "'She's the girl who operates a gun-barrel lathe or beats out a riveter's tattoo on an airplane body. She does a man's work as capably as many a male, though she seldom collects as much pay. Because she's pitching in to do a vital job that must be done by women, with more and more men being called from the factory front to the armed forces, the girl in slacks is emerging as something of a national heroine.' That's you, Léa!"

"Give me that," Léa says, and keeps reading, in a tone of false concern. "'But one day the war will end—and then what? What if they refuse to be stripped of the pants and deprived of the pay envelopes? What if they start looking round for some nice little chap who can cook and who'll meet them lovingly at the door with their slippers in his hand?'"

She slaps the magazine on the kitchen table.

"How have we managed all these years without a nice little chap to bring us our slippers at the door?" Léa says, but she is worried. "You know, the boys are still in charge. All the foremen at RCA are men, even though the girls are plenty capable. They'll let us build the planes, but they sure as heck aren't going to let us fly."

She leans back in the kitchen chair, nibbling a ragged cuticle. Her hands are a mess from the line, and they've run out of gloves.

"Listen to this. 'As one girl said of her lathe, with a look of amazed delight on her face, "Why, it's easier to run than a sewing machine.' Nobody has ever told these girls they're good at anything in their entire lives. It's a travesty."

"Eat up," her mother says, "it's getting cold." Léa flosses her teeth with a fingernail, moves the liver around her plate.

"Come on, Léa," Mama says, "it's full of iron, you're getting too thin again."

Léa coughs, and her mother, alarmed, stands up, ready to pound her on the back or to call an ambulance, but she's not choking, she's laughing.

"Listen to this putz: 'Women make poor foremen because they are likely to abuse authority'—said one plant manager, 'They're cats.' They're cats! And he's a pig!"

"That's enough," Mama says. "We have peaches for dessert. Can you fetch the can opener?"

Léa can't figure out if everything is changing or if nothing will ever really change. Shaking her head, she moves to the kitchen drawers, palming the rest of the liver into her napkin as she gets up, before her mother can catch her. It is a sin to waste food in this war. But God knows she can't eat it. She'll put it out later for the cats—the real cats—who are also hungry.

Soon it will be the longest day of the year.

32.

Léa gets 25 cents an hour building radios for the war. If she is a minute late, they dock her pay fifteen whole cents. The skin peels off her fingertips and she has a dull headache from morning until night. The girls do the dirty work on the line and the men get paid double and keep their hands clean and this is what it means for women to join the workforce. The war makes it worse; there is not much sympathy for the unions, when everyone is being asked to sacrifice, and new legislation makes it harder to strike. But they do have an advantage, which is that they are needed.

Her real job at RCA is to organize the workers. She is an expert by now. She leaves pamphlets in the toilets, she lingers on the sidewalk after hours, she gets to know the girls and asks about their families. She puts menstrual pads on top of her bag so she can smuggle the literature into the factory and when the security guards ask her to open her bag they blush and tell her to close it back up again.

The International Brotherhood of Electrical Workers is just starting up in Montreal; she goes to see the local officer, Monsieur Beaudry, to introduce the possibility of RCA joining under the umbrella of the larger union. He is sitting in a nice office, his chair pushed back to make space for his big belly, and he is smoking a cigar.

"I speak for the workers at RCA," Léa says. "Our pay is poor. Our workplace is filthy and unsafe, and the workers are angry. I believe the conditions are right to vote on the union."

Beaudry waves his cigar. He is wearing a gold pinky ring, and it flashes in the light. He looks more like a mob boss than like a union organizer.

"I appreciate what you young ladies are doing," he says. "But you have to understand, women's work is not our first priority."

His response is disappointing but not surprising. Just another fat cat at the top, more concerned about his own power than about his mission. Just another man who has never learned to take women seriously.

Léa stands up and slams her hands on his desk.

"No, *you* have to understand," she says. "We'll go straight to the head office in Washington if you won't work with us. We're organizing, and we don't need your damn permission."

"I should have plucked that cigar right out of his fat face and put it out on his fancy desk," she tells the girls over coffee at Georgette's. But the message has gotten through: Beaudry backs down and they join forces. In the end, they don't even have to strike. By September, the International Brotherhood of Electrical Workers signs an agreement with RCA, and the workers vote it in, ten to one.

It's the easiest win she's ever had. By January, their new local is up and running and Léa is elected the grievance officer.

"You'll be good at that, Léa," Gilles says.

"What, complaining?" Léa says, ready to take offence. She's never been a whiner.

"Not at all," Gilles says, "I mean, you could have been a lawyer. I've never seen you lose an argument. You're not always right—it's just that you won't ever let it go."

"That's not much of a compliment," Léa says.

Her first case is Nicole Roy, fired after a hysterectomy. Nicole is the main provider in her family. It drives Léa wild that the factory treats the women employees like silly girls earning pocket change for lipstick. Women run the place, they need to feed their families, they are in every way essential.

The boss has hired a Dr. Barrette to testify that Nicole is no longer fit to work. "Tell me, Doc," Léa says, "what do you use to solder wire? Your hands or your ovaries?"

"I've never heard anything so vulgar," Dr. Barrette says, and storms out of the office.

Léa sits calmly, looking the boss, Mr. McCallum, straight in the eye. Ever since she was a girl, she has been famously good at staring contests. She never blinks, never breaks. Mr. McCallum doesn't last nearly as long as her little brothers once did, and as he looks down, he stammers, "Miss Roback, you mustn't think we don't have a heart."

"I'm not interested in your heart," Léa says, "I'm interested in justice."

She's not sure how she feels when she gets a merit decoration for distinguished service on the home production front. She is cited for "outstanding ability, initiative and devotion as a war worker in defence of our country and freedom." The certificate is dated March 15th, 1943. Ability, initiative, devotion, yes. But not for this war. Not for any war.

Even Henri has a new job, only he claims he can't tell her anything about it. Something to do with researchers at McGill, which seems anodyne enough, except that one night over a bottle of wine he leans towards her and whispers that they are working on a new weapon. "What kind of weapon?" she says, and he crosses his arms over his chest and refuses to say anything else. They are all working for the war; his confession does not surprise her. She might be building weapons at RCA, and she wouldn't even know it.

The union is worried that a new flood of workers from Europe will destroy their working conditions. In her role as union representative, Léa writes a statement that gets printed in the newspapers. "We must be careful that we do not allow in economic immigrants who will undermine the cause of labour while we still battle for fair treatment of our own workers."

For the capitalists, every disaster is an opportunity. "Come to Quebec, where labour is cheap and plentiful!" the province advertises, preparing for a postwar boom.

"Plentiful, because they take it out of our hides," Henri grouses.

"Not if I have anything to do with it," Léa replies.

At Sabbath dinner, Rose is furious about Léa's statement. "For shame, Léa," she says. "What are those poor people supposed to do? Where are they supposed to go?"

The sisterhood at Rose's synagogue is trying to speed the applications of Jewish immigrants, and they are meeting resistance everywhere. Deaf ears in government, silence in the media. And now, even Léa, putting her shoulder against the closed door.

Léa is stubborn, resolved. "I'm not talking about refugees," she says. "I'm talking about our people."

"You might want to think about who you mean by that," Rose says, and won't speak to her for a month.

33.

Just in time for Valentine's Day, the brothels get shut down. The war years have been good to Ontario Street. Kids go down to the port and hand out business cards—business cards!—to the sailors getting off the ships, and they walk uphill straight to the red-light district. Henri has a friend in city hall. He says the army sent the mayor a letter warning him that he had better do something about the whorehouses, or else the whole city will be declared off limits.

"They're lousy with VD," Henri says. "Five times the rate of the soldiers in British Columbia. It's an honest-to-God health emergency. We're endangering the war effort. From the waist down."

He's laughing, but Léa is sober. "Those poor girls," she says. "How are they going to eat? How are their families going to eat?"

She sees a group of the girls on her way home, sitting together at Beauty's luncheonette, pouring liquor into their coffees from a little flask.

"How are you girls doing?" she says, and the tallest of them, she thinks her name is Sophie, in her fur coat and a bright red dress, lifts her little cup of coffee as if to toast Léa.

"No problem!" she says. "My customers know where to find me! We're all working for ourselves now! Fuck the madams and the landlords! Fuck Anna Beauchamp!" she says, and the girls look around, just in case one of her spies is there, and laugh as they clink cups. "Fuck Blanche Allard and Marcel *les Dents en Or*! And fuck the police!"

"Or don't fuck the police," Sophie amends. It's a betrayal, the end of this long open secret, the alliance between the brothels and the morality squad.

"You let me know if you need help, girls," Léa says, and Sophie laughs loudly, a badge of red lipstick on her prominent front teeth.

"And you let me know, Léa, if you need help! With your outfits, maybe. You have nice legs and you can show them a little more. I know a guy with a stocking factory!"

Léa laughs and straightens her skirt. There's no point in taking it personally. Anyway, she knows she has nice legs.

The newspaper reports on a health emergency that day, but it's TB, not syphilis. A no-strike bill is passed in the house. And Lottie comes back from the Hadassah convention at the Mont Royal Hotel fired up about a speech by Rabbi Stern which claimed a Jewish state must be established in Palestine for the postwar refugees.

"They need a haven, Léa," she says. "In Eretz Israel." Her tongue stumbles a little on the Hebrew. "He said it's going to be a dangerous time for the Jews even after the war. You think the socialists are on your side, Léa, but they hate us. We need our own country."

Léa laughs. "You're kidding me." Typical of a rabbi to libel the socialists when right here in Quebec we have our own little führer.

The soldiers stay and the bars and gambling joints just get busier. Marcel of the golden teeth might be missing out, but Charlie the Horse, Oscar the Hammer, Albert the Syrian, and Moishe the Electrician are doing just fine. The brothels shutter in a day, but in a week a few houses are open again, in new locations and with a little more discretion.

Léa hears that Sophie has gone west with an admirer, and she's happy for her, though a little concerned—sometimes that phrase is just a euphemism for disappeared.

34.

And yes, she is beginning to believe that one day this war really will be over. After two years of energy conservation, the lights go back on downtown. New neon signs flash traffic-light red outside the cabarets and theatres. The city is bustling again. They are all so hungry for normalcy.

Some of the action is chaotic. In Verdun, there are fights between the kids and the sailors. They call them the zoot suit riots. She's seen those boys, with their padded shoulders and long, sloppy coats, their big bow ties and high-waisted pants, and it's true that it's against the law—all that fabric and no frugality—but she doesn't really see the harm in it. Just kids playing dress-up, that's all. But it drives the sailors wild, and one night at the dance hall they storm the pavilion and strip the poor kids naked, even a couple of girls.

The fights break out all weekend. The city says it is the Navy's fault, and the Navy says those kids are entirely to blame, those fascist blackshirts and Italians.

"They're not blackshirts," Léa says, laying the paper down. "That's ridiculous. They're just kids trying to have a good time. And anyway, Italy's on our side now, was the Navy not informed?"

She does not like the way the soldiers and the sailors think they own the streets. Good for them, fighting overseas, but it's too much to bring the fight back home. Why, they're even talking about martial law in Montreal. Martial law! What kind of freedom are we fighting for?

In the end, the city does not declare martial law, but they also don't restrict the sailors to the boats. The fights peter out but mostly because the kids disappear, in their clown pants with their oversized watch chains and wide brimmed hats. They've given up, or they've gone underground. She is surprised to realize she misses their swagger—not that she approves, exactly, you can't work in those clothes, they advertise your uselessness—but also, well, they are so young. She remembers boys dressing a little like that in Berlin, ten years earlier; she remembers being careless like them, and foolish like them. Youth is not an excuse; it is a glorious state of exception.

But then she thinks of the boys their age overseas, in their hot uniforms, and she feels confused. No exception has been made for them.

Michael and Leo have been training in Canada, and they leave for Europe in the summer of 1944. They pose with Mama in their uniforms on the sidewalk in front of the house, their arms linked, Leo still holding his cigarette in his other hand. Mama is beaming with pride and, standing between her boys, she is small and squat. Their little mother. They look like schoolboys who have outgrown their suits, their wrists raw and exposed in the sun.

The allies have landed in Normandy and are pushing towards Léa's beloved Paris. She still hates war on principle, nonetheless, is bursting with pride for her brothers and convinced that they are fighting the good fight. Though she also desperately wants them to come home so she can burn their uniforms instead of washing them.

It has been a dreadful summer. Hot, so hot that before she gets to the corner, she has damp circles under the arms of her shirtwaist, she has beads of sweat rolling down her neck.

Paul Robeson comes back to town, this time on his tour of *Othello*, with Uta Hagen as his Desdemona. He looks monumental on the stage, in a striped silk robe, but also a

little silly, as if he has come out in his dressing gown. He is…
not great, if she is honest. As he moves across the stage, he is
a little stiff, but he is adequate in the monologues, which he
intones almost as if he is singing. And he does look the part of
the general, despite the robe. When he kisses Desdemona on
stage the audience gasps.

Fred has told her to come over the next day, that he has a
surprise. And there is Paul, large as life and twice as natural—
actually, twice as large as life, she has heard he played football
when he was in college. Fred's apartment is full to bursting
with her friends. People sit on the tables and on the floor,
and the room can barely contain their voices as Paul stands
to sing.

I could die right now, Léa thinks, perched on the edge of
her chair, and I would be perfectly happy. Right here, in my
own city, I have seen the promised land.

35.

When conscription is finally enforced in the fall, it's a bust; the volunteers outnumber the conscripts by a factor of ten, and those zombie soldiers rounded up with force do credit to no one. Mackenzie King needn't have bothered. He has lost credibility, flip-flopping from the promise never to conscript to this late and lame attempt, and now sending these dregs, these fifteen thousand overseas. If anything, conscription has empowered the nationalists, and there are riots in Quebec City and Montreal.

People say the war will be over soon, but the closer they feel to the end the more difficult it becomes to be patient. Their thoughts start turning to ordinary things, to the life that has been interrupted. To the end of rationing, to real nylons, to a new car. To the return of husbands and sons. There is no end of things to desire. The politicians keep promising abundance, and don't they all deserve it? New bicycles for the kids, a new car for dad, and for mom? Isn't her dream a shining white electric refrigerator?

Léa reads the ads, laughs it off, feels a little refrigerated chill. They let those fair Amazons in overalls out of the house, but sure enough they'll have them back in aprons in the kitchen as soon as the war is over. There were just a few thousand women in the work force in 1914. Now there are well over a hundred thousand, and most in industry. Almost half the women of Quebec between the ages of twenty and forty are unmarried. It is suddenly a nation of spinsters.

The countryside is abandoned. Why be a farm wife and work from sunrise to sunset when you could have your own smart little apartment in the city? Why be a slave in an apron with shit on your shoes when you could have your freedom?

Léa reads the paper every morning, charting the final battles in nearly real time. Each day, she anticipates the end, and each day, is forced to wait just a little longer. What she is most afraid of is the knock on the door. Just because the end is near, doesn't mean her brothers are not at risk.

Crocuses poke up in dirty residual piles of snow, flare yellow, and fall back; scylla blooms in the handkerchief front yards of the Plateau, fly their indigo flags, and wilt. The creamy louche cups of the magnolias swoon open, they droop, they drop, then litter the yards. The cherry trees and the crab apples have just begun to bloom when the news comes; it is as if the whole city holds its breath, waiting for confirmation, before swarming out on the streets. Balconies and windows put out flags like tulips opening on a sunny day, you cannot think for the ruckus of horns and whistles, strangers embrace, and children run in circles because there is nowhere else for their energy to go.

Léa heads to the action at Peel and Sainte-Catherine. She likes to be where the people are, in the benevolent chaos of the streets. She walks her feet sore and then goes home to Mama, who is both pleased and panicked, so flustered Léa finds her sitting on the steps in her housedress, her feet dirty and bare, watching the parade of celebrants walking down the street.

"Ma, at least let me get you some slippers," she says.

Embarrassed, Mama pulls her robe to cover her feet and announces, "But I'm not going to sleep a wink until the boys are home."

"It's going to take a little while," Léa says, "but they'll be back soon." She offers her mother her arm back up the steps, who knows how long she'll be able to manage them? This is not a city built for old age. Léa makes her herbal tea and helps her mother wash her feet, bringing a warm basin of soapy water to the couch, and despite her promise, Mama falls asleep early that night, Léa sitting beside the bed to reassure her.

The older she gets the more she feels a mother to her own mother.

In the morning, a great black banner across the front page of the paper announces the war is over. She laughs out loud, even though she already knows. It's really something to see it in big capital letters, in black and white. She stays home until nine to listen to the broadcast on the news, and when she gets to work the factory is half-empty, everyone has chosen to treat the day like a holiday. This sacred day of peace.

36.

When Fred runs for office again Paul sends him a recorded endorsement. "Your boys in Canada have fought a brave fight, they have died on many fronts to establish a people's world," he intones. "We have that kind of world in our grasp but dangerous forces have again arisen..." They listen together, and Léa feels afraid, though she's not sure what Robeson means. Which forces? Whose world?

Fred's platform this time is uncontentious. Help for the boys coming home, family allowances, postwar reconstruction. They print his face over a map of the neighbourhood so voters know that they are inside the constituency, and just like last time, they layer the posters on every surface. They didn't have to try so hard. The election is a cakewalk; he wins by a large majority. There is none of the suspense of the last vote, and maybe less euphoria.

Other than Fred and a few independent candidates, it's a Liberal sweep across the island. "We should celebrate," Fred says, but Léa is bone-tired, she has been knocking on doors all day and into the night. Winning for a second time must mean they have arrived, but the only place she wants to go is her own bed.

Also, this is the end for her, she has already decided. Her last campaign. It is good the war is over—well, almost over, the Pacific drags on—and it is good the election is won, but she's going to have to get up in the morning and go to work.

There is a last victory celebration for Fred in early August, at the home of a Party member Léa barely knows. She arrives, carrying a bottle of wine by the neck; it takes its place among the other bottles, glittering in the back courtyard by candlelight. The air has been heavy these last few days and they are expecting rain. She keeps glancing up at the pretty paper lanterns hung across the yard and at the tables laden with food. When the rain comes, they will need to move quickly so it does not all get ruined. In the distance, she can hear the thunder roar.

Fred is looking prosperous. His buttons strain a little at the stomach, and his colour is high. He is surrounded by admirers, and Léa is surprised at how few of them she recognizes. She lifts her glass in his direction, and he meets her eyes, then looks away quickly, something evasive in his glance. Those ears like jug handles on each side of his head—even if he becomes prime minister, nothing will make them dignified.

Henri is in a dark corner of the garden, sitting by himself. He is drinking wine straight out of the bottle, and Léa wanders towards him, looking for some company. The thunder is getting louder. What a warm, velvet, blue-black night.

All these brothers and sisters, and she feels so lonely.

"Are you drinking to victory?" she asks. "And to our bright future?"

The phrase a code they no longer need now that they are in government.

"To our bright future," he says, and lifts the bottle, tilts it back. When he puts it on the ground, she can see his face is wet.

"Henri," she says, "are you crying? If you cry when you win, what do you do when you lose?"

"Léa, did you read the news today?" he says, clasping her hands.

She squats down so she is on his level.

"I did," she says, "I read it every day." She remembers skimming the headlines that morning. The war in the Pacific stumbling to a bloody close, and negotiations at Potsdam, and new restrictions on alcohol sales in Canada. "Henri, what are you talking about?"

He sinks his head between his knees and then raises it again. The party around them is a riot of light and sound, and they are in his little antechamber of shadow and grief. She cannot think what is wrong.

"Did you read about the bomb?"

There was a little article, she remembers, about a new weapon, used somewhere in Japan, she can't recall. No reports yet on the damages, and she has become so numb to the continual stream of military updates she had not registered it.

"Another bomb," she says.

"No Léa, not another bomb. This changes everything."

She would like her hands back but he is holding tight. He pulls her closer and she feels off balance on the grass. His breath is warm and wine-thick.

"They've been working on this bomb for months, Léa," he whispers loudly, and she pulls her face away a little though he is still holding onto her. "This is the most destructive weapon known to man. They aren't saying yet, but it's a massacre. A city, destroyed. Civilians, thousands, hundreds of thousands, who knows how many. Remember the weapon I told you about?"

Henri stops talking and lets her go without warning, and she tumbles into the grass. Fred is standing over them with a candle, the fire mirrored in his eyes.

"Won't you join the rest of us?" he says, jovial. He pulls her up by her free hand, and she wipes the back of her skirt. If she is lucky, it will not stain. She follows Fred to the centre of the yard, but she can't spot Henri; he has slipped away.

"I didn't want you to miss the toasts, kid," he says, slipping his arm around her waist. "This is your victory too." Someone hands her a glass.

"To peace," Fred says.

Gilles says, "To the man of the hour!"

Santé, *lechayim*, and *za zdarovje*.

The sky opens and the guests rush to the door, holding plates of cocktail franks and bowls of potato chips, dips made of mayonnaise and blue cheese and celery stuffed with egg salad, wine bottles under their arms and glasses in their hands.

Fred pauses at the half-open door. Léa is just standing there in the rain.

"Aren't you coming?" he says.

"I think I'm going home. I have to work tomorrow."

She's not sure why she hesitates to follow him inside, where they will all dry off and keep drinking in the humid air, sitting on towels to protect the couches and talking over each other until the early hours of the morning. Suddenly, all she wants is to walk by herself in the street, in the warm rain, under the night sky, so cloudy you can't even see the moon.

"Are you sure?" he asks. "You're going to get wet."

She tilts her face to the sky. "I can't get any wetter."

When Fred is arrested, not even one year later, she remembers the storm that night and Henri's labile despair. At the commission, Fred refuses to testify. By then, Henri has disappeared, and no one knows where he has gone. She believes in Fred's innocence. She visits him in jail and writes him letters of support. She stands by his wife and daughter as others shun them and when he is released, she is among the very first to greet him.

But in a private, hidden room inside of her she wonders: how far did they go? The bride and groom have glass eyes, and many a man has ruined himself for what he loves. One day in 1958 she slides her membership card into an envelope and sends it to the head office, a gesture of quiet resignation. At her first march against the proliferation of nuclear weapons, she thinks of the day she learned about the bomb. In Hiroshima and Nagasaki, the light of the blast created silhouettes of ladders, windowpanes, water valves, bicycles, even people, incinerated in an instant, their imprints burned onto the sidewalk. History is a light that burns so brightly it cannot be witnessed. Memory is a shadow that leaves an indelible stain. None of this is understood in the moment, lost in the blast of the action.

She will leave the Party, but all her life, she will embrace the struggle.

Afterword

Léa Roback was born in Montreal on November 3rd, 1903, and died on August 28th, 2000. Her life, which nearly spanned the century, was exceptional. She lived freely and travelled broadly, especially in her youth, and became a member of the Communist party while living in Berlin, leaving shortly before the Nazi seizure of power. She was a polyglot, fluent in English, Yiddish, French, and German, and was as skilled at navigating communities as she was at languages. Upon her return to Montreal, she managed the city's first communist bookstore and played a leading role in early victories for the labour movement and for women's suffrage. She was indefatigable in her activism and expansive in her causes: votes for women, workers' rights, access to contraception and abortion, pay equity, social housing, and free education. She campaigned against the Vietnam War, Apartheid in South Africa, and the proliferation of nuclear weaponry, to name just some of her many causes, and was an activist until nearly the end of her life. Léa Roback was a *farbrente yiddishe maydel*—a fiery Jewish girl—whose audacity challenged and changed her times.

I learned about Léa Roback on a Jane's Walk led by her relative, Melanie Leavitt. To learn more, I turned to Sophie Bissonnette's film *A Vision in the Darkness* and Nicole Lacelle's longform interviews with Léa and fellow labour pioneer Madeleine Parent (1988), to Merrily Weisbord's indispensable *The Strangest Dream: Canadian Communists, the Spy Trials, and the Cold War* (1983), and to books about the history of Montreal, especially William Weintraub's wonderful *City Unique: Montreal Days and Nights in the 1940s and '50s* (1996). Following Léa, I found myself immersed in a mostly forgotten history, the stories of the socialists and suffragettes who organized during some of the darkest years in the 20th century, and who won crucial and heroic victories. I spent a season in the Léa Roback archives at the Jewish Public library, leafing through her own collections of newspaper clippings and documents, and discovering her brief but tantalizing attempts to write her own life story. I thought about writing a biography instead of a novel, but the form of a novel allows more intimacy and a little bit more freedom. Historical novels are a hybrid and tricky form, straddling the worlds of actuality and of fiction. Bits of historical dialogue and reportage have found their way into my book, like the train tickets and calling cards modernist painters used to pastiche into their artworks. I have tried to be both faithful to history and daring in imagination. The more I wrote, the more I felt like I was channeling not only the past but the present.

This novel tells the story of nearly half a life: Léa Roback's childhood in Beauport through her formative years in Europe and her first great victories, the successful garment industry strike of 1937, and her work for Fred Rose's campaigns. But Léa never faded. She went on from strength to strength. Her mission and her name live on: in the Léa Roback Foundation, which offers scholarships to economically disadvantaged and socially committed women; in the Léa Roback Research Centre, which focuses on inequality and public health; and in the Maison Parent-Roback, which advances the causes of women and social justice through linking hundreds of different community organizations.

I will donate half my proceeds from this book to the Léa Roback Foundation.

Thank you to the Canada Council for their invaluable support of this project. Thank you to Carlos Oliva for permission to use the beautiful mural featured on the cover, and to Archie Fineberg for the photograph. Thank you to Linda Leith, Elise Moser, Leila Marshy, and the entire team at LLP. Thank you to my dear friends and first readers, Bill Tipper, Sandie Friedman, and Julie Shugarman. Sivan Slapak read more versions than anyone should be expected to read, and so did Jeremy Wexler, who was indefatigable. Ben Wexler contributed editing skills and intimidating discernment. Lev Wexler is, as ever, my number one fan.

Ariela Freedman
Montreal